From the Grey Tunnel to the Green Tunnel:

A 9/11 Firefighter's Journey from Despair to Hope

By

Rob "Sleepwalker" Weisberg

DEDICATION

I would like to dedicate my book to my family, Kathy, Justin, and Shane, for supporting me when I wasn't being me, even when they couldn't understand me.

TABLE OF CONTENTS

INTRODUCTION

One night, I was listening to the radio, and fellow Long Islander Billy Joel was talking about his career. He talked about when it was starting to really take off. Between his "Turnstiles" and "Stranger" albums, things were transitioning for him. He knew what his life was like, and he was beginning to see where it was headed. He was beginning to taste success. It wasn't like he didn't like his life the way it was, but he knew he wasn't going to be able to go back to it once his fame came to stay. It made me wonder if he was a "stranger" to himself as he headed towards his new self.

What Billy was sharing resonated with me. I could tell that when I came home from the Appalachian Trail (AT), my life was going to be different. I wasn't the same person who started hiking 1,852.5 miles ago. How could I be? I just spent 5 ½ months reflecting on and finally taking the time to process what I had been through on September 11, 2001, as a firefighter at the World Trade Center, being a survivor when so many others perished, and the impact that horrific experience had on my life. I thought about the self-imposed, unnecessary, unearned blame and guilt I was secretly carrying. I thought about how my Post-Traumatic Stress Disorder (PTSD) negatively impacted so many of my relationships and all the apologies that I owed.

Literature uses the metaphor of a Phoenix rising from the ashes to symbolize someone who had the opportunity to gather themself from their lowest point and move forward in some kind of positive direction. One could say I'm a living Pheonix. This is my story

CHAPTER 1
Growing Up

I grew up on Long Island in the late 60's, 70's, and 80's in a growing town called Commack which was transitioning from a farming community to a New York City suburb. The land beneath my childhood home used to be a potato farm, and our post office had a hitching post for horses. My street was part of a typical middle-class neighborhood where the fathers worked, and the mothers watched the kids. Some of us, including me, became latch-key kids when we got a little older and our mothers went to work. During our school breaks, the kids in the neighborhood would be out early, finding things to do together. We would play kickball in the street and use the manhole cover for home plate or second base. Car doors became first and third base. We headed home for lunch when the Commack Fire Department's 12 o'clock whistle sounded. I don't know if the fire department knew it, but their whistle was an integral part of our childhoods. Around 1 pm, we would all meet up in the street again, find something else to do, and then return home when the first father came home from work.

My home was located close to the firehouse. Like most kids, the thought of being a firefighter was the coolest thing ever. When I was about 4 or 5 years old, being a firefighter was my Halloween costume. It consisted of my rain jacket and snow boots and a plastic firefighter's helmet someone gave me. I vividly remember being in the car with my father, and I always looked at the firehouse when we drove by. Open bay doors meant I could see the trucks that were parked inside, and I was going to have a good day.

When I got a little older, I joined the local baseball and soccer leagues. Playing both sports at the same time made my schedule a bit hectic and my mother a bit nuts with all the driving from field to

field. Sometimes, I had to wear my soccer uniform underneath my baseball uniform since there was no time to go home and change between games.

I also joined the Cub Scout Pack 405 at my school, Old Farms Elementary School. While I enjoyed playing baseball and soccer for many years, Scouting became an obsession for me. It allowed me to be outside; I didn't have to wait for the next season to start the following year, and I was exposed to so many different activities. I remember as a Webelos; there were 15 different activity pins that we could earn. They covered so many topics, including sports, science, citizenship, art, and of course the outdoors. In my first month, I earned 7 of them. One of my friend's parents asked why I did so many of them at once since I had a year to earn all of them. I thought it was a funny question. I responded with my own question. Why should I wait?

As a Cub Scout, I was invited to an Eagle Court of Honor. This is the ceremony where a Boy Scout who completed all the requirements to become an Eagle Scout receives his rank. This ceremony is quite impressive and rare. Only about 4% of all Boy Scouts make it to Eagle. The Honor Guard brought in the American and troop flags and then everyone recited the Pledge of Allegiance. Afterwards, the troop recited the Scout Oath and Law. I remember looking around the room and seeing the troop's members sitting in the audience wearing their merit badge sashes. Then, the Eagle Scout and his parents were escorted to the stage. I immediately thought, "Wow! Look at how many merit badges this guy had." The ceremony continued with a lot of speeches, including one from a member of the Police Department. This made it clear to me how highly respected this rank was. Then, the Scoutmaster read a letter that really grabbed my attention. It may have been short and to the point compared to the other letters, but it left such an impression on me. It came from the White House. President Jimmy Carter sent this Scout from my hometown a congratulatory letter. This confirmed to me how significant this achievement was. At 9 years old I just set my first long-term goal!

I loved my Cub Scout pack, partly because of the friends my family made with other families in the neighborhood. Our families didn't just see each other at the weekly and monthly Pack Nights meetings. Each 4th of July weekend meant we were going camping with four other families. Camping with our neighbors was my family's first exposure to family camping. After borrowing gear for our first trip to see if we liked camping and to see what was needed, we were all in. The parents would have a planning meeting, look at different camping guidebooks, and make phone calls, trying to find that year's perfect spot while all the kids were in the basement making a ton of noise. I couldn't wait until it was time to go. There would be ten adults and around 15 kids since we could bring friends too. The campgrounds always had something to do. We could go fishing, play softball, or just have a catch, do arts and crafts, or go boating. I will never forget the time one of the other kids and I took out a sunfish sailboat. We caught a really nice breeze and were skimming across the smooth-as-glass lake. The next thing I knew, the wind changed direction, the sail came swinging across the boat, the boat flipped, and we went flying into the water. I remember quite clearly the panic I felt when my feet got tangled in the lake's vegetation while I was underwater, watching the bubbles I made rise above me. I kicked frantically to free myself so I could get to the surface to grab my next breath of air! The funny thing about this situation is that it made me wonder how long it would have taken for any of the adults to notice if anything bad had happened since they really didn't know where any of the kids were. For example, later that day, I was exhausted and went into my family's tent to lie down for a while. I fell asleep for a few hours, and when I came out, I saw one of the fathers grilling chicken over a campfire. I thought it was bizarre that we were about to have chicken for breakfast. When I asked my father why we were having chicken for breakfast, he had a very perplexed expression on his face. After my ridiculous questions continued a while longer, he finally asked me where I had just come from. I told him that I had just come from the tent after sleeping all night. He couldn't stop laughing after he realized what had happened. My nap was so deep and relaxing that it felt like I slept through the night. What I thought was breakfast time the following morning was actually dinner time the same day my friend and I flipped the sailboat!

The food we ate was always amazing. The hard part was finding something 25 people enjoyed. One night, we were going to have spaghetti and meatballs. One of the kids asked the mother who was cooking if there was wine in the gravy. She asked why they were asking, and they replied they didn't like wine in the gravy. She told them not to worry since she wasn't using any. The kid liked the response and walked away. A little while later, another kid came by, also asking if there was wine in the gravy. She asked this kid why they were asking, and they replied that they loved wine in the gravy. She told them there was a lot of wine in the gravy, and that kid walked away incredibly happy with the response. While I can't remember if there was wine in the gravy or not, everybody loved it!

I looked forward to the nights at the campground. Each night, there was a different activity. One night, the campground would show a movie. Another night, there might be square dancing. Other nights, we would sit around the fire or at the picnic tables with lanterns and talk about our day or whatever else was on our minds. Sometimes, the kids would do skits we learned on Scout trips for our parents. They loved watching our performances.

These campouts were so important to me for another reason. One of the kids in our camping clan was deaf. Whenever I wanted to talk to her, I needed to communicate with her through her parents or siblings. I hated the idea that she probably felt excluded since there was so much going on; she missed out on things frequently or was delayed in knowing what happened until someone translated to her what was said and why we were laughing. I remember how we would watch the translation and then the laughter, and then we would all laugh again together. It became so important to me that I could communicate with her directly. As a high school freshman, I enrolled in American Sign Language (ASL) classes. It was such a wonderful opportunity for me. My classes were in the evening as part of an adult education program. My classmates were in their 40's, 50's, and 60's, and I was just 14. At the end of each term, there was a party, and members of the deaf community were invited. We prepared some skits to entertain them, and afterwards, we shared refreshments while we practiced our signing skills with them. It was gratifying to see how much they appreciated our interest in their community.

As my brother, sister, and I got older, and my family became more experienced campers, we were able to do longer trips. We even did a cross-country trip, which took about six weeks. Pulling into a campsite in the evening was like a NASCAR pit crew going to work. My dad, brother, and I pitched our tent and unrolled our sleeping bags while my mother and sister made dinner. Within 10 minutes, the camp was set up and we were eating a hot dinner. We visited numerous national parks which were so impactful on my life. Part of me wanted to become a ranger with the National Park Service when I got older. How could I not? Think about how amazing it would be to have Yellowstone National Park as my "office." While zoos are a cool way to see animals, seeing them in their natural environment doesn't get any better. Even now, seeing a tiny chipmunk can totally make my day!

I moved up to a Boy Scout troop when I was old enough. I looked forward to the weekly troop meetings and the monthly campouts and hikes. As a young Scout, I was amazed that I hiked up a mountain that was part of the Appalachian Trail, built a fire to stay warm and cook my food, and hiked back down the mountain the following morning.

My Scouting career provided me with so many opportunities to see other parts of our country. For example, I went to Washington, D.C. and stayed at Andrews Air Force Base. In 1981, I went to the National Jamboree in Virginia. It was held at the army's Fort A.P. Hill in Virginia. I also hiked through Boston, learning about the American Revolution, and stayed at Hanscom Air Force Base.

The Scout trip that had the biggest impact on my life was my trip to Philmont Scout Ranch in 1982. Philmont is a working cattle and horse ranch in the Rocky Mountain wilderness of Cimarron, New Mexico. It is approximately 214 square miles. I was 14 years old and was one of the youngest members of a 12-person crew. My friends and I flew into Denver, Colorado, a few days before our trek started to acclimatize ourselves to the elevation change from Long Island's 100 feet above sea level to the Rockies 5,000+ feet above sea level. Our time in Colorado included a white-water rafting trip on the Arkansas River and a tour and stay at the U.S. Air Force Academy.

Philmont offers numerous trekking options. To be clear, none of the options are easy. They are classified as either challenging, rugged, strenuous, or super strenuous. The Philmont staff admits the treks are designed to be difficult on purpose. The ranch is set up with a base camp. A crew reports to the base camp on its scheduled day, is assigned a ranger, completes its final medical review, picks up the last of its gear, and attends an opening ceremony. The following day, the crew boards a school bus, which drives along a mountain road and stops. At a predetermined point in the middle of nowhere, the bus stops, and their ranger instructs the crew to get off the bus and prepare for its first hike. Over the course of about ten days, the crew hikes from point to point without returning to the base camp. The ranger stays with the crew for the first few days, teaching the crew members the "Philmont way" of doing things and observing the crew as a whole to confirm it has the skills required to remain alone in the wilderness safely. Some days, the trail would take the crew to a sub-camp where the Philmont staff provides an activity. For example, the crew may learn how to pan for gold or experience what it was like to be a lumberjack in the 1800's. Crew members may also have the opportunity to learn how to rock climb and repel. On other days, a crew may set up camp with nobody else nearby and just enjoy the solitude the wilderness provides. On the last day of the trek, the crew hikes to a rendezvous point where a bus picks up its members and returns them back to the base camp for a closing ceremony.

We knew we were in the wilderness because our ranger kept stressing the fact that we needed to remain bear aware. Cooking needed to be done away from our tents, and food and other smell-ables needed to be secured in a bag hanging from a tree at night. The one thing we couldn't control was where the bears actually were. One day, my crew was hiking up a switchback along the side of a mountain. The next thing we knew, a bear cub was chasing us! While it was "only" a cub, we had a bigger concern. Where was

Momma Bear? The worst place a hiker could be is between a mother bear and its cub. We could only run further up the switchback since the terrain up and down the side of the mountain was too steep. While most of us were running, one of our guys decided to take off his pack, find his camera, and take a picture of the playful creature. Needless to say, he was the only one who got a picture of it. Fortunately for us, the cub got bored chasing us and stopped on its own and Momma never showed up!

I must share that I was blessed with the opportunity to return to Philmont 40 years later to complete another trek with my older son, Justin. I'm also looking forward to returning again soon to complete my third trek with my younger son, Shane!

Just to give you an idea about how much I enjoyed Scouts as a youth, I earned my Eagle Scout when I was 15 years old. While most Scouts don't make it to Eagle, those who do complete their journey close to their 18th birthday, which is just before a Scout becomes too old for the program. These years had such an influence on the rest of my life. For example, this is where I learned about the value of community service. I also developed my passion for the outdoors, honed my outdoor skills, and acquired a solid foundation in first aid.

As a senior in high school, it was time to go through the college selection process. I don't think my parents were surprised when I told them that I wanted to get back to the Rockies. After all, they knew the impact Philmont had on me and how much I loved being around the Rocky Mountains. In the fall of 1986, I was accepted to the University of Denver, where I earned my bachelor's and master's degrees in accounting.

Even as a college student, the idea of becoming a firefighter was in the back of my mind. I worked for the university as a resident assistant in one of the school's dormitories. The dorm I lived and worked in consisted of two ten-story buildings connected by a common ground floor. One night, my partner and I were doing rounds, checking each floor in the dorm, making sure the students were safe, and enforcing policies when necessary. We would start on the top floor of one tower and work our way down to the ground floor. Then, we would check the other tower. After completing the first few floors in one of the towers, my partner and I noticed the slightest scent of burning wood. We picked up our pace, checking each floor, and the scent strengthened as we completed each floor. My partner and I agreed that we needed to pull the fire alarm. We did so and started banging on bedroom doors as we proceeded to the remaining floors. When we got to the ground floor, the building director saw us and asked what was going on. I explained that we could smell something burning, so we pulled the alarm. When the fire department arrived, I was asked to help their guys locate the room where the smokey odor was coming from. Once we identified the room, we knocked on the door, and nobody answered. The firefighters used their forcible entry tools to quickly rip the door off its hinges. What we found was some unattended burning incense. Fortunately for us, we prevented a potential catastrophe. Unfortunately for the students who lived in the room, they had to pay to replace the busted door!

When I moved back home after graduation in 1991, I found a job as an accountant. After getting my career going, I felt like I needed to get involved in my community. I needed to do something that didn't involve sitting since I was doing enough of that at work. I enjoyed working out and was in decent shape, so in mid-1993, I decided the time was right to submit my application to become a volunteer firefighter. In December of 1993, I was sworn in as a Commack Fire Department firefighter. The next several months were insanely busy. I was completing county and in-house fire academy classes, attending fire department and fire company meetings and drills, learning where the equipment was located on each rig, how the department and company operated, including chain-of-command, and most importantly, how to make a good pot of coffee for the senior guys.

The training I received and continue receiving today is simply the best. My county and in-house instructors were tough, but patient, which made sense. A lot of these guys worked for FDNY and were more than willing to pass along their knowledge. There is a banner hanging up in my firehouse's truck room. It says, "You Can't Train Too Hard For A Job That Can Kill You." These can't just be words when you consider what each alarm can potentially throw at you. The thing with fire and other emergencies is you can't have the "that will never happen in my neighborhood" mentality. There is no such thing as routine. Many times, an alarm came in that sounded like a situation we handled before, but when we got there, there was something unique that required outside-the-box thinking. For calls like that, the best tools we have on our rigs are our brains!

I have over 30 years of experience protecting my hometown. Over that time, I have gone on numerous alarms and interacted with my community in so many ways. I love hearing the dispatcher announce over the intercom that there is a family here to have a tour of the truck room. I couldn't help but think about how much I loved seeing the trucks when I was a kid. The most memorable tour I gave was for a child who was about five years old. I introduced myself to the boy and his mother and then asked the boy what his name was. The mother replied instead, informing me that her son was deaf. I said that wasn't a problem and switched to using my rusty ASL skills. I must have done a good enough job since my young visitor's face lit up. His eyes got huge as I watched him sign excitedly to his mother that a firefighter knew how to sign. I really couldn't tell who had more fun during that tour. Maybe my little friend? Maybe me?

CHAPTER 2
September 11, 2001

September 11, 2001, was my generation's December 7, 1941, or November 22, 1963. Most Americans who were alive in those days knew where they were when the Japanese bombed Pearl Harbor or when President Kennedy was assassinated. I will never forget where I was when the Al-Qaeda terrorists attacked the World Trade Center that day. I was there.

I didn't go to work on Monday, September 10, 2001, since I wasn't feeling well. As the financial controller for a software company, I didn't want to miss a second day in a row since I had a lot of work to do. I exited the subway train at the World Trade Center's station as I was completing my two-hour commute. I heard the deafening sound of an enormous explosion while I was walking along the subway platform to the stairs that would lead me up to Church Street. The ground shook, and the shock wave sent those already on the stairs ahead of me tumbling back down to the platform. I immediately thought the Trade Center experienced its second car bombing. However, when I got to the street, I saw the destruction the first plane inflicted on the North Tower.

While I still had no idea as to what exactly happened, it was obvious that whatever happened was awful. I called my wife and told her something terrible happened, but I was ok. As a firefighter, I knew where the firehouses were in the immediate area and knew there weren't enough guys to take on this tragic event. I got to my office and shared my concerns. I told them that I wanted to respond to the nearby firehouse located on Liberty Street, which is the southern border of the World Trade Center complex. They knew my background and supported my request. I told them that if I wasn't needed, I would come back. Needless to say, I never went back to the office that day.

When I arrived at FDNY's 10 House, the engine and truck companies weren't in quarters. My understanding was they had responded to a gas leak. Over 20 years later, I found out they responded directly to the World Trade Center, which was just across the street. I introduced myself to Captain Paul Mallery, Ladder Company 10, who was in quarters alone. I told him that I was a firefighter and that I was available if he needed me. He looked at me squarely and told me I was all he had. He immediately accepted my assistance. My assignment was to convert the firehouse into a triage location. This would be either one of the first or possibly even the first triage location for all of Lower Manhattan. I immediately knew this was an enormous responsibility since there were so many injured people already in the firehouse, and more kept coming in. I needed to bring order to a totally chaotic environment. It wouldn't be until later that I fully comprehended the magnitude of this responsibility.

I spent the next few minutes literally running from the truck room throughout the rest of the firehouse to see what resources were available. One of my old Scoutmasters taught me many years ago how important it was to know my resources. That lesson totally applied here. The ground floor consisted of the truck room, and behind it was a hallway with a bathroom and then a kitchen with tables and chairs to the left and a small alcove with a pay phone and a TV room to the right. At the end of the hallway, there was an exit door. On the right side of the ground floor, there was also a staircase leading to the two upper floors. The second floor had the firehouse's weight room. I didn't see anything there that would be of much use. On the third floor, I found the bunk room. Bingo! I grabbed as many blankets and pillows as I could carry and brought them downstairs.

I laid them on the floor of the truck room and then ran back to the bunk room for more. There were already chairs in the truck room, so the injured could now either sit or lay down depending on their injuries.

My next concern was finding first aid supplies. The captain told me any first aid supplies they had would be in the grey cabinet in the truck room. I opened the cabinet door and felt like Old Mother Hubbard. The cupboard was almost completely bare. The supply of rubber gloves and everything else was minimal at best. I could maybe find four pairs of gloves in total. Ideally, I would have put on a fresh pair of gloves as I went from victim to victim to avoid any cross-contamination issues. Unfortunately, this wouldn't be an option.

While I was setting up the truck room to provide the injured with a comfortable place to rest and looking for first aid supplies, everyone in the firehouse could hear the roar of an accelerating jet engine. It was the second plane used in the attack, flying directly over the firehouse just seconds before it slammed into the World Trade Center's South Tower. Moments later, Captain Mallery told me that it was no accident; we were being attacked and needed to keep our eyes open.

The number of people showing up at the firehouse was overwhelming. Some were injured, some were scared, and some just didn't know where else to go, so they just stood outside the firehouse, watching as the horrifying scenes continued in front of them. Little did we know things would get much worse.

There were two victims that I will never forget. Both were already in the firehouse when I arrived there. The first was a woman from Japan who was sitting on a chair. She started her day by putting on an elegant dress. Unfortunately for her, she would later be standing near one of the elevator banks and get caught in a fireball. She had 3rd-degree burns covering about 70% of her body, and what was left of her dress was scorched. Her ability to speak English was minimal, and my Japanese was less than that. I used the phrases I knew to make her smile. At least I could provide her with some psychological first aid. I would later return to her with a ring cutter to cut her beautiful diamond ring off her blistered finger. I didn't want to damage her ring, but she needed relief from the pain it was causing her. I found a small envelope and placed the pieces into it, so she had everything. It was the least I could do for her.

The other victim was a man from China named Fu. When I met him, he was lying on the truck room floor, his suit pants were mostly torn from his body, and he was resting his head on his briefcase. He was injured in one of the explosions and had a broken pelvis. He was at the World Trade Center, picking up a loan from the Chinese government for his import business. Gratefully, he spoke English clearly, so we didn't have any communication issues. Ironically, he was at the World Trade Center when Al-Qaeda set off a car bomb in the North Tower's parking garage on February 26, 1993.

New York City immediately activated its recall process. All available emergency personnel needed to report to their respective firehouses or police precincts forthwith. All shifts that just ended were extended. If you were home, you left your couch. If you were on vacation, you cut it short. Two EMTs, Brian Smith and Brian Gordon, assigned to an ambulance in Brooklyn just finished their shift. They looked at each other and decided to take a spare bus (slang for ambulance) over the Brooklyn Bridge to 10 House. I was thrilled to see these guys. The experience, help, and supplies I needed had arrived. I was just as thrilled to find out they were both named Brian. This meant I only had to remember one name! I had them back their bus into one of the bays in the firehouse. I figured we could load the ambulance with as many victims as possible and then see if they could come back with more EMS support.

As more firefighters reported to 10 House, I heard Captain Mallery was putting together a search team to look for victims in the South Tower. I found him and told him that I was a truckie. He knew that meant search was one of my specialties. I also mentioned that the EMTs were here so they could take over the triage assignment. He told me that he was happy with the job I was doing with triage and instructed me to continue doing it. While I was disappointed that I wasn't re-assigned, I didn't complain. I was given my orders, and that was that.

As I mentioned earlier, there were people who showed up at the firehouse because they didn't know where else to go. I told them to go to the kitchen at the back of the firehouse. Many people listened, which was great since I figured they were now in a safe place, and they weren't in the way while the EMTs and I were trying to treat the injured. I used those who stayed in front of the firehouse as my eyes to the outside. At one point, my "eyes" started screaming, "They're jumping!" At first, I started making my way to the front of the firehouse to see what they were talking about. Then I realized they meant people were jumping out of the windows from the higher floors of the 110-story Towers since leaping to their deaths seemed to be the better option than burning from the tremendous heat from the flames they were facing. I stopped myself from getting any closer. I knew I didn't need to see what was happening outside, and I couldn't help any of these people when they landed on the concrete sidewalk below. Having those images in my head for the rest of my life was something I just didn't need.

Shortly after, the search team the captain assembled headed across the street to the Towers. I remember watching those eight guys leave the firehouse, still thinking that I wished I were going with them. About 5 minutes later, my "eyes" started screaming again, but this time, they also came running inside the firehouse. "It's coming down!" I asked them, "What's coming down? The plane?" They frantically shouted back, "No, the building!" Immediately, everyone in the firehouse started running to the back of the firehouse towards the kitchen. As Smith was passing Fu, Smith dragged Fu further into the firehouse while Fu maintained his vice-like grip on his briefcase. After several seconds of the loudest sound anyone could ever try to imagine, we were wrapped in complete darkness and silence, suffocating from the grey dust cloud that used to be the South Tower. We were trapped in the firehouse, and the entire search team that I so wanted to be on was dead.

I quickly realized I was being crushed in the panic-filled firehouse. I was caught between those in the kitchen and the injured in front of me and my "eyes" behind me. I couldn't understand why people weren't going out the door in the rear of the firehouse. In the complete darkness, while I was still holding my breath so I wouldn't breathe in the dust-filled air, I first pushed those behind me off my back. I couldn't hold my breath any longer. I gulped in the dry dust which coated the inside of my mouth and throat and filled my lungs. It was so difficult to breathe with all that dust clogging my respiratory system I started gagging and dry heaving. I wished I could have puked just so it would have given my mouth and throat some form of moisture. Once I was no longer literally being crushed, I started moving those in front of me out of my way. Fortunately, I had enough time in the firehouse before the collapse to create a map in my head. As I worked my way forward, getting past the people in front of me, my right hand was on the right wall of the hallway leading to the back of the firehouse. I had a pretty good idea where I was since I found my telephone alcove and TV room landmarks. When I made it to the doorway at the end of the hallway, I tried to push the door forward to gain access to the street behind the firehouse. I couldn't understand why the door wouldn't open. Then, like muscle memory, my training kicked in and I felt around the sides of the doorway. Hinges! The hinges that I felt told me that the door didn't open away from me as I had expected it to do. The door needed to be pulled towards me to open it. A storm door was placed in front of an emergency exit door in a firehouse, of all places! Problem solved, right? Well, not exactly. There was so much debris on the other side of the door that I couldn't open it at first. After slamming my shoulder into it a few times, I was finally able to open it.

Afterwards, Gordon attempted to check the truck room for survivors. This was challenging since it wasn't only filled with debris from the Towers but there was also a jet engine from one of the planes that crushed their ambulance. Gordon was able to find the radio in the ambulance and transmitted a "mayday." That is a radio transmission announcing to everyone listening to that channel that there are firefighters in a life-threatening situation who need assistance immediately.

Looking back, I remember specifying to Smith and Gordon which bay they should use to park their rig. Who would ever think that the seemingly meaningless decision as to which bay to use would turn out to be such an important one? After all, the ambulance was used to save lives. It just wasn't how we intended to use it!

When I looked through the doorway into the street it was quite an eerie scene. The thick grey dust was still hovering in the air. It reminded me of the scene in the movie "Titanic" when the submersible approached the sunken ship. All I could see was grey, and as I walked a few feet down the street, I could see the outline of a motorcycle parked behind the firehouse. As I got closer to it, I could see it more clearly.

I could make out the silhouettes of a group of police officers in the distance. I called them over to help us evacuate those who needed assistance from the firehouse. The victims included civilians as well as firefighters. Then, gratefully, on the other side of the blown-out kitchen window, the guys from Ladder Company 124 appeared. We started passing the injured through the gaping hole to those guys, too, so we could evacuate as many victims as we could as fast as possible.

With the firehouse nearly empty, Smith, Gordon, the remaining victims, and I heard another set of rumbles filling the air. Here we go again. It was the North Tower's turn to collapse. It was the North Tower's turn to get us. The sound and wind were, like with the South Tower, insanely intense. Only this time, we weren't starting out with a clean set of lungs. Gordon and Smith were able to make it to the bathroom to protect themselves from the next violent dust storm and pray. We all thought there was no way we were going to be lucky enough to survive the second collapse, too. Gordon told Smith how much he enjoyed working with him while Smith tried to keep Gordon's spirits positive. I just kept thinking to myself, "Keep working until you drop." Amazingly, we all made it, including Fu. I'm sure heaven is our destiny since hell just sent us back!

I later heard estimates that the wind where we were was about 140 mph. I don't doubt it at all. I was blown off my feet and hit the cinderblock wall in the back of the truck room. Smith was also sent flying to the back of the truck room. Gordon was also blown off his feet, thrown to the ground, and had several people land on top of him. The intense wind even blew out the window in the kitchen. While I was pretty banged up with cuts and bruises, Smith suffered a cut to his head and a concussion, and Gordon sprained his shoulder and ankle. In front of the firehouse, body parts and pulverized concrete covered the street, and cars were flipped over on their sides like a child got tired of playing with them.

The structural integrity of the firehouse was severely compromised. The possibility that the firehouse was going to collapse was a real concern. Captain Eugene Kelty, Engine Company 10, who made it back to the firehouse, ordered everyone out of it. After Smith, Gordon, and Captain Kelty climbed through the opening that had once been the kitchen window, they were astonished to see Fu and me. Captain Kelty broke off from us to work with his men while Smith, Gordon, and I focused on getting Fu the medical attention he needed.

Just moving Fu was a challenge. We didn't have any equipment to carry him, so we had to go "old school". Like an injured football player being carried off the field by his teammates, Smith and Gordon got Fu upright off the ground and placed themselves underneath each of his shoulders while Fu wrapped his arms around their necks and maintained his grip on his briefcase. I followed behind them, carrying a first-aid bag from the ambulance and Smith's backpack with some of his personal items. As we walked away from 10 House, we rotated our positions, taking turns carrying Fu and his briefcase. After getting hit in the head numerous times with the briefcase, we stopped for a moment and begged him to leave it behind. He told us that he couldn't, so we asked him what was in there that was so important. He told us that he was at the Trade Center picking up a loan for his business. When he told us he had $1,000,000 in there, we just looked at each other, stunned. Then we all agreed, his briefcase was coming with us!

We walked a few blocks and found ourselves at 2 Rector Street. It was an office building with a clean lobby and fresh air. Inside its offices, it was business as usual. Having heard about the attack on the Pentagon, Smith and Gordon decided to evacuate this building.

I found a landline and called my mother to tell her that I was alive. I told her I couldn't stay on the phone very long since I still had a lot of work to do. I then waited in the lobby with Fu while Smith and Gordon went floor by floor, instructing everyone to meet me in the lobby. I will never forget seeing people's reactions when they looked outside the lobby's windows and saw Broadway blanketed with several inches of the Towers' powdered concrete. They were obviously clueless about the nearby death and destruction. After everyone assembled in the lobby, Smith stood on top of the security desk, telling everyone that we were going to help them get home. Our plan was to walk single file south on Broadway to the Staten Island Ferry, near Battery Park, where city buses were being staged to evacuate Lower Manhattan. I will never forget when one of the women in the lobby came up to me before we left the building. She told me that she needed to be in Brooklyn the following day. I told her that if she didn't work with us today, she didn't have to worry about tomorrow. It was at that moment that she started to realize how serious things were outside.

As everyone got ready to make their way downtown, I asked if anyone was pregnant or had any other issues that we needed to know about. Three women told me they were pregnant, so I had them stay with me in the front of the line. I was concerned that what they were about to see outside could be stressful to them and send them into premature labor. I told them that they needed to tell me immediately if they started having any issues.

We were on our way. About 90 of us headed down Broadway. As we made our way to the buses, people saw me leading our line and carrying emergency gear. Some came up to me and asked me what they should do or where they should go. I told them they could come with me, and they would get out of the city, or they could be on their own, and I had no idea what would happen to them. They all decided to join our line. As we made our way further downtown, I saw a McDonald's. I stopped our line and told them that I would be right back. I entered the McDonald's and announced that Lower Manhattan was now closed, and everyone needed to come with me. The size of our line continued to grow. When we arrived at the buses, a police officer came up to me and asked me what I had. I told him I had about 125 people who were ready to leave Manhattan. They just needed buses. The police officer waived over a line of buses, and my line quickly boarded them. When the end of the line had boarded the bus, I was beyond surprised. Smith, Gordon, and Fu weren't there. I immediately wondered where they were and what happened to them. I backtracked my way back to 2 Rector Street, hoping to find them resting somewhere along the way. I couldn't find them anywhere. Worse than that, I was alone.

I found out later that Smith and Gordon placed Fu into a police car that was damaged from the collapses and was brought to a hospital. Afterwards, Smith and Gordon were able to get a ride to 100 Wall Street and then a police boat took them across the East River to the Brooklyn Navy Yard. They then made their way back to Battalion 31. Smith's plan was to drive to a hospital on Long Island so he could be treated for his concussion and Gordon could be treated for his shoulder. The problem with this plan was I had his car keys. Therefore, brothers from their station brought them to Kings County Medical Center. Sadly, Smith would soon find out that his father, a member of FDNY's Haz-Mat Company 1, was killed in the North Tower's collapse.

As I made my way back to the ferry terminal, I met a group of fire marshals. They saw the gear I was carrying and asked me where I was coming from. I mentioned 10 House, and they were like, "Wow, that place got hit pretty hard!" I then told them how I couldn't find my guys and asked if I could join their group so I wouldn't be alone. Of course, they allowed me to join them, and we made our way to Battery Park to set up a command post. This seemed like the perfect place to do so. It was close enough to Ground Zero to operate, but it was also far enough away from there to get some "fresher" air. The reality was there wasn't any "fresh" air. The dust and acrid smell of smoke was still in the air and would be for weeks. The area was also very open and spacious. This seemed nice since we really didn't want to be very close to tall buildings.

When we got to Battery Park, I saw a small building that was a restaurant serving lunch. I thought to myself that I found more people completely oblivious to what happened not so far away. I tried several doors to enter it. They were all locked as I made my way around the glass walls until I found the main entrance. I walked through the restaurant looking for the restroom since I desperately needed to flush my burning eyes with clean water. People were looking at me coated in dust as I walked through the dining room. I entered a restroom and made my way to the sink. The cold water on my face felt amazing. I could feel relief in my eyes immediately. As I was washing my face as best I could, a livid waitress stopped me. She felt the need to ask me if I knew that I was in the ladies' room. While I honestly had no idea, I felt the need to tell her that I really didn't care. I probably could have handled that interaction better!

I was getting some rest and listened to the fire marshals asking each other why they thought the attacks took place on that day. They explored different theories. Was that day an important day in history? It didn't seem to be. Then they pondered about the date itself. September 11? 9/11? Maybe that was it. 9/11 could be seen as 911, the emergency number so many people would be calling as their plan unfolded.

As the discussion continued, the next frightening part of that day was about to start. We started hearing the roar of more planes.

However, the planes we saw that were quickly approaching from the south weren't commercial airliners. They were fighter jets! We all believed this was the next wave of the attack. There was no place for us to hide. We instinctively put our arms up in front of us to protect ourselves from the soon-to-be incoming rockets and bullets. We realized that wasn't going to do a thing. We just looked at each other and braced for the worst. When the lead plane was nearly on top of us, it turned to its right, heading east. I will never forget seeing the star on the side of the plane. These were our planes! I will never forget how low and close those planes were. I could clearly see the pilot's white helmet. They were securing the airspace around New York City. Later that afternoon, they were supported by Blackhawk helicopters and Apache gunships.

In the afternoon, the fire marshals decided to walk the perimeter of Ground Zero, so we headed back to where the Towers once stood. After walking along the east side of "the pile", we walked along the north side of it. As we headed south along the west side of it, a huge crowd came running towards us. We were clueless as to what was happening. Then we heard people screaming that Tower 7 was coming down. We just looked at each other and kept walking south. We were wondering what everyone was so worried about. After all, Tower 7 was only about 50 stories. That is the kind of day we were having.

By now, it was about 4 pm. I was exhausted and needed to start thinking about myself. What was I going to do, and where could I go? I called my buddy, Frank Verderosa. We have been friends since the 5th grade. He lived in New Jersey but had his own sound-recording company in Manhattan. I called him to see if he was at his studio. I was hoping he was there so I could come by and get some sleep since the trains to Long Island had been shut down. He told me that he was home since he was watching from his balcony what had transpired earlier that day. But there was some hope. He told me that I could stay at his place. I just needed to find a way to make it across the Hudson River to New Jersey. So, it was back to Battery Park and the docks by the Staten Island Ferry.

When I got to the docks, I met a fishing boat captain. He could tell I was a tired, beaten-up responder who could use some help. He asked me where I needed to go, and I replied, "New Jersey." He told me that wasn't a problem, so I dropped the gear I had been carrying all day onto the deck of his boat. I then lowered myself down the high seawall to his boat, too. When we made it to New Jersey, we arrived at a pier that was much higher than the one in Manhattan. I threw the gear up onto the pier and started looking for a way to climb it. Fortunately, there were at least 100 police officers there who were being reassigned from New Jersey to Manhattan. They were waiting for a boat to take them across the Hudson. When I reached up the cement wall, two officers on each of my arms lifted me up onto the pier. I asked them where I was, and they told me I was in Jersey City. While I did make it to New Jersey, which was good, it meant that I had another problem. I needed to get to Hoboken!

I reached for my cell phone to call Frank so I could let him know where I was. That was when I realized I needed to add another problem to my list of problems. My battery was dead. My face made it clear that I was having an issue, so a concerned man asked me what the problem was. He was eager to provide whatever assistance he could. I told him that my cell phone was dead, and I needed to make a call. He generously offered me his phone. But that only identified another problem. I never memorized my friend's New Jersey number. He was always speeding dial "7" on my phone. If I used it now, I would have had no idea who I was calling. I begged my new friend to ask if I could make two phone calls. One to my wife to get the needed number and the second to Frank so I could tell him where I was. He laughed and said I could surely make whatever calls I needed to make. Progress, right? Not exactly. I had nothing to write with. The next thing I knew, a woman who was watching everything that was happening with me dumped her pocketbook on the sidewalk, found an eye liner, and offered it to me. I called Kathy, got Frank's number, which I wrote on my arm, and called Frank to tell him the intersection where I was. Now I just had to wait for him to find me. By the way, it turned out that the nice man who shared his cell phone with me was the mayor of Jersey City!

While I was solving my problems, Frank's problems were just starting. He was pretty new to Hoboken and totally lost when it came to Jersey City. As he came across police officers at various locations on his way to me, he would ask them for directions. They were just as lost since everyone was being reassigned to cover unfamiliar areas so those closest to New York City could respond there. Around 7 pm that evening, Frank found me exactly where I said I would be waiting for him. He took one look at me and was able to formulate some sort of idea as to what I had been through.

When we got to Frank's apartment, the first thing we did was place a black sheet over his couch so we could keep his furniture as clean as possible. Next, we ordered pizza and chicken parmigiana heroes. I was absolutely famished since I hadn't eaten since the night before. Typically, I don't have cheese on my sandwiches since I watch my calories, but on that day, I ordered my hero with extra cheese. When I got off the couch to pick up our food, Frank just looked at the couch and then at me. I could tell something was off. He showed me the ghostly image I left on his black sheet. It was easy to see where my arms, legs, and back were resting. I have to admit, it was more than spooky.

Frank and I made our way to the shop where we were picking up our order. I took my wallet out of the back pocket of my jeans and opened it. Frank and I looked at each other dumbfounded. Between the bills that resided securely in my wallet was more dust from the Towers. The dust storm that I managed to survive was so intense, the dust not only sandblasted me it also made its way through the denim pocket of my jeans, inside my leather wallet, and between each of the bills inside it. Frank and I were blown away, no pun intended. By the way, Frank picked up the tab!

While Frank and I ate, I filled him in on what my day had been like. The adrenaline that I had been running on wore off, and it was replaced with exhaustion. I was ready for some sleep. I shouldn't have planned on sleeping through the night. Just after midnight, someone was banging loudly on the door. I was out of it and didn't know what I was hearing or where it was coming from. Then I heard it again. I went to the door and asked who it was before opening it. It was the FBI, so I opened it. They asked me if this was my apartment. It told them it was my friend's apartment. It was pretty easy for them to believe what I was telling them when they saw my clothes and the gear by the door. They asked if they could speak with Frank. I knocked on his bedroom door to wake him up, and he asked me if I was ok. I told him I was fine, but the FBI was here, and they wanted to speak with him. At first, he probably thought I was joking, but when you consider what the day had been like, we should almost have expected it. As it turned out, people were seen on the roof of his building watching the attacks on New York City and cheering. Therefore, the FBI was canvassing the building to obtain any relevant information that could identify who those people were. They knocked on doors and determined who owned the cars in the parking lot. I believe they confiscated at least one car. Then it was back to bed!

My next morning started pretty late. After all, I was exhausted from the previous day and where was I going? Public transportation had been shut down. I was sitting on Frank's couch in his living room, where we were having a conversation. While we were talking, a construction crew was clearing a nearby lot. Their heavy equipment dropped debris into an empty metal dumpster, and the echo filled the air. In mid-sentence, I jumped, and Frank almost had to scrape me off his ceiling. Immediately, he asked me in a joking manner if I was feeling a bit jumpy. Already knowing the answer, I asked him if he saw that. He replied, "How could I not?" We both laughed it off, but inside, I thought this wasn't good. I knew things weren't right with me. This was the first time I recognized and acknowledged that I had PTSD.

That afternoon, the PATH train connecting New Jersey to Manhattan had re-opened, and the Long Island Railroad was running from Penn Station back home. I didn't know if this was a temporary opportunity or not, so I had to give it a shot. Frank drove me to the train station and wished me luck. I had no idea how I looked to everyone else, but it soon became very clear.

I stood in the middle of a crowded train car as I rode the PATH train from New Jersey back to Manhattan. I was wearing my clothes from the day before, still covered in the World Trade Center's grey dust and Brian Smith's personal backpack. One hand was holding onto a strap while some of the emergency gear salvaged from the ambulance that was demolished the previous day was set on the floor between my feet. It was pretty easy to look at me and figure out my situation. The seats that ran along both sides of the car were filled. In the seats next to where I was standing were two elderly women. I would guess they were in their late seventies or early eighties. They both got up and told me to take their seats. I thanked them but refused their offer. I told them that I was ok, but then they demanded that I sit down. I must have looked awful for these two elderly women to give up their seats to someone half their age.

The public's generosity didn't end there. After making it back to Manhattan, I transferred to the Long Island Rail Road. I sat by myself in an aisle seat. Across from me in the same row was a husband and wife who were also heading home. They each had a personal pizza and were about to enjoy their dinner together during their commute home. What happened next completely surprised me. The wife turned to me and offered me her dinner. Again, I refused, but she and her husband insisted that I take it. The outpouring of support complete strangers showed me the day before and that day shocked me. Then, it started to make sense. Everyone wanted to help during this dark time, and those who couldn't help just wanted to say thank you.

Kathy picked me up from the train on Long Island. However, it wasn't my usual stop. Her cousin's mother-in-law passed away, so she picked me up in Nassau County so we could pay our respects. When we arrived at the funeral home, I decided to wait in the car since I wasn't dressed properly and what I was wearing was still covered in dust. She told me not to worry about how I looked since everyone wanted to see me. I entered the room where the wake was taking place, and suddenly, all the attention was on me. This was the last thing I wanted. I just wanted to express my condolences, talk for a bit, and leave. So many people came up to me instead of visiting with the grieving family. I will never forget the hug Kathy's father gave me. That was a very special moment for me since I can't remember seeing him hug anyone.

When I finally got home that night, I was already aware of how the thought of being in the dark truly horrified me. Darkness brought me back to being trapped in the firehouse, not being able to see or breathe. Each night, the sun set, the darkness returned, and my anxiety continued to increase until the sun rose the following morning. Exhaustion granted me short bursts of relief during the day, but the nightmares wouldn't allow me to sleep for very long.

My midnight hours were spent alone in my den while Kathy slept upstairs. I sat on the couch with most of the lights on throughout my house since sleeping at night wasn't an option. Hour after hour, I watched CNN and other news broadcasts, trying to find the latest developments relating to how and why my country was attacked and what and when would be my country's response to those who did this. Those hours were spent thinking some of my friends were either dead or missing, and I needed to find some way to get involved with the rescue effort that was happening at Ground Zero.

On Thursday, September 14, I called my firehouse for the first time. When the dispatcher answered the phone, I heard my friend Tommy Cornell's voice on the line. I told him it was me calling and before I could get another word in, I heard him screaming, "I got Weisberg on the phone!" It turned out that I was the last guy on our department's missing list. Then I asked him the question I really wasn't ready to hear the answer to. I said to him, "Tommy, how bad is it?" I needed to know who survived and who didn't. We had so many guys who were also members of FDNY and NYPD. I braced myself for what I was about to hear. I couldn't believe his response. Everyone made it. I was the only guy who was a question mark. I was overcome with relief. I'm not afraid to share that my relief made me cry.

Later that day, I went to my firehouse and saw my brothers for the first time. Everything I went through the last two days was hitting me pretty hard, physically and mentally. I saw some of the guys and just started crying. They could easily see I was in bad shape. From a clinical perspective, I was a mess. After some of the guys calmed me down a bit, Chief John Engberg brought me to Huntington Hospital. This was my first visit with a mental health counselor. We spoke for a while, and then I went home.

I returned to Huntington Hospital's emergency room on Saturday, September 15. This time, I was having trouble breathing. While I was sitting in the waiting room waiting to be seen, a little boy about four years old was also there. He was keeping himself busy with his coloring book and crayons. We talked for a bit as he created his masterpiece. When he was done, he gave it to me. I still have it. It was nice being appreciated, especially by someone so innocent.

My friends were genuinely concerned about me. One friend was Al Groveman. He was a local school district's superintendent. We went through our training together as probationary firefighters. By September 11, 2001, Al was a captain. He invited me to lunch with his very understanding wife, Lynne. I got a Coke when I ordered my lunch since I don't drink alcohol. When I was finished speaking to the waitress, Al gave me this look and reminded me that I was almost killed. He then ordered me to get a beer. He told me that having just one would help me relax. Since I couldn't ignore a direct order, I had a beer.

Please allow me a moment to share some funny stories about Al to lighten the mood of this chapter. They may also clarify why I refer to Lynne as "understanding." I think you will agree.

The first story is more of a life-lesson than a story. Al taught me, "It is easier to ask for forgiveness than permission." Fascinating! I applied this lesson a few times in my marriage since it sounded simple enough. So far, the results have been mixed. I still haven't figured out what I'm doing wrong. While I may not recommend this approach to every part of one's life, feel free to blame Al for the consequences. I have!

The other story is when Al, Lynne, Kathy, and I were at an annual awards dinner for the Commack Volunteer Ambulance Corps, where Al and I volunteered. During the dinner, Al intentionally said something that really upset Lynne. I heard it, too, and just looked at him in amazement. I couldn't believe what he said. Al could tell from my face exactly what was going through my mind, "Al, what were you thinking?" He then explained to me that even if he didn't make that particular comment, he surely would have said something else unintentionally that would have upset her. He figured it was better to get her being angry at him behind them sooner than later so they could both enjoy the rest of the evening. All these years later, I still haven't tried this strategy with Kathy. Al is so much braver than I am!

Shortly after my first hospital visit, my dear friend Rebecca "Becky" Fishman, who was a therapist, reached out to me. She knew I was having a tough time and offered her assistance. I had known her most of my life and was very comfortable with the idea of seeing her professionally. I saw her for the next six weeks. Besides just helping me to verbalize what I went through and how I was feeling, she used a technique called Eye Movement Desensitization and Reprocessing (EMDR) therapy. During this therapy, Becky instructed me to move my eyes back and forth quickly. These movements mimicked how my eyes would move if I were in REM sleep. Basically, this therapy allowed me to dream while I was still awake, and together, we would process my nightmares. I found this therapeutic technique helpful, and I recommend it highly. I can never fully express my gratitude to her for all of the love and support she showed me.

I had never seen a therapist before, so I didn't know what to expect. I didn't know how long I was supposed to see her or how to tell if I had actually made it to the finish line. Looking back, what goes through my mind is, "Dude, what were you thinking? There is no way you were better!"

My co-workers and I didn't go to work for a few weeks since the building we worked in was severely damaged. Windows were shattered, and our office was contaminated with asbestos. Our company's senior management team realized how important it was for everyone to get together in person, so they arranged a company-wide meeting. They also understood how important it was to hold the meeting on one of the lower floors of a building. Our office was located on the 40th and 41st floors and being that high up wasn't appealing to many of us since the ability to evacuate any building quickly was on everybody's mind. We met on the second floor of a building where the company's president gave a reassuring speech. While it was comforting to hear that everyone from our work family survived, it was difficult hearing that a former employee, who was also a dear friend of mine, was killed. A plan was laid out for getting the company running again and everyone back to work. My responsibilities were deemed critical, so I was part of the skeleton crew supporting the company until a longer-term, temporary location could be secured, and we would all be working together again. As it turned out, it was almost a year before we returned to our office.

My teammates and I reported to our sister company's office in Westchester County, just north of New York City. The commute itself was arduous since a significant portion of the city's displaced workforce was being reassigned to the same area. One day, the traffic to get off Long Island was so horrible that I called my manager to apologize. Even though I had just spent 5 hours trying to get to work, I was barely half-way there. He praised my effort and told me to turn around and go home. Shortly after that, the company provided me with a hotel room near the office.

The idea of being in a hotel for the week was appealing since I would have a much shorter commute during the week. However, I soon realized that being left alone in a hotel room, away from home and my wife, was the worst place I could possibly be. I was working during the day and not sleeping at night. When I needed to take a break from watching the news, I would find a movie on HBO. One night, I ended up watching "Saving Private Ryan". While this is a fantastic movie, there couldn't have been a worse choice considering my recent experience in a war zone.

I previously mentioned my "work family." That accurately describes my office's environment. We were a very close team. I'm still honored to have been associated with this exceptional group. We knew each other's "home families" since there were so many opportunities to interact outside of the office. We knew each other's spouses and watched the kids grow over the years. My friend, Stacey Simonelli, was offered the opportunity to stay in the same hotel as me, but she had a much better offer. She stayed with her sister Sally's family in a nearby town in Connecticut. I was friends with Sally and her daughter, Alexandra, and they all invited me to stay with them. I don't know how to express in words how much I appreciated the love they showed me, especially when I was getting the earliest glimpses into how my life was changing.

One night at Sally's home, Stacey was telling me about how she and her other sister, Suzy, who I was also friends with, were volunteering at Ground Zero. They were part of a team preparing food at one of the restaurants located downtown for the rescue workers. She gave me the details about how to get involved. I was in!

I got a spot on the team Stacey told me about. I worked the overnight shift from Friday night to Saturday morning for several weeks. This made for long days since I was still taking care of my responsibilities as the company's controller. Around the time Thanksgiving came around, those overseeing the operations at Ground Zero decided it was time to cut back on the number of volunteers supporting the rescue and recovery effort. I was informed that the team I was on was no longer needed. During my last shift, I needed some supplies, so I went to the Red Cross team that I became friendly with. After they gave me what I needed, I thanked them, and they gave me a cheery "See you soon." I told them that, to my disappointment, this would be my last night at Ground Zero. I informed them that my team was one of the teams being cut, but I still wanted to work. They told me not to worry about anything. They were impressed by how hard I worked and made me a member of their team.

Around the same time I started working with my new team at Ground Zero, my office relocated again. We returned downtown, just a few blocks away from our contaminated headquarters. We took up residence in the historic Woolworth Building at 233 Broadway. Ironically, this was the tallest building in the world back in the early 1900's. Gratefully, we were on the second floor. Returning to the old neighborhood meant I would be trying to sleep in my own bed. Being in familiar surroundings and my own bed may not seem like much during typical times, but for me, these were small steps back to normalcy.

During the next several months, my physical issues continued to present themselves. I developed asthma and GERD, which is a horrible form of acid reflux. It gave me some insight as to what it would be like to be a fire-breathing dragon. Additionally, breathing through my nose became nearly impossible. I met with an ear, nose, and throat specialist. The doctor planned on inserting a camera up my nose to look at my damaged sinuses. However, my sinuses were so swollen that we needed to postpone the procedure. After a week of taking an anti-inflammatory to reduce the swelling, the doctor could see a thick layer of scar tissue that was preventing air from flowing from my nose down to my lungs. To correct this, while I was awake, the doctor used electrified wires to burn holes through the scar tissue. I will never forget the smell of my own burning flesh.

My first holiday season after September 11 was approaching. One Saturday morning, after finishing my shift at Ground Zero, I went to the local CVS to purchase Christmas lights and other decorations and returned to the office. I strung the lights around the windows and strategically placed the other ornaments around the office. I was hoping that my co-workers would appreciate my attempt at another step towards normalcy. The attacks took place just over three months before, and it was still easy to smell the destruction and see the pain and sorrow in my friends' eyes, even if we weren't talking about it. I just wanted to make everyone smile, even if it lasted for just a moment.

Christmas Eve at Ground Zero was special. I was assigned to a crew charged with getting St. Paul's Chapel ready for Midnight Mass. There were three services that night. The first two were crowded, but the mass at midnight was packed. Every seat was taken, and the front pews were filled with city and state dignitaries.

I was debating with myself whether to include the following story or not. I decided to do so since it provides a glimpse of what things were like down there, even on Christmas Eve.

Christmas Eve dinner was special. We were about to share this special meal as members of a new family. Everyone was working so hard, either on the pile or doing some type of support function. The work was depressing and gruesome, but it was extremely important. So many families wanted and needed closure. It was the least we could give them, considering what they were going through and continue to go through today. When the workers (firefighters, police officers, tradesmen) were ready to eat, they would enter St. Paul's Chapel and join the food line. Another firefighter and I were standing in line next to each other, waiting to make our plates. We had never met before, but we just started talking. That is just how the brotherhood is. We got our food and started looking for a place to sit so we could enjoy our holiday meal. But then he stopped, changed direction, and dumped his plate into a nearby garbage can. I was stunned. I didn't understand what just happened. I asked him why he did that, and he pointed at his boots. There were human remains clinging to them. His Christmas Eve meal was over before he even had the chance to take his first bite.

I continued working at Ground Zero while the air continued to blanket Lower Manhattan with its distinctive, acrid stench. In February 2002, my life started to go into a tailspin. Being near Ground Zero every day when I went to my office and working my weekly shift supporting the recovery effort was taking its toll on my mental health. The worst case of burnout imaginable was setting in. I was quickly becoming someone others, including Kathy, would easily find difficult to be around. I needed to get away from everything. This included every aspect of my life. Getting away didn't mean staying at home and isolating myself. I needed new surroundings. I needed to get away from the sights and smells that were significant components of my life 6 days a week. I needed to totally clear my mind. I remember my parents telling me about how much they enjoyed their eco-tourism trip to Costa Rica a few years prior and about how much I would have loved it. I called their tour group and asked if there was any space available on their next trip.

While I had their representative on the phone, I asked Kathy if she wanted to go with me. She told me she couldn't give me a decision since she would need to check with her manager. I told her I needed an answer immediately so she told me she couldn't go. I then told the tour representative that I would take one of the remaining spots and I left for Costa Rica shortly after. I honestly didn't know if she would be waiting for me when I got home.

My parents never told me that their trip to Costa Rica was with a tour group that was geared towards retirees, so I obviously didn't fit the demographics this tour operator focused on. I celebrated my 34th birthday with my tour mates and was easily the youngest person in our group by 30 years. Everyone in our group was curious why someone my age wouldn't want to go on a vacation with others who were closer in age to me. When the question was finally asked, I explained what I went through on September 11 and after that day. I told them about the burnout I was experiencing and how I needed to take some time for myself. Everyone was so supportive in helping me acquire the temporary peace I was seeking before heading back to Ground Zero.

I have always said age is just a number. It shouldn't dictate how someone is supposed to behave. You can ask my kids. They are always asking me, "When are you going to grow up?" My travel buddies exemplified what young-at-heart meant. We enjoyed daily programs, which included hiking, white-water rafting, horseback riding, and zip-lining in the Costa Rican rainforests. I was so proud of them. Nobody ever said they wouldn't try any of these activities. Not once! Seeing my friends in their 80s wearing their safety helmets and harnesses as they prepared for their zip-lining adventure was exciting. Hearing them screaming and laughing as they crossed the rainforest's canopy from platform to platform while suspended from a pulley and thin cable was absolutely inspiring. I wish the world could have seen them. Not only was my group adventurous, but each night, one of my tourmates put together a slide presentation using the pictures she took with her digital camera. As it turned out, she recreated herself in her retirement. She started a business creating websites. This may not seem like a big deal today, but in 2002, this was new to many of us. We were fascinated!

My second favorite part of my tour was when we stayed at a ranch. After my friends and I came back to the corral after some horseback riding, one of the wranglers asked me if I saw the waterfalls. I told him that I didn't. Before I knew it, we had two fresh horses and headed back out. The waterfalls were spectacular. My favorite part of my trip, however, was seeing my wife still there waiting for me.

I have to share a situation that caught me off guard one morning at Ground Zero. I was exhausted after working all day at my office the day before and then working my shift overnight, supporting the recovery effort. Cots were available in St. Paul's Chapel to get some rest, so I decided to take a nap before driving over an hour home. When I woke up a few hours later, I tried standing up, but it was extremely difficult since my back had tightened up. Some nurses saw my eyes almost fall out of my head, so they came over to provide their assistance. They helped me get to a massage table and get my shirt off so one of the masseuses could try to help me not resemble a pretzel. While I was lying face down on the massage table that was next to the chapel's altar, I heard the sound of chimes. They indicated mass was starting, and there I was, shirtless, getting a massage, next to the altar. I told the masseuse I appreciated what they were trying to do for me, but I felt very weird and needed to leave!

At the end of May 2002, the recovery effort came to an end. It was time to say goodbye to those who I worked with for so many months, doing whatever needed to be done to support the effort. Before we all went back to our previous lives, we shared one last, very special moment together. A barbeque was held at St. Paul's Chapel. Our families were welcome, which was so important. It provided them with a chance to put faces with the names they often heard when we shared stories about those who we were working with. There were too many of us to fit inside the sanctuary, so it was held in the cemetery behind the chapel. It seemed strange, but at the same time fitting, since we just spent so much time around death.

In July 2002, the World Trade Center Health Registry was created to track the health of those exposed to the 9/11 toxins. Then, on December 30, 2005, the World Trade Center Medical Monitoring and Treatment Program was created.[1] The mission of its compassionate staff is to provide those who were impacted by the attacks in New York City, Washington, D.C., and Shanksville, PA, with medical monitoring and treatment free-of-charge. I registered for the program and go for my medical monitoring annually. I encourage everyone who was in any of these locations to register for this program. While I can only speak to the New York City location, I know a lot of great people who succumbed to some of the over 300 possible cancers that can be directly linked to that lethal environment.[2] The early detection of these diseases will at least give the participant a chance to spend more time with their loved ones.

One story that I need to share took place about a year after September 11. I was back in my office on Cortlandt Street, and my friend, Laureen Yang, knocked on my door. She is Chinese and was

---

[1]https://www.cdc.gov/wtc/history.html#:~:text=July%202002%20The%20WTC%20Health,and%20Disease%20Registry%20

https://journals.lww.com/oncology-times/Fulltext/2020/01200/Cancers_Related_to_9_11_in_Responders___Survivors.2.aspx holding a copy of a New York City-based Chinese newspaper. She asked me if I was looking for a man named Fu. Her question shocked me. I couldn't say yes fast enough. She told me that there was an article in her newspaper about him and he mentioned that he was looking for me! I asked Laureen to come sit down in my office. I closed the door, and we searched for the newspaper's phone number on the internet. Once we found it, we called the newspaper and asked to speak to the reporter who wrote the article. After we were transferred to her desk, Laureen told the reporter that she had seen her article and knew Fu was looking for me. Then she told the reporter that I was looking for him as well. What transpired was magical. The reporter set up a surprise reunion at the Wading River Volunteer Fire Department, where Brian Smith was a member. Besides the reporter and her cameraman, the only people who knew about the reunion were Fu's wife Fei, Brian's wife Karen, Brian Gordon, and me. Unfortunately, Brian Gordon wasn't able to make it. When Brian and Karen arrived, Brian was kept in a secluded room and was told he couldn't come out until Karen said he could. Fu, Fei, their 13-year-old daughter Danni, and I arrived at the same time, so part of the reunion started early in the parking lot. Fu recognized me immediately. As he limped towards me using a cane, I walked to him, and we hugged. It was a very emotional moment for us. The four of us then proceeded into the firehouse, where we saw Karen, the reporter, and her cameraman. Once the reporter and her cameraman were ready, Karen brought Brian into the room, and the tears started flowing. I will never forget what Fei said to me. She told me that if I decided to leave Fu behind, she would have understood. The only thing that I could think of when I saw the three of them standing there as a complete family was everything Smith, Gordon, and I went through together was worth it. So many families were missing a loved one. We made a difference that day!

I still keep in touch with Fu and his family. They came to my home for family parties and attended my father's funeral in 2012. There is a photo that I kept on my desk at work which includes Fu, Fei, Danni, my mother, father, and sister, Kathy, and me. People who saw it for the first time would ask me who everyone was. I would simply tell them it was a picture of my family.

Fu with his wife, Fei, and daughter, Danni, my parents, Larry and Lynne, my sister, Stephanie, my wife, Kathy, and me.

CHAPTER 3
What is PTSD?

"First responder" is a broad term for individuals tasked with keeping the public safe in dangerous, high-risk, high-stress environments. These professionals include law enforcement officers, firefighters, emergency medical service providers, and emergency telecommunication operators. They are the first people called for assistance during an emergency. They may engage with the public or directly address some type of dangerous or terrifying event or natural disaster. Unfortunately, these individuals, like our military service members, see, smell, and/or hear things that will haunt them. While our local heroes and heroines may encounter these situations often, the general public will most likely never have such experiences in their entire lifetime.

The impact these emergencies have on the members of the first responder community can be devastating. Their traumatic experiences may negatively impact them immediately or sometime after a specific event. It is also possible that the effects can be felt after the accumulation of numerous events. Each first responder's reaction to the same event is unique to them. Their response to the same event may also be unique.

According to the Mayo Clinic, Post-Traumatic Stress Disorder (PTSD) is a mental condition resulting from a frightening or stressful event. PTSD may present itself immediately or years later, and how it presents itself can fall into four symptomatic categories. These categories include intrusive memories, avoidance, negative changes in thinking and mood, and changes in physical and emotional reactions.

Intrusive memories may include recurrent, unwanted thoughts about the event, flashbacks, nightmares, and severe emotional

distress or physical reactions to something that is a reminder of the event.

Avoidance may include not thinking or talking about the traumatic event. It may also include avoiding places, activities, or people that are reminders of the event and avoiding similar situations.

Negative changes in thinking and mood include a wide spectrum of issues. For example, it may include negative thoughts about oneself, others, and the world's hopelessness about the future. Memory issues, including not remembering important aspects about the traumatic event, difficulty maintaining close relationships, feeling detached from family and friends, lack of interest in activities once enjoyed, difficulty expressing positive emotions, and feeling emotionally numb are other symptoms that may be encountered.

Changes in physical and emotional reactions (also known as arousal symptoms) may include being easily startled or frightened, always being on guard for danger (hypervigilance), self-destructive behavior, such as drinking too much or driving too fast, trouble sleeping or concentrating, irritability, angry outbursts or aggressive behavior, overwhelming guilt, and shame.

PTSD comes with several types of complications. Besides negatively impacting personal relationships, those suffering from PTSD may experience depression and anxiety, which may lead to suicidal thoughts and actions, drug and alcohol abuse, and eating disorders.[3] Others may experience hypnopomic or hypnogogic hallucinations. These are hallucinations that occur in the morning when one is waking up (hypnopomic) or at night when one is falling asleep (hypnagogic).[4]

Numerous studies have been published on suicide. For example, the Surgeon General issued a report called "Call to Action to Implement the National Strategy for Suicide Prevention". It identifies suicide as one of the top 10 causes of death in the United States. The report includes staggering statistics from a 2019 national survey, which notes in the prior year alone, approximately 47,500 people committed suicide, an additional 1.4 million people attempted suicide, 3.5 million people reported making plans to commit suicide, and 12 million adults had serious suicidal thoughts. The report also notes that the national suicide rate increased 32% from 1999 to 2019. During that time period, it went from 10.5 to 13.9 people for every 100,000 people. The report further notes that those impacted by a suicidal crisis, or an actual suicide are far-reaching. Sadly, when a person loses someone to suicide, it may increase their risk for suicidal behaviors. Such behaviors include preparing for, attempting, and committing suicide.[5]

The Substance Abuse and Mental Health Services Administration's "Disaster Technical Assistance Center Supplemental Research Bulletin First Responders: Behavioral Health Concerns, Emergency Response, and Trauma" report issued

---

[3] Mayo Clinic Staff, December 13, 2022, https://www.mayoclinic.org/diseases-conditions/post-traumatic-stress-disorder/symptoms-causes/syc-20355967

[4] https://www.sleepfoundation.org/how-sleep-works/hypnopompic-hallucinations

[5] The Surgeon General's Call to Action to Implement the National Strategy for Suicide Prevention, 2019, https://www.hhs.gov/sites/default/files/sprc-call-to-action.pdf

in May 2018 focuses on mental health and substance abuse in the first responder community. It noted that 30% of first responders experience behavioral health issues such as depression and PTSD, compared to 20% of the general population. It also notes that when it came to suicide, firefighters had higher rates of attempted suicide and suicidal ideation than the general population, and for law enforcement, somewhere between 125 and 300 police officers commit suicide annually.[6]

This may be due to the environments in which first responders work, their culture, and stress, both occupational and personal. Occupational stress in first responders is associated with an increased risk of mental health issues, including hopelessness, anxiety, depression, and post-traumatic stress, as well as suicidal behaviors such as suicidal ideation (thinking about or planning suicide) and attempts.[7] Even during routine shifts, first responders can experience stress due to the uncertainty in each situation. During emergencies, disasters, pandemics, and other crises, stress among first responders can be magnified. Relationship problems have also been linked to a large proportion of suicides among the general population (42%).[8] Because first responders can have challenging

---

[6] SAMHSA Disaster Technical Assistance Center Supplemental Research Bulletin, First Responders: Behavioral Health Concerns, Emergency Response, and Trauma, May 2018, https://www.samhsa.gov/sites/default/files/dtac/supplementalresearchbulleti n-firstresponders-may2018.pdf

[7] SAMHSA. May 2018. Disaster Technical Assistance Center Supplemental Research Bulletin First Responders: Behavioral Health Concerns, Emergency Response, and Trauma.)

[8] Petrosky E, Ertl A, Sheats KJ, Wilson R, Betz CJ, Blair JM. Surveillance for Violent Deaths — National Violent Death Reporting System, 34 States, Four California Counties, the District of Columbia, and Puerto Rico, 2017. MMWR Surveill Summ 2020;69(No. SS-8):1–37

work schedules and extreme family-work demands, stress caused by relationship problems may also be magnified in this worker group.[9]

Law enforcement officers and firefighters are more likely to die by suicide than in the line of duty.[10] Furthermore, EMS providers are 1.39 times more likely to die by suicide than the public.[11] Studies have found that between 17% and 24% of public safety telecommunicators have symptoms of PTSD, and 24% have symptoms of depression[12]. While telecommunicators are often the very first responders engaged with those on the scene, research on their suicide risk and mental health has lagged.[13]

Even given the high number of suicides, these deaths among first responders are likely underreported. The data regarding suicides and mental health issues among these workers is insufficient. Many first responders may consider stress to be 'part of the job' and feel that they can't or shouldn't talk about traumatic events and other occupational stressors. The perceived stigma around mental health problems or concerns over the impact on employment (i.e., being labeled "unfit" for duty) may lead first responders to not report suicidal thoughts. Additionally, occupational data may be incomplete or difficult to capture for first responders, who often have multiple jobs and/or work in a volunteer

---

[9] https://blogs.cdc.gov/niosh-science-blog/2021/04/06/suicides-first-responders/#_ednref4

[10] https://rudermanfoundation.org/white_papers/police-officers-and-firefighters-are-more-likely-to-die-by-suicide-than-in-line-of-duty/

[11] https://www.tandfonline.com/doi/full/10.1080/10903127.2018.1514090

[12] Lilly, MM & Pierce, H. 2013. PTSD and depressive symptoms in 911 telecommunicators: the role of peritraumatic distress and world assumptions in predicting risk. Psychological Trauma: Theory, Research, Practice, and Policy, 5(2):135-41)

[13] https://blogs.cdc.gov/niosh-science-blog/2021/04/06/suicides-first-responders/#_ednref7

capacity. More complete data are needed to identify risk and protective factors and design evidence-based suicide prevention programs for first responders. In addition, prevention programs should reflect the differences among first responder groups and be tailored to each population.[14]

I want to touch briefly upon vicarious trauma. This is where an individual is indirectly exposed to a traumatic event and is then impacted so greatly by what they were exposed to their mental health is negatively impacted. Typically, empathy allows an individual to feel another's feelings, and that is a healthy response. However, it becomes unhealthy when the empathy experienced causes symptoms similar to PTSD. As previously mentioned, this includes feeling guilty, angry, or hopeless, having difficulty managing one's emotions, becoming detached from others or things one used to enjoy, nightmares or difficulty sleeping, and hypervigilance. This is particularly concerning for those like police officers who review crime scene photos, mental health professionals who listen to their clients' traumatic events, and emergency room personnel who interact with those injured by natural disasters or violent acts. One should also realize anyone can suffer from vicarious trauma. For instance, someone seeing a terrible situation on the evening news can also be negatively impacted.[15] It is extremely important for one to remember that they are in a safe place and, except for situations like watching live television, what occurred is in the past when being indirectly exposed to these types of situations.

---

[14] https://blogs.cdc.gov/niosh-science-blog/2021/04/06/suicides-first-responders/#_ednref4

[15] https://health.clevelandclinic.org/vicarious-trauma

CHAPTER 4
Living With PTSD

I believe the first time I really became aware of PTSD in the first-responder community was after the Oklahoma City bombing on April 19, 1995. Approximately one year after it happened, one of the police officers who saved lives that day committed suicide. There have been countless other suicides since then, including 4 Capitol Police officers after the January 6, 2021, riot at the Capitol.[16] When I was sworn into the fire department in December of 1993, I never imagined I could possibly have come so close to being part of those statistics.

After 9/11, my friend, Pete Witte, from my fire department, reached out to me. He was a Vietnam veteran who clearly understood where I was and, worse, where I was headed. He gave me a lot of articles to read about PTSD. He tried to give me the tools needed so I could manage it before it managed me. Sadly, while he was trying so hard to help me, his demons won, and he killed himself. I was devastated, sad, and terribly angry. I couldn't understand why someone who was trying so hard to help me couldn't help himself. I discussed this during one of my therapy sessions. Possibly, he didn't have access to the help that is available today. Without the necessary treatment, his situation was never really addressed like mine is being addressed now. While it is only a theory, it does make sense, at least to me. I miss you, my friend. I could have dedicated every mile I hiked in your memory.

---

[16] https://www.newsweek.com/3-capitol-police-officers-have-died-suicide-since-january-6-insurrection-1615452

PTSD is unique to the individual. My PTSD experience and how it has impacted my life may be similar to how some people

experience PTSD but can be vastly different from how others experience it. Someone may exhibit some or all of the symptoms I already mentioned. Some symptoms may present themselves, subside, and then present themselves again, while other symptoms may remain present all the time or never present themselves.

One or more symptoms can be brought on after being exposed to a trigger. A trigger can be anything that serves as a reminder of the traumatic event. For example, I don't like loud noises. That shouldn't surprise anyone since the exploding planes and the collapsing towers were deafening. I don't think I ever experienced sounds louder than what I encountered that day.

Triggers don't have to be anything significant. Surprisingly, a symptom can be triggered by something that would otherwise be seen as pleasant. Who would ever think that the scent of a flower could be a trigger? For me, fragrant flowers remind me of the numerous funerals and memorial services I attended after 9/11. Cooked bacon is another one of my triggers. When I see or smell it, I'm reminded of the woman from Japan who I helped in the firehouse. Without getting too graphic, I will just say she was significantly burned after being caught in a fireball. I also don't like smelling the sheetrock dust when I go to places like Home Depot or Lowes. That distinctive odor reminds me of the gray cloud that sandblasted me during both collapses. Darkness is a trigger that I'm doing much better with. When I was trapped after both collapses, besides suffocating from the pulverized concrete, there was absolutely no light allowing me to see anything. I was in a sea of black. For months, the sun would set, and my anxiety would increase throughout the night until the sun rose the following morning. Can you imagine what it was like for someone who was 33 years old to be afraid of the dark? I would sit in my den watching TV all night with a lot of lights on since the idea of going to sleep and then having my nightmares wake me up wasn't an attractive option. One more trigger that I'm aware of is being in crowded places since I was getting crushed by the panicking crowd of people in the firehouse. I still have more work to do with this one.

Dealing with triggers is a bit like playing hide-and-seek. If I know that I'm going to be exposed to any of my triggers, I can prepare myself for them. For example, if I know that I'm going to go to Home Depot, I know I'm going to be exposed to sheetrock dust. I would tell myself that everything is fine and that I'm in a safe place. The problem came when I didn't know I was going to be exposed to a trigger. Talking myself down in real-time when I'm adrenalized isn't easy, at least not for me.

The worst for me, however, is when I get exposed to a trigger that I'm not aware of. Unidentified triggers are extremely challenging. All I know is something set me off. Then, I had to try and figure out what it was so I could prepare myself next time. Unfortunately, there are times when I can't figure out what the trigger is. I just have to keep moving forward, knowing these gremlins are lurking out there.

I can distinctly remember one instance when I experienced a hypnagogic hallucination. I was upstairs sleeping in my bedroom and could swear to this day that I heard several voices downstairs in my den. I grabbed a large Maglite flashlight to see who was in my house. As I came down the stairs, I continued hearing the partygoers. I then heard someone say to the others that they heard me coming, and my patio door close. I checked out the house, didn't find anyone, and confirmed the patio door was locked. I went back to bed, and the next morning, Kathy found the Maglite in the bed next to me.

She was wondering why it was there, and I told her what I heard. I'm sure she thought I was nuts!

There are coping strategies that some sufferers may find helpful to potentially manage their PTSD. These strategies are categorized as learning about trauma and PTSD, talking to others for support, practicing relaxation methods, distracting yourself with positive activities, and talking to a doctor or counselor about trauma and PTSD.

Learning about trauma and PTSD allows the survivor to understand what a normal response to trauma is and when professional help may be necessary. It also allows the survivors to understand that they aren't alone. What they are experiencing is quite common among those who experienced a traumatic event.

Talking to others for support can be helpful. Besides talking through what the survivor is going through, having someone listen to them prevents the survivor from feeling isolated and misunderstood. Survivors may also get help with the problems they are having.

Practicing relaxation methods may also help the survivor with PTSD. Some methods include muscle relaxation exercises, breathing exercises, meditation, swimming, stretching, yoga, prayer, listening to quiet music, and spending time in nature. It is important to realize that some survivors may feel their stress increase when they first try relaxation techniques because they may be focusing their attention on disturbing physical sensations. Mixing relaxation techniques with music, walking, or other activities may help to minimize the stress brought on during relaxation exercises.

Distracting yourself with positive activities means spending time doing hobbies and other pleasant endeavors. Hobbies are a terrific way for a survivor to improve their mood and reduce the harm PTSD causes. Many trauma survivors use art to express their feelings positively and creatively.

Talking to your doctor or a counselor about trauma and PTSD means using available resources. It is important to reach out to professionals when self-coping exercises aren't working effectively enough for the survivor. Getting professional support is important if symptoms don't go away or worsen. Medications can be prescribed to improve sleep, anxiety, irritability, and anger.[17]

Another coping technique is adopting a healthy lifestyle. PTSD can be physically challenging. Therefore, taking care of oneself can be an important part of managing PTSD. This includes exercising, spending time in nature, taking time to relax, avoiding drugs and alcohol, eating a healthy diet, and getting enough sleep.

Exercising is very beneficial. Besides releasing endorphins and improving one's mood and outlook, it allows one to focus on how one's body feels. It helps their nervous system to become "unstuck" and allows the sufferer to exit the immobilization stress response.

There are so many activities that allow one to spend time in nature. Such activities include hiking, camping, mountain biking, mountain climbing, whitewater rafting, and skiing. Nature's relaxing, secluded, peaceful environment can be very beneficial.

Relaxation techniques can be used to ease PTSD symptoms. Such techniques include meditation, deep breathing, massage, and yoga.

It is common for those suffering from PTSD to self-medicate. Drug and alcohol abuse makes PTSD symptoms worse, not better.

---

[17] U.S. Department of Veteran Affairs, <u>Coping with Traumatic Stress Reactions - PTSD: National Center for PTSD (va.gov)</u>
https://www.ptsd.va.gov/gethelp/coping_stress_reactions.asp

They contribute to emotional numbness, social isolation, anger, and depression. It can also interfere with treatment and negatively impact social relationships.

Eating a healthy diet is a simple way to manage PTSD symptoms. Omega-3s play a vital role in maintaining emotional health. Fatty fish, flaxseed, and walnuts are excellent sources to get them. Limiting processed food, fried food, refined starches, and sugars can exacerbate mood swings and cause energy level fluctuations.

Getting enough sleep is critical for managing PTSD symptoms. Sleep deprivation can trigger anger, irritability, and moodiness. Getting 7 to 9 hours of sleep each night is considered ideal. Some find developing a bedtime ritual effective. It may include listening to calming music or an audio book, or reading something light, and making the bedroom as quiet, dark, and soothing as possible.[18]

As I mentioned, breathing exercises can be performed to help someone relax to either prevent or minimize the effects of PTSD. One such breathing exercise is called "box breathing." Those with high-stressed jobs, such as soldiers and law enforcement, use this technique to clear the mind, relax the body, and improve focus. Box breathing is an easy-to-do, four-step technique.

Step 1 - Inhale for 4 seconds.

Step 2 - Hold one's breath for 4 seconds.

Step 3 - Exhale for 4 seconds.

---

[18] Melinda Smith, M.A., Lawrence Robinson, and Jeanne Segal, PhD., https://www.helpguide.org/articles/ptsd-trauma/ptsd-symptoms-self-help-treatment.htm

Step 4 - Hold one's breath for 4 seconds.[19]

This technique is in my toolbox of strategies for managing my PTSD. I like it because it is simple; I can perform it anywhere, and most people don't even notice when I'm doing it. I find this technique to be effective and recommend it to anyone with PTSD. Those who just need a moment to reduce the stress they are experiencing in their everyday lives can do it, too.

I have been asked numerous times to describe what it is like living with PTSD. I believe there will be similarities among those who have it. However, each person's experience is different. While it is difficult for me to articulate what living with PTSD is like, I will try my best to describe what my experience has been like.

For me, PTSD is multifaceted. One part is being in a chronic state of anger. My PTSD makes me feel like I'm a pot of water on a stove that is constantly heated to 210 degrees. I'm not quite boiling over yet, but I'm really close to doing so. Then something insignificant happens. What happened wouldn't be considered a big deal for most people. However, for me, that little nothing incident would be just enough to add the missing 2 degrees, causing me to boil over. My reaction wouldn't be appropriate for what happened, but I was already primed to explode. My simmering anger would become visible to others. The angry outbursts aren't me. My Michael Douglas "Falling Down" moments are definitely not me. When I'm in a public setting, I have to work hard to control them. Most of the time I can, but maintaining that control can be exhausting. It is frustrating when they do come out since the anger is being misdirected to whoever provided the missing 2 degrees, and they aren't the source of the original 210 degrees. Unfortunately,

---

[19] Adrienne Stinson, October 19,2023, <u>Box breathing: How to do it, benefits, and tips (medicalnewstoday.com)</u>

that has mostly been my family. I know it hasn't been easy for them to live with me and my PTSD. I hope someday they can understand what it is like being me.

The chronic nightmares were a significant part of my PTSD-related issues. Fortunately, after 21 years, I found the right therapy that worked for me, and I can now sleep through the night. That being said, it doesn't mean that I no longer have them. They still happen from time to time. They just occur less frequently. They may come back after being exposed to a trigger or as the calendar gets closer to the next 9/11 anniversary.

Hypervigilance is something else that I'm compelled to deal with. I'm keenly aware of my surroundings. My eyes are constantly scanning for something unusual. I find myself looking at people's hands a lot. I also scan their bodies for unusual shapes underneath their clothes. If I see empty hands and don't see anything unusual about how a person's clothing lays, I quickly determine the person isn't a threat and move onto the next person. I used to work in Manhattan. Can you imagine how exhausting it was for me to walk to and from Penn Station and my office? One time, I was at a McDonald's in Penn Station with my family. We ordered our food and found a table tucked away in a corner of the restaurant. In that same corner was a large, unattended suitcase. I immediately asked those nearby if the suitcase was theirs. Nobody claimed it. Then, I became much more vocal, trying to find its owner. Finally, someone said it was theirs. I then proceeded to explain to that person that only idiots and morons leave suitcases unattended in New York City. I guess I still need to work on my social skills!

Another facet of my PTSD is survivor's guilt. While I was able to save a lot of people on September 11, one person died in the firehouse. While logically, I understand I'm not responsible for their death, I held myself accountable for over 20 years. I kept asking myself what I could have done differently that day, where did I make a mistake? I couldn't see the lives I saved that day. Instead, I was only focused on the fact that I failed to bat 1,000 that day. It is important to reiterate here that it took me years of therapy to finalize and realize that I wasn't responsible for that person's death. It was impossible to bat 1,000 that day. I need to focus on the fact that the Brians and I saved a lot of lives that day, including our own.

Another part of the survivor's guilt has to do with my denied request to be on the search team that went into the Towers. I remember watching the team leave the firehouse, thinking how I wished I were going across the street with those guys. Less than 5 minutes later, they were all killed in the first collapse. The difference between my being killed and surviving that day was the simple difference between my request being approved or denied. Instead of feeling grateful for my second, third, and fourth chances in life, I felt tremendous guilt.

Depression is another component of my PTSD experience. This is a tough one to manage because I can't control what causes the episode or how long each one will last. Sometimes, it may last a day or two. Other times, it can last several weeks or months.

Apparently, I have a way of subconsciously broadcasting when I'm feeling depressed. I wasn't aware of this until both my sons mentioned it to me. They can tell when I'm in a depression by how much ice cream I buy. If I buy two half gallons of ice cream, it is no big deal. After all, we each have a different favorite flavor. However, if I buy an amount where my wife asks me if I lost my mind, my sons are thinking, "This isn't good."

With my depression, there is also a sense of detachment from whatever is going on around me. I could be hosting a party in my house where I'm about to be surrounded by family and friends. While physically in the room, I can feel like I'm not connected to what is happening around me. Sometimes, it can even feel like things are going on in slow motion around me.

Other times, my wife will come upstairs to let me know guests have arrived. I will come down a few to several minutes later after pumping myself up to be in a public setting, even though I'm in my own home. I feel like I'm getting ready for a performance. When I finally appear on stage, the forced smile on my face is really just hiding what is going on inside me. After the party is over, so is my performance, and I'm beyond exhausted.

I have kept this totally quiet until recently, but sometimes the depression and guilt got so bad I really wanted to kill myself. It wasn't just the thought of doing it. It got to the point of knowing exactly how I was going to do it. I will never forget a particular day when I needed some alone time to reset my head. Usually when I have a day like that, I would go to a park where I could spend a few hours in the woods hiking a trail. On this particular day, the anticipated couple of hours turned into several hours. When I finally came home Kathy told me she tried calling me numerous times, but I never answered her calls since my phone was turned off. She thought that was the day I killed myself. I never meant to upset her.

When I was trapped in the collapses, I was getting crushed by the crowd of people around me, so now I feel extremely uncomfortable when I'm in crowded places. For example, I feel my heart rate accelerate, my chest tightens, and my hypervigilance kicks into high gear. I can be in my firehouse on department meeting nights. We may have around 60 members there. Being in a room with that many people is still overwhelming for me. It is hard for me to make sense of this, considering this is a safe place filled with friends. Another example is when I'm in a restaurant with my family. I need to be in the outer seat when my family is seated at a booth. Over 20 years later, I still need to ask my sons to slide into it so I can have my preferred spot. They don't understand that with my hypervigilance, I'm very aware of my surroundings, watching for a less-than-desirable situation. I don't want to have to climb over them to get involved should one of those situations arise. They will never get it.

For those of you who aren't familiar with the Commack Fire Department, we have headquarters and three other stations. I'm an immensely proud member of Truck Company 1, which responds out of headquarters. Headquarters has offices upstairs for the Chiefs, Commissioners, and other administrative positions, as well as a large meeting room. The main floor has our truck room, the dispatcher's room, and the Company 1 room. The Company 1 room is where my company's members have meetings, share meals, and watch TV while waiting for alarms. Our members take a lot of pride in maintaining it. All around our room are pictures of our members and pictures of past alarms. Included in those pictures are the annual Company pictures taken at our installation dinners where the Department's officers are sworn in. These dinners are held in dimly lit catering halls and are attended by a few hundred people. I have tried attending these dinners several times since 9/11. Fortunately, I was able to hide that I was totally stressed out. After a while, I just stopped going since the anxiety was so intense. When Kathy saw the invitations to the dinners that came in the mail, I would tell her that we weren't going. She would ask why, and I would make up an excuse. A couple of times, I told her I just didn't feel like it. That was my lamest excuse, considering she knows how much I love the Department. I hope my fellow Company 1 members understand why I'm not in a lot of our Company pictures. I hope they never saw it as some kind of disrespect, as that was never my intention.

My PTSD stole something from me that I will never get back. Kathy and I always wanted to have kids when the time was right.

When she told me we were going to have our first child, I could definitely see how excited she was. However, she saw my reaction didn't match hers. She even asked me if I was excited. All I could think was, how could I take care of a baby when I was having so much trouble taking care of myself? I was so afraid that with my life being such a mess, I wasn't going to be able to be the father my children deserved. While I have done my best with both of our sons, I never had the opportunity to enjoy the excitement of that moment that I deserved to experience.

My PTSD has made me feel like I have been in a state of mourning for over 20 years. I just couldn't get past that day. I would find myself feeling guilty if I were enjoying myself. How could I be happy when so many people were hurting? How could I be happy when so many families were left incomplete and could never have the closure they craved since their loved ones were never found? To me, being happy seemed disrespectful.

I also continue to deal with gaps in my memory. My brain locked away certain grotesque things that I saw. Occasionally, one of those images will escape and appear in my mind's eye. I can't control when an image appears before me, and I don't know how I will react when it does. I won't describe what those images are, but you can trust me. They aren't anything you would want to see or remember. I can understand why my brain is trying to protect me, and I really don't want to know what else I'm hiding from myself.

Unfortunately, for first responders or members of the military, we know in the back of our minds that we will see things or deal with things that "normal" people typically go their whole lives without seeing or dealing with. This is why when people asked me what I wanted to do when I got home from the AT, I told them that I wanted to join my county's Critical Incident Stress Management Team. This team responds to fire departments, ambulance stations, and other first-responder agencies around the county that recently handled some kind of disturbing situation to perform debriefings and lets the responders know about the resources available to them. I figured my real-life experience would help me relate to those who just had a potentially life-changing negative experience. I could share with them what I experienced and things they should watch for. It would be a real shame for anyone to unnecessarily go through what my family and I have gone through. I love the concept of responders helping responders.

Hopefully, this provides an idea of what living with PTSD has been like for me. To provide some other perspectives on what living with PTSD is like, let me tell you about a couple of my friends who are veterans. I won't disclose their names or their units to protect their privacy.

One friend is a marine who proudly served our country in the early 2000s. He was deployed to Kuwait and stationed along the Iraqi border. I won't go into the details of what he was required to do or what he saw after he entered Iraq. However, what I will share is both were horrific. As a result of his combat experience when he was 23 years old, he has a traumatic brain injury, a back injury, and lives with severe PTSD.

His PTSD has negatively impacted his civilian life. For example, it has taken my friend on a self-destructive path. Besides self-medicating heavily with alcohol and cocaine, he also considered hurting himself in numerous other ways. For instance, he seriously contemplated wrecking his car. He also didn't shave for months since he didn't want to tempt himself with a sharp object near his neck. Fortunately, a doctor recognized the seriousness of his dark state of mind and checked him into a VA hospital. He remained there until he was no longer a danger to himself. That was approximately seven months later.

While my friend has lost his ability to smell, he can still smell something burning. Unfortunately, that burning smell can easily trigger flashbacks. When they happen, my friend needs to "ground" himself. He finds comfort in lying on the ground, feeling the grass underneath him. He will then coach himself back to his feet by reminding himself that he is home and no longer overseas. He reassures himself that he is in a safe place and that what he is "seeing" in front of him isn't real.

Loud noises are another source of anxiety for my friend. As one can imagine, he sees the 4th of July as a source of stress instead of a national celebration. He can enjoy a professional fireworks display since what he is about to see and hear is anticipated. However, when a rogue neighbor sets them off unexpectedly, they are far from enjoyable. When this happens, he wears noise-canceling headphones to minimize the unwelcome intrusions. It is important to share that the anxiety doesn't end after the last firework goes off. It may take several days or even weeks before the anxiety associated with that one day has dissipated.

My friend also deals with a chronic sense of anger. This has led to extreme responses to minor situations. It even led to instances of road rage with discourteous motorists. My friend took jobs doing personal protection details, fugitive recovery, and being a bouncer at clubs after returning home from Iraq. These jobs were appealing to him since his violent acts were rewarded as he released his anger.

Interacting socially is another challenge my friend faces. He often feels disconnected or isolated when he is around people. In fact, at one point in his life, he isolated himself from the world for almost 4 years. This is particularly difficult for him since he is married and has five children.

My friend is also very protective of his family and friends. When he is home and hears a noise, he checks the doors and windows of his house to make sure they are locked and the yard for anything unusual. He also has a strict rule with his family that nobody leaves their home after 9 pm.

Being in crowds and hypervigilance are other issues that he needs to address. To manage them, he often goes to stores to do his shopping very early in the morning or late at night to avoid those peak times when the stores are the most crowded. One time, my friend was invited to an organization's dinner event. When he arrived at the venue, his anxiety became so severe he couldn't get out of his car. After sitting in his car for over an hour and a half trying to calm his mind, he called his host and told him that he wasn't going to be able to attend the event. When he is able to be in crowded environments, his time is limited. Anything more than two and a half hours is an impossibility. During that time, the anxiety builds up inside him to the point where it becomes unbearable, and he needs to leave. While he prefers to be polite and excuse himself, finding the exit and trying to slip out unnoticed is a common occurrence.

What I found most interesting about my friend's PTSD experience is what he refers to as his "moral injury." He is quite religious and considered becoming a minister. He was and remains conflicted when he tries to reconcile his responsibilities as a marine performing his duties in a war zone to someone who is trying to follow the Ten Commandments, especially the Sixth Commandment, "Thou shalt not kill."

My friend uses several strategies to help him get through those days when his PTSD symptoms become overwhelming. For example, he may simply take a nap or a walk on the beach. Sometimes, a little rest or connecting with nature is all he needs to get himself back into a good state of mind. Unfortunately, he usually needs more than that to accomplish his mental reset. Taking walks with his dog helps him to calm down. These walks are particularly effective in the middle of the night after waking up from one of his disturbing nightmares.

Besides my friend taking various medications to help manage his PTSD and anxiety, he watches comedies and avoids war movies, drinks water and avoids caffeine, eats a healthy diet, does yoga, guided meditation, and gardening, listens to classical music, plays his saxophone, and colors and other art projects. Finding the time to focus on himself is a challenge since he has many responsibilities. I hope he finds the time to focus on himself and makes his well-being a priority.

The most beneficial moment of all for my friend is when one of his marine buddies calls to check in on him. Regardless of whether he can honestly tell them things are going well or share with them when things really suck, the fact that they took the time to say "hi" is invaluable to him. Their concern for him comes through clearly over the phone. Knowing that others care so much about him is greatly appreciated.

My other friend is an army veteran. He comes from a family where numerous men and women served in the marines and the navy. Sadly, his father passed away when he was only 14. His grandfather couldn't have been prouder when my friend told him that he enlisted.

This friend's background is different from my other friend's but equally interesting. After completing his studies at the prestigious culinary school Johnson and Wales, he enlisted in May 1998. The early part of his military career included serving with the 82nd Airborne division. During an 850-foot jump from a C-141, the soldier who followed him out of the plane got tangled in my friend's parachute, and they free-fell the remaining 150 feet to the ground, hitting tree branches along the way. My friend's injuries included a broken ankle, and the other soldier broke his back. The State Department told my friend that he had 120 days to get better, both physically and mentally, from his injuries, or he would be discharged for medical reasons. He wanted to continue his military career. However, remaining with the 82nd wasn't an option since his body was too badly injured. Fortunately, he was able to put his skills as a chef to work. The army reassigned him to be the personal chef for Generals Casey and Petraeus when they were in Iraq and Afghanistan.

My friend was 38 years old at the end of his deployment to Iraq in July 2012. He was looking forward to returning home to attend a wedding. During the drive to the airport, an IED destroyed his vehicle. My friend and the driver were severely wounded. They barely survived the attack. The three other servicemen in the vehicle perished.

It shouldn't surprise anyone that my friend suffers from PTSD. Like many others with PTSD, he turned to alcohol and then started including pain medication to numb himself. One could only imagine the impact that was having on his family. When his wife had him choose between his booze and pills or his family, he courageously stopped self-medicating cold turkey.

My friend also experiences chronic irritability. This aspect of the PTSD experience must be much harder for him than for most others who also deal with it. I say this because his son has special needs, which brings additional challenges to any parent. Pairing chronic irritability with a situation that requires the highest amount of patience seems to be the making of a perfect storm. I want everyone to know that my friend is an amazing person and an even more amazing dad!

Actively participating in entire conversations is another challenge my friend faces. He often finds himself "checking out" in the middle of them. It is easy to understand how frustrating this can be for both sides of those conversations. The other person feels like they are being ignored while he feels disconnected from what is happening around him. To address this, my friend tries reading the other person's lips when they are speaking to help him focus and remain connected and engaged in their conversation.

My friend also has gaps in his memory and has difficulty remembering basic information. For example, he knows that he needs to go to the supermarket to pick up a few items. However, when he gets there, he has no idea as to what he is supposed to buy. Written lists help to minimize his frustration.

Loud noises are triggers my friend is still learning to live with. For example, the siren at his local firehouse reminds him of the in-coming sirens during his deployments. When it goes off while he is sleeping, he wakes up and immediately "hits the deck." One time, he threw himself to the floor so violently that he tore his sutures after one of his many surgeries and needed to go back to the hospital to have them redone.

My friend's situation is a recurring thought in his mind. He contemplates the "what ifs" often. He wonders what his life would have been like if he didn't enlist in the army. He wonders what his life would have been like if he didn't get injured during his last jump with the 82nd Airborne. He wonders what his life may have been like if the IED hadn't destroyed his vehicle. He wonders if he would have been killed another time if he wasn't injured this time. These are just some of the "what ifs" that haunt him.

Like so many of us with PTSD, my friend hasn't been able to elude the thought of suicide. On three separate occasions, it seemed like an attractive option for him. He would debate with himself the pros and cons of going through with it. Ultimately, he recognized suicide as being a selfish act and decided not to do it. Being there myself, I can't express how proud I am of him for pushing through those bad days and staying in the fight!

Finding ways to cope with PTSD that aren't self-destructive isn't an easy task. What works for one person may or may not work for someone else. I'm relieved that my friend was able to find "his" ways. One coping strategy he uses is spending time with his service dog and his other three dogs. He may watch them run around in the yard from his porch, or he may sit with them and pet them. Dogs are great stress sponges. I'm always amazed at how they can absorb our stress and negative thoughts without asking for anything in return!

Another coping mechanism my friend uses is turning the lights off in the bathroom and taking a shower while listening to music. The darkness, hot water, and gentle music create the soothing environment my friend craves to help him reset mentally.

One other way my friend manages his PTSD is when he turns his cell phone notifications off from 10 pm to 7 am. His phone is on in case of an emergency. Other than that, everything else can wait until tomorrow. His day is over, and it is time to relax!

It was interesting talking with my friends about our PTSD experiences. It allowed us to see how certain aspects of our lives are very similar. The biggest commonality we share is how much we appreciate our families for the support they have and continue to provide us, especially on those days when we aren't someone anyone would want to be around!

I learned some very important lessons while living with PTSD. I would like to share them with the hope they will make someone else's life a bit easier and inspire them to stay in the fight. The first is for someone who is new to living with it. Find a way to reset your state of mind when you start feeling overwhelmed. For me, spending time in nature is very calming. I'm not saying everyone with PTSD should attempt to hike the entire Appalachian Trail like I did. That is a pretty extreme undertaking without PTSD. Some people like to go fishing. The peacefulness one can feel while sitting on a rocking boat or standing in a river can be very relaxing. The key is to find what works best for YOU since it is YOUR resetting activity. Try different activities if you don't know what that activity is. You will know when you find it!

Rebecca Stromski, my dog trainer from Paws of War, taught me so many valuable life lessons. The one that applies here is I can always restart my day. It doesn't matter what time of the day it is. This simple concept makes so much sense. With or without PTSD, we all have bad days. However, we don't have to let what remains of our day suck. We just have to find something positive and go for it. Rebecca is so wise beyond her years!

The most important advice that I can give to anyone suffering from PTSD is to put your pride aside and GET HELP! Don't be ashamed to ask for it! Find a therapist that you can connect with. This may sound a bit obscure, but you will know after a few sessions if you are making that connection or not. You may know by asking yourself, "How comfortable am I sharing some of my most private thoughts and feelings with them?" If you aren't feeling that special connection that will lead you down the right path to peace, find another therapist. Don't feel awkward about telling your current therapist that you would prefer to work with a different one. They are professionals and will understand. It is important to mention that your therapist should also be monitoring the connection between the two of you. Quite possibly, they are the one who feels that the two of you aren't a good fit for each other. Maybe they feel you aren't comfortable fully opening up to them, or they don't have the right experience in the type of support that you need. I'm not saying your therapist needs to suffer from the same condition or disorder as you, but they do need to really understand you. If the sessions are ineffective or not as effective as they should be, they may recommend another therapist who they believe can better help you achieve the results you deserve.

My therapist, Ernie Leuci, LCSW, has helped me tremendously to manage my PTSD. Fortunately for me, he is a former police officer. He totally understands where I'm coming from. He has a good idea about the things I have seen because he was at Ground Zero and saw his own share of gruesome sights throughout his law enforcement career. He doesn't ask me to tell him some of my war stories because he has plenty of his own. I firmly believe if your therapist can't somehow relate to what you experienced, then making that good connection will be very difficult to impossible.

One other lesson that I want to share is for employers. People with PTSD can live very productive, successful lives. Without trying to sound arrogant, I'm comfortable saying I had a successful career, and I believe others would agree. Employers shouldn't miss out on an extraordinary talent pool. Those of us with PTSD can contribute to the success of your enterprise.

As I mentioned earlier, I was very close to committing suicide. Suicide is a permanent solution to a temporary problem. You can't quit the fight. You are going to have bad days, but you will also have good ones. It is imperative that you keep fighting so you can keep having them! The key is DON'T QUIT!!!

I want to make sure that everyone is aware of the Suicide Prevention Hotline. You can call 988 just like you would call 911.

Please share it with anyone who you believe may have the slightest need for it. You may never know the impact it could have!

CHAPTER 5
Horses

As I mentioned previously, I disappeared from everything and everyone in my life for a couple of weeks when I went to Costa Rica. When I returned home, I also returned to my stressful life working at Ground Zero. I knew I had to find ways to relax locally. I couldn't keep doing my disappearing act. Besides being expensive, it was impractical. The demons I was literally running away from were in my head. No matter where I went, they came with me.

Horseback riding and just being around horses has been a passion of mine since I was a kid. There was a horse farm just a short car ride away from my home growing up. I loved being in the car when we drove past it, seeing the horses grazing in the pasture. My favorite weekend campout with my Scout troop was our annual trip to South Haven Park, which had a stable. It meant I would spend my weekend camping and horseback riding. Can it get any better than that? During the summers, my troop did its week-long trip to Baiting Hollow Scout Camp located on Eastern Long Island. Besides camping for the week, my brother scouts and I were working on merit badges, swimming, canoeing, rowing, shooting rifles, doing archery or arts and crafts, or learning outdoor survival skills. Basically, we did just about anything but sleep! One year in particular stands out so vividly in my memory. A local farmer made his stable and horses available to the camp. This provided us with the opportunity to learn about horses and earn the Horsemanship merit badge. We didn't just spend time riding. We learned about a horse's anatomy, different breeds of horses, and the equipment used to take care of and ride them. I earned 42 merit badges during my scouting career. Horsemanship and Wilderness Survival were my two favorites, for sure!

It became obvious to me that I needed to spend time around horses. I found a family-owned stable near Belmont Lake State Park on Long Island's south shore. Private lessons were expensive, so I decided to go with a group lesson package. When I got home from my first lesson, Kathy could see a big smile on my face. She asked me how it went, and I started laughing. She was a bit confused at first. Then I explained to her that my classmates were very sweet. My class consisted of kids ranging from 4 to 6 years old. The 4 of them and their parents welcomed me into their group. Another time, I came home from my lesson, and again, she asked how it went. I told her I felt a bit left out; like something was missing. Again, she was a bit confused. This time, I explained to her that the lesson was held in the indoor arena because it had been raining. The parents sat together in the viewing stands. Each time we completed a lap around the arena, my classmates waved to their parents, and they waved back. I told her I had nobody to wave to, and nobody waved to me. She started laughing and told me she would come to my next lesson. I told her that would be weird and wasn't necessary. She gave me this look, which expressed, "This is the only thing here that seems weird?"

My fondest recollection about this stable was when the owner's son and I decided to take some horses out for a trail ride. As we rode, talked, and enjoyed the trail, the sun started beating down on us, the temperature kept rising, and the horses were getting hot. The lake in the nearby park provided the perfect solution. We cut through an opening in the fence that separated the trail from the park and rode our horses right into the lake. For the horses, the water wasn't very deep. It came up to their bellies, and we held our legs out so our stirrups wouldn't get wet. The horses loved it, and I had the most memorable ride of my life!

In the early 2000s, I helped a therapeutic riding organization in Connecticut with its annual fundraising event for a few years. While I never saw the horses, I was fascinated by the services this organization provided for children. It wasn't until September 2021 that I had the opportunity to spend time around horses on a regular basis again. A stable near my home, Pal-O-Mine Equestrian, runs various therapy programs and they were hosting an open house. I had been curious to know more about this facility, so I decided to take advantage of their event. It was impressive. The horses were well cared for, and their 13 acres were immaculate. They explained the numerous services they provided. They didn't just provide physical therapies. They also provided therapies to address mental health issues. They really had my attention when they talked about the programs they provided to veterans and first responders to address their PTSD. After their presentation, I spoke with the presenter to get more information and discuss my situation. As would often happen, I got choked up during our conversation. It became quite obvious to them that I needed to be in one of their programs.

Shortly after the open house, I started their 12-week program. I met once a week with a therapist, Mary Ann, and a wrangler, Christine. Mary Ann would give me different tasks to do with the horse and Christine was there to keep me safe in case I did something incorrectly that put me in a dangerous situation. After all, my new 4-legged friends were over 1,000 pounds!

Mary Ann asked me if I had any goals that I was hoping to achieve from our sessions. She wanted to know what success would look like so we could tell if we were making progress. I answered her immediately since I knew what I desperately needed. I told her my vision of success was simple. I just wanted to be able to sleep through the night. That was my priority. Just sleeping was challenging for me. I couldn't remember the last time I slept through the entire night without disturbing images waking me up. The chronic lack of sleep not only made me tired but also intensified my PTSD-related anger. If I could just sleep through the night, then I would be less cranky, and I would be able to think so much more clearly. The impact that a peaceful night's sleep would have on so many other parts of my life would be immeasurable!

My program started with me working with a horse named Mack. He and his paddock-mate, Zie, were from Canada. They used to pull a milk wagon, making deliveries to the local townspeople. After a few weeks, I worked with both horses together. I was controlling over 2,000 pounds of horse! Even though I started my therapy with Mack, Zie and I made a special connection, an incredible bond. He would see me coming towards his paddock and meet me at the gate. After I entered it, he would follow me around wherever I went. Sometimes, when I stopped walking, and he was behind me, he would place his head over my shoulder and rest his neck on my shoulder. Other times, he would lie down, and I would sit on the ground next to him. During one of my sessions, Mary Ann gave me an assignment to do with Zie. She and Christine stood to the side and observed as Zie and I completed it. During that time, Zie started licking me. This totally surprised me. I had never heard about a horse licking a person. When my assignment was finished, I asked them if it was normal for Zie, or any other horse for that matter, to lick a person. They both started laughing and told me that they were asking each other if they saw Zie licking me. They were just as surprised. I'm proud to say that by the time I completed my program, with everyone's support, including Mack and Zie's, I was sleeping through the night. Success!

After I completed my program in December 2021, I wanted to give back to the organization. In March 2022, I started volunteering at the stable. I completed my training on how to take care of the horses and how to be a sidewalker during therapy sessions with the clients. As a sidewalker, my job is to walk along the right side of the horse, making sure the rider doesn't fall. I love interacting with the kids during their sessions. Sometimes, I will have a catch or play basketball with the child while a therapist holds them in the saddle. I love seeing their smiles. I can tell they are having fun even if they can't articulate that they are. My favorite part of our sessions is when I hear a non-verbal child tell the horse to "walk, please." That is always a special moment for me.

CHAPTER 6
Paws of War

Paws of War is an amazing not-for-profit organization created in 2014. It is funded entirely by the generosity of its donors and supported by a dedicated professional and volunteer staff. Its mission is to honor and support veterans, active military, gold star families, and first responders by providing support or companion animals. It rescues dogs and other animals from shelters within the United States and around the world. Animals may also be rescued from areas that experienced a natural disaster or are a war zone. These animals are placed with adopters so their new owners can live productive, independent lives.

Paws of War's motto is "Helping Both Ends of the Leash." For the rescued animal, they are placed in a new home where they receive the love and attention they are desperate to receive. For the adopter, what they receive is unrepayable. Animals improve their owner's cardiovascular health, reduce their stress, decrease their loneliness and depression, and facilitate social interactions.

A qualified individual can receive a rescued animal from Paws of War through one of its numerous programs. One program is its Service Dog Program. This program focuses on providing veterans, active military, and first responders with a service dog to help them manage service-related physical and mental health issues. Some issues adopters may be dealing with include traumatic brain injuries, PTSD, depression, anxiety, and drug and alcohol abuse. The support that a trained service animal provides can be life-changing. For example, a service dog can be trained to assist their adopter by performing tasks like opening and closing a drawer or turning lights on and off. These activities may sound simple, but for an amputee, these skills are appreciated enormously.

A service dog may also be trained to wake up their sleeping adopter who suffers from PTSD when they display signs indicating they are having a nightmare. While their service animal may not be able to prevent the nightmare, they can stop it before it gets out of control.

Another program is its Companion Dog Program. This program matches rescued dogs and cats with veterans, active military, and first responders and their families. These animals aren't trained to perform specific tasks. However, just having one of them has a positive impact on their adopter's home environment. I believe most would agree that taking a walk with a dog or sitting on a couch petting a dog or cat are very relaxing experiences.

Paws of War even has a Therapy Dog Program. Adopters bring their dogs to various locations in their communities, allowing those in facilities, such as nursing homes, to interact with their dogs and enjoy their company.

Paws of War also has a War-Torn Pups and Cats Program. This program reunited military personnel with the animals they rescued and bonded with during their overseas deployments. Countless dogs and cats have been reunited with their heroic service members.

When military working dogs complete their service, they retire from the military like any other service member and may need someplace to live. Paws of War's MWD Mission Well Done Program focuses on these dogs. Paws of War works with the military to either place the dogs with their former handlers or new families since they deserve loving forever-homes. After all, they earned it!

Paws of War also has a Foster Program. Families living near a Paws of War location can host a rescued animal until it can be suitably matched and placed with its adopter. Fostering services may also be provided in emergency cases, such as when an adopter is hospitalized.

An adopter is never charged an adoption fee when they receive their new best friend. They also receive everything necessary to ensure a great start together. They go home with a collar, harness, leash, food, and car seat belt. They may also receive other items, including a crate, toys, and bones. Besides the physical items needed to make the new addition comfortable in their new environment, Paws of War also provides training for the dog and their new owner in a group setting, free of charge. It is important for people to understand that the dog and the adopter are trained together since they need to work together as a team.

Paws of War understands there are veterans and first responders who are on fixed incomes and could benefit from additional support. Therefore, it provides veterinary care free of charge for their pets. It also provides the veteran and/or the dog with food, fencing around their home to keep their dog safe, any other items that the dog may need, and assistance in obtaining outside resources.

My family rescued our dog Chip in September 2019. He is a Treeing Walker Coon Hound. When we first rescued him, he was untrained and had a ton of unharnessed energy. That October, I was first introduced to Paws of War during my town's street fair. Numerous local vendors from the community set up tents along the town's closed-off Smithtown Boulevard. I was with both my sons at one vendor's tent when my wife saw Paws of War's tent. She went over to them to see what they were all about. While she was listening to them, she was thinking of me and my 9/11-related issues. Afterwards, she shared my situation with them, thanked them for their time, and then went looking for me. When she found me, she told me that I needed to go to their tent. What she didn't realize was that the volunteer who she spoke with followed her. Immediately after my wife told me to go to their tent, the volunteer told me that Chip and I were accepted into the program and could start immediately. I knew this was going to be a bit of a challenge for Chip and me since he is a hound who follows his nose everywhere, but I saw his potential. I had no idea how my life was about to change so much for the better!

I was amazed by so many things when Chip and I went to our first class. For example, I couldn't believe how quirky he was. For instance, he was afraid of entering the training room since the texture of the floor was a new sensation on his paws. Another part of Chip's quirkiness was he didn't like the sound coming from the vent in the ceiling above the training room. Whenever I tried to walk with him in that corner of the room, he would tell me to forget it. What really amazed me was our trainer, Rebecca Stromski. She has this remarkable ability to quickly diffuse Chip's fears. She held a treat to his nose and led him around the room. She totally controlled him. Wherever she went, he followed. I asked her how she did that, and she laughed. She said that since he was a hound, he would always follow his nose. Besides that, she told me that she speaks "dog!"

Chip and me, visiting Competition Subaru of Smithtown for an event with Paws of War.

Chip is still working on his water bowl issues. In his mind, he has certain requirements. For instance, he doesn't like bowls that are made of metal. He is afraid of the clinking sound his dog tags make when they hit it while he drinks. To deal with this, he will stand about two feet from the bowl, stretch his neck, making him look like a giraffe, and lower his head down to the bowl so he can quench his thirst if he hears that scary clinking of his tags against the bowl, he runs away. It is funny to watch, but I don't tell him that since I don't want to make him self-conscious. Other times, he will just stand near his bowl and start barking. That is his way of letting me know that he wants me to pick up the bowl from the floor and hold it in front of him while he determines when he will be ready to drink.

I always have plenty of water available in my home for Chip and my other dog, Star. I bought a water bowl that comes with a 5-gallon jug that refills the bowl automatically. This way, I don't have to worry about them getting thirsty when I'm not home. Apparently, Chip also believes water bowls must be located in a specific place for them to be deemed acceptable. After a month of trying to get him to use this water bowl without any success, I donated it to Paws of War. I figured they could use it since they have so many dogs either training or waiting to be adopted. They were thrilled to receive it and set it up in the training room. The first time Chip saw it there, you guessed it, he went right up to it and started drinking from it!

I love having my canine partner. We are a team. He knows my physical cues when I'm having a PTSD episode. He will whack me with his paw when he sees them. It is his way of saying we should go for a walk, or we need to change what I'm thinking about before I head too deeply into the episode. He knows when he is working and gives me his best. He also knows when it's time to relax. He will just lay his head on me to pet him. He is my friend and just wants me to be happy. By the way, on December 6, 2024, Chip and I passed our final assessment so he could be my certified service dog!

Chip with his sister, Star.

While Paws of War provides so many noteworthy services relating to animals, it provides me with something even more important. When I'm having a PTSD moment, I will tell my family that I'm having a bad day, and they will give me some space to settle things in my head. I can explain to them what I'm experiencing or what I'm feeling. However, they will never understand what I'm going through. This isn't their fault. What I experienced on September 11 is something so unfathomable; there is no way they could. However, if I go to Paws of War and say to my friends that I'm having a bad day, they understand what I mean. We are all members of this special club. We all won a lottery that nobody wanted to win. Paws of War provides me with a safe place where I can be me.

CHAPTER 7
Maybe I'll Hike the AT?

In 2020, I was working as an accountant for one of Warren Buffet's subsidiaries, which had its headquarters on Long Island. The people I worked with made this an incredibly special place. There is a reason some of my colleagues were with the company for 30 to 50 years. Everyone was so welcoming. As the new guy, I fit in nicely with them and enjoyed the team environment. I don't think anyone would object if I called it a family environment. Nobody had the "not my job" attitude I had seen in some other companies. If a report needed to be run or the water cooler bottle in the breakroom needed to be changed, everyone helped where they could. In my mind, I made the decision that this would be the last company that I would ever work for. I found the place where I was going to work for the next 10 to 15 years. Or so I thought.

In 2021, the senior management team in Ohio decided to relocate the company's headquarters to Columbus, so much for my long-term plan. While I was offered the opportunity to relocate, it wasn't a viable option for me when I considered my family's situation. My sons were both midway through high school, and I didn't think it would be fair to them if I just pulled them away from their friends. I was also taking care of my mother, who had significant health issues. She had too many doctors to leave behind, and finding replacements would have been a significant feat. Therefore, I committed to management that I would assist them with its transition. I spent the next year and a half teaching the newly hired financial team in Ohio how to perform my responsibilities. During this time, I wondered what my life would look like. I wondered what I was going to do next. As the months passed by, I was also feeling the stress in my life steadily increasing. Taking care of my mother became much more demanding. She started needing more care, and the type of care she needed was outside of my skillset. My mental health was also deteriorating. Between my PTSD and the additional stresses from my pending job loss and taking care of my mother, it was becoming obvious to me that I was heading to a very bad, very dark place. The idea of ending my life started becoming an extremely attractive option. It got to the point that I planned out how I would do it. My plan included a note to the first responders that would be called, apologizing to them that they had to deal with me. What I really needed was an alternate plan. I needed something that would provide me with the opportunity to reset how I was thinking about myself and my future.

On May 20, 2022, my mother passed away at about 1:15 am. A few hours later that same morning, I was supposed to be at my annual World Trade Center Health Program appointment. As I mentioned earlier, this program provides free-of-charge an extensive medical evaluation, follow-up services, and medications to the first responders involved with the September 11 rescue/recovery effort and individuals who either worked or resided in lower Manhattan since the area was so toxic for several months following the attack. Each year, I could feel the stress building during the few weeks prior to my evaluation. I would start thinking about everything I went through during the scariest day of my life. Before working with my equine buddy, Zie, the little sleep I did get was reduced by my thoughts. I would quietly start wondering, is this the year they find something? Was I about to win the lottery nobody wanted to win? So many responders were already sick or had passed away from one or more of the maladies included on the enormous list of 9/11-related illnesses, conditions, and disorders. I had already prepared myself for it mentally. I convinced myself that everything was going to be fine and hopefully, if something serious was detected, it would be caught early enough to treat. Waiting for my rescheduled appointment would have been an ordeal, so I kept it.

As one of the program's original participants, the staff always comments on the low participant number assigned to my file. The medical part of this year's evaluation went as expected. I completed various tests to check my heart, lungs, and memory, and provided my blood and urine samples. I was asked if I was self-medicating and truthfully responded negatively as I always did. Then it was time for my psychological evaluation with a social worker. I had to complete a multi-page questionnaire that included numerous general inquiries about my feelings over the last several weeks, while other questions specifically asked how I valued my life and self-worth, and how I felt about suicide. I knew my responses weren't going to be too well received. In prior years, my less "code-red" responses attracted plenty of attention. I was positive they were about to freak out. Honestly, I couldn't have expected anything else. Afterall, they were looking directly at someone who wasn't only telling them that the idea of checking out sounded more than appealing but also knew exactly how he was going to do it. Let the freakout begin!

After the social worker reviewed my responses, they asked me if I needed to be anywhere, or if I could stay for a while. I told them that I could. I didn't tell them that I had already planned on staying since I had been through this so many times before and knew what to expect. Then, the real fun began. They asked me if I would be willing to see a therapist, and I agreed. Turning down this opportunity would have been a bad move. They had a specific therapist in mind and made numerous attempts to contact him. They thought he would be the best one to take me on as a client because he was a police officer for several years prior to changing careers. Unfortunately, they couldn't reach him while I was still at my evaluation, so the social worker left urgent messages to have him reach out to me directly. After some more discussions between the social worker and me, it was about time for me to go home. However, we didn't just stop talking and say goodbye. I had a few more questions to answer. For example, did I promise that I wasn't going to hurt myself? Another was, did I have someone who I could call if I changed my mind, no longer wanted to keep my promise, and was going to carry out what I had planned? I provided acceptable answers to these questions and was free to go. It was time for me to be in a less stressful environment, so I went home and planned my mother's funeral with my brother and sister.

Shortly after my mother's funeral, I started seeing the therapist the social worker recommended, Ernie Leuci. I had my initial 45-minute telehealth session scheduled, and we started on time. The first 45 minutes went by very quickly. Then I noticed my therapist was texting, and he apologized. He told me that his next client was trying to reach him since their session didn't start on time. He responded to them that they needed to reschedule since he was dealing with an emergency. I was his emergency. Our first session went on for over an hour and a half. I appreciated his candor when he told me that he took over 12 pages of notes on a legal-size pad. This confirmed to me that I was a mess and had a lot of work in front of me. When I thought about my two boys, I couldn't be selfish. I knew they needed me. I knew I needed to be committed to this effort.

Over the next several months, I continued meeting with my therapist weekly. During that time, I was also quite active as an Assistant Scoutmaster in the Scout troop my sons and I belong to, Troop 349 in Smithtown, NY. In July 2022, after a year of planning and training, our troop sent two crews, totaling 16 Scouts and 7 adults, to Philmont Scout Ranch in Cimarron, New Mexico. Philmont is one of Scouting America's (formerly known as Boy

Scouts of America) high adventure bases. The ranch covers approximately 215 square miles in the Rocky Mountain's Sangre de Cristo range. It provides Scouts with the ultimate back-country hiking and camping experience. It also provides Scouts with the opportunity to create memories and stories that they will share with their kids.

My wife, Kathy, my sons, Justin and Shane, and me at a Scout function.

Philmont treks are designed to be tough on purpose. Participants are pushed to their physical and mental limits. I told our guys before we left that this trip was going to be life-changing. I had no doubt they weren't going to be disappointed.

This was my first time returning to Philmont in 40 years. Reflecting on my trek as a Scout, I couldn't wait to see what this one had in store for us. What was even more exciting for me, however, was the fact that I was returning to Philmont as the adult advisor for my older son's crew. We were embarking on a memorable experience that we would share together.

Being in the Rockies, or anywhere in nature for that matter, enjoying the wilderness and its challenges, is my happy place. This trek was exactly what I needed: 10 days on backcountry trails in the Rocky Mountains. As the adult advisor, I was responsible for keeping the Scouts safe and building them up when they hit those mental roadblocks. I knew there would be times when the Scouts were going to be cold and wet. I just needed to make sure they weren't cold, wet, and miserable. And if they were, my job would be to get them back to just cold and wet. Other than that, I was on vacation!

When we landed at the airport in Denver, I thought it was the perfect time for a practical joke. I reached out to an old friend of mine, Mark Nagel, who was one of the top people in the airport's Security Department. Luckily, he was working that day but had a few minutes to see me and meet my son. I told him my idea about the joke and was all in. He met our guys by the baggage claim, and I acted like I didn't know him. He told us that contraband was found in one of our backpacks and announced to everyone that my son, Justin, needed to identify himself. The color drained from his face. The other fathers and all the Scouts were so concerned. They were asking what they found and what would happen to him. After a few minutes of chaos, our bus arrived, and we needed to leave the airport, so I announced, "Gotcha!" I introduced everyone to my friend. We couldn't stop laughing. Mark and I had a blast. Justin, not so much!

As I mentioned, I was responsible for keeping my Scouts safe and building them back up when the trail worked its way into their heads. It only took a couple of days for some of the crew members to hit their first mental wall. The trail already presented some of its challenging terrain, and they didn't get their hiker legs yet. It was easy to hear them sharing their frustrations. They were heading down the wrong trail mentally. They needed a distraction that would change their thinking. I took out my cellphone to play some music to motivate them. I thought Journey's "Don't Stop Believin'" would be the perfect choice. Having electricity to power cellphones in the wilderness is considered a luxury. Saving my cellphone's electricity was important so I could access help in case we had an emergency and take pictures of the crew and the breathtaking scenery. However, helping the crew get over its first mental hurdle became a priority. Maintaining a positive mental attitude throughout this adventure was the key to everyone's success. Shortly after some sounds from civilization, their conversations changed back to their typical teenage nonsense!

Each day we were on the trail, we were at the mercy of Mother Nature and whatever mood she was in. Boy, was she moody! On the fourth consecutive day of hot, dry weather, we had the opportunity to wash our clothes. We figured we could hang our wet clothes on our backpacks so they could dry while we continued hiking in the sun. This plan sounded great, except it rained for part or all of the next 6 days. Our clothes never really dried out.

One night, we set up camp in Flume Canyon, on the other side of a small stream from the trail we hiked that day. We could see a storm in the distance coming directly at us. The sky got dark, except for the lightning bolts, and the rain started to pour down and we were getting drenched. Signs of a flashflood began presenting themselves. Three of the four stream crossings that we could access were now underwater. Our other crew was downhill from where we were. I shared our concern about the potential flashflood with them. I don't remember sleeping that night. If conditions deteriorated any more, we needed to be ready.

Philmont specifically instructs the Crew Advisors to let their crews make and correct their mistakes. At one point, the trail we were hiking came to a T. We had to turn right or left. Some of the crew looked at the map and determined that we needed to turn left and head down the mountain. Knowing that this wasn't the correct decision, I gently asked the entire crew if everyone agreed. After everyone responded affirmatively, I followed the crew for two miles down the mountain. When the error was identified, they looked at the map again and confirmed we needed to turn around and hike back up the mountain. Before we started the second half of our 4-mile detour, they all asked me if I knew they made the wrong decision. The look on each of their faces was priceless when I told them "Of course I did." This group of extremely respectful Scouts sent visual daggers my way. Then, they asked me why I didn't say anything. I asked them if they remembered when I asked them if they all agreed with the initial decision and they said yes, even though only a handful of them actually looked at the map. Needless to say, the next time the map came out, everyone was around it!

During our trek, we spent some nights on the trail and other nights in a sub-camp tucked away in the wilderness. Besides resupplying crews with food, the sub-camps provided crews with the chance to learn some of the skills pioneers in the area needed over 100 years ago. Some of the skills included rock climbing and repelling, panning for gold, and lumberjacking. When we got to one of the sub-camps, the Scouts met with one of Philmont's female staff members to complete a team challenge. They needed to get everyone in the crew across a 6-inch-wide bridge that they were about to build without touching the ground. To do this, they needed to strategically place planks into brackets in front of them to build it, but if someone fell off the bridge or dropped the plank they were trying to secure, that person or plank would be removed from the resources available for them to use. After one of the planks was removed from their stockpile, they did have one option available to them to get the plank back. They were told that they could sing a song. The poor young woman had no idea what was about to happen, but I saw it coming a mile away. She didn't know that the Scouts had a repertoire of songs they liked to sing. Then next thing she knew, she was in the middle of a reenactment of the bar scene from Top Gun and was serenaded to a moving and lively version of "You've Lost That Lovin' Feelin'". The other fathers and I were laughing so hard. I thought I was going to pass out. Our Philmont Ranger, Josh Quarterman, who was temporarily assigned to our crew to confirm we had the skills to roam the wilderness, was sitting on a rock when the show started. After a few measures, he was on the ground laughing hysterically as well! After she stopped blushing, the crew got the missing plank back and completed the bridge. It was a real team effort!

The most challenging day on our trek was the day we were supposed to summit Baldy Mountain. It is the highest peak at Philmont and the second-highest peak in New Mexico, reaching 12,441 feet above sea level. Our hike started with some beautiful weather and exquisite views, which inspired us to march up the mountain in front of us. As we covered the uphill miles, we were able to catch some glimpses of the summit. They were motivating us even more. I loved hearing the Scouts sharing their thoughts about how cool it was going to be when we made it to the top. Some of these boys have been waiting for this moment since 2020 when their original trek was put on hold due to the Covid epidemic. Then, like what happens so many times at high elevations, the weather began to change, and it changed rapidly. Our perfect views were becoming blanketed with thick clouds. The cairns that we were following up the mountain were becoming difficult to find. Instead of seeing the next two or three, locating just one was challenging. I was becoming more concerned the further we ascended the mountain.

My son, Justin, and me at Philmont with Baldy Mountain in the background.

Conditions continued to worsen and were becoming precarious. The time came for me to be the advisor and take everyone's safety into account. I spoke to the two other fathers in our crew to hear their thoughts. They both agreed that the conditions were deteriorating, and it was becoming too risky to continue. I gathered our crew and told them that continuing our hike was becoming too dangerous. I knew I was making a very unpopular decision, but it was the correct one based on the limited information we had. The disappointment these Scouts were feeling was tremendous. Seeing their disappointment turn into tears was heartbreaking. We used the next half hour remaining where we were obtaining additional information. Our other crew was ahead of us. Fortunately, we were able to contact them via cellphone to see how they were making out. They told us that the weather was tough, but summiting the peak was still possible. I gathered the crew again and shared with them the newly received information. I told them that we could continue, but I needed to know that the entire crew agreed to do so. After an initial vote, everyone agreed to move forward, except for one. My son. We stepped away from the crew for a private conversation. I told him nobody could stay behind alone. I also assured him that we would be together, and that I could help him if he thought he needed it. He agreed to continue. Watching the crew work together as we all made it to the top of the mountain was inspiring. They made me so proud. Everyone was encouraging each other, cheering each other on, and telling each other how great their success was going to feel. This is exactly what these kids were supposed to be getting from this adventure. The top of the mountain was above the tree line, and the treacherous terrain consisted of rock pieces that were ready to slide down the mountain. The wind was phenomenal. I could stand at a 45-degree angle, and the wind would prevent me from falling. As expected, visibility from the peak looking down into the valley was non-existent. We were just looking out into a sea of white. Judging from the celebratory screams of summiting the mountain, the view was less important than what these guys had just accomplished!

Our chartered bus ride home from LaGuardia airport in Queens back to our quiet Long Island neighborhood was another significant part of our adventure. It wasn't strenuous or challenging, but it still managed to create memories. I spoke with my crew about what they accomplished and presented them with their Philmont Scout Ranch arrowhead patches. These patches couldn't be purchased in the ranch's trading post. They could only be earned by completing at least half of their trek and the crew's assigned conservation project. Separately, one Scout and one father got injured during our hike. Gratefully, their injuries weren't serious, and they only had to spend one night at the ranch's medical facility. They were able to join us back on the trail and earned their patch.

After being home from our expedition for exactly one month, I sent my crew a text telling them how proud I was of what each of them accomplished individually and collectively. I reminded them that when we were planning our trip, this was going to be life-changing. I asked them if this experience delivered what I promised. I wanted to know if they were pushed beyond what they thought they were capable of doing as individuals. I wanted to know if they were put in situations that made them question if they could succeed as a team. I also wanted to know how they liked being outside of their comfort zones. Their responses were exactly what I expected them to be. They thought about and recognized their accomplishments. They knew what they went through was tough and, at times, dangerous. They appreciated their opportunity to test themselves physically and mentally. My favorite part about their feedback was each one of them wanted to return to New Mexico for another trek, As I predicted, each of these boys returned home as a young man!

This trip was invaluable to me for so many reasons. Sharing this experience with my son will always be the most valuable reason, of course. After all, look at what we just accomplished together. However, there is a close second. Hiking the Appalachian Trail was one of those ideas that bounced around in the back of my head for decades. How romantic was the idea of hiking about 2,200 miles, embracing everything that Mother Nature would lay out in front of me? The terrain. The weather. The wildlife. The scenery. I knew my accounting job was ending the following February, and I was quite aware of how my mental health issues were worsening. My research was telling me this was something I had the experience to do, so I started to seriously consider attempting the hike. After spending that time in the Rockies and seeing how much better I felt when I came home, it was becoming quite clear. For me, the Appalachian Trail was changing from something I always wanted to do to something I needed to do. I knew for sure that I was AT bound!

CHAPTER 8
The AT's Unique Culture

The Appalachian Trail covers 14 states, including Georgia, North Carolina, Tennessee, Virginia, West Virginia, Maryland, Pennsylvania, New Jersey, New York, Connecticut, Massachusetts, Vermont, New Hampshire, and Maine. Periodically, the trail is modified slightly for conservation purposes. In 2023, the trail covered approximately 2,198 miles of the east coast's most rugged terrain.

The AT community is its own sub-culture in American society. It has its own approach to life, its own food, and its own language. If anyone is looking to get their PhD. in sociology, you may want to meet some hikers and see for yourself what I'm talking about.

Let me give you some examples of the language. There are thru-hikers and section hikers. Thru-hikers attempt to hike the entire AT in less than 12 months. Section-hikers cover a piece of the AT at a given time and hope to complete the trail at some point in their lifetime. It could be years before a section hiker completes the entire trail.

There are also NOBO, SOBO, and Flip Flop hikers. NOBOs start their hike in Georgia and will hike the trail northbound to Maine. SOBOs hike southbound from Maine to Georgia. A Flip Flop hiker starts anywhere in the train, hikes in any direction they please, and then changes directions as needed until they complete the entire trail.

Hikers will encounter trail angels and trail magic along their trek. Trail angels are people who volunteer their time and resources to support the hikers. What they provide is referred to as trail magic.

This could include anything from food to a ride to/from town, a comfortable place to sleep, a shower, or laundry facilities.

One of my favorite terms is slack packing. This is when a hiker leaves most of their gear behind and uses a small backpack, similar to the type students may use, for the day to just carry the basics. This would include things like their cell phone, food, water, a water filter, rain gear, toilet paper, a shovel, and a first-aid kit. For example, I could be staying at a hostel, and someone from the hostel would drive me to a drop-off point somewhere along the trail. I would then hike to a pick-up point, and someone from the hostel would then bring me back to the hostel. This would allow me to crank out the miles without the extra weight of my tent, sleeping bag, and the rest of my gear on my back!

Hikers leave their real-world life behind and assume new identities on the trail. This includes having a trail name. A hiker may name themself, or another hiker may give the un-named hiker their name because they have a unique characteristic about themself, or they did something that was memorable or totally bonehead that warranted the given name. For instance, my friend earned her name "Flash" because when she arrived at a shelter one evening, she was drenched and freezing. To warm up quickly and prevent hypothermia, she stripped down in front of everyone so she could don some dry clothes. I'm sure this was a memorable moment for everyone in the shelter that night!

My trail name was "Sleepwalker" since I was a firefighter at the WTC on 9/11 and had PTSD. It took me over 21 years to find the right therapy that finally allowed me to sleep through the night. For those 21 years, I did what I needed to do, but I was always exhausted and felt like I was sleepwalking through my life.

CHAPTER 9
Why Hike the AT

Those who know how much I enjoy the outdoors were probably not all that surprised when I first started sharing my idea about hiking the AT. However, I found their common reaction interesting. So many people wanted to know why I wanted to do it. What was it that I was personally looking to get out of hiking the trail? After all, this was a monumental challenge. I was going to be facing months in the woods, experiencing who knows what, under unknown conditions. I could easily understand their question since so many people attempted it for so many reasons. I also knew that they had no idea about my suicidal thoughts. I thought for a long time about what my "why" truly was. I thought about the times when I was hiking, camping, fishing, canoeing, or doing some other outdoor activity with my friends. Quite often, they would tell me that they never saw "that smile" on my face anywhere else. For such a profound question, the answer was actually pretty simple. I just wanted to be happy.

My PTSD has had such a negative impact on my life. Just trying to control my uncontrollable chronic anger has been an exhausting task. It also damaged so many relationships. This is especially true with my immediate family. Just being happy would significantly improve my relationships with them. It would eliminate their need to be on eggshells around me, afraid of setting me off. I was hopeful that as part of my mental reset, I was going to reduce the internal rage that I was carrying. How great would it be to have reactions that were appropriate for whatever transpired around me?

I told my sons numerous times that I wished they knew how I was before 9/11. There is a clear line drawn in my life, separating it from before that day and from that day forward. It would have been

naïve of me to think my hike was going to miraculously free me from all the demons I have been fighting. The anger, the sorrow, the guilt, the suicidal thoughts. I understood that, but I had to try.

As I was preparing to use the AT to address my mental health issues, another thought entered my head. How cool would it be to turn my hike into a fundraiser for Paws of War? While I could never adequately repay or express my gratitude for everything its team has done for me, maybe this could somehow. At least just a little bit. I presented my idea to Rob Misseri, Paws of War's co-founder and president. He loved it and shared it with his co-founder, Gary Baumann. He loved it, too. We all saw this as more than just a fundraiser. It would be an opportunity to shine a spotlight on the mental health issues so many members of the military and first responder communities face. Rob generously offered to reach out to Corbett Public Relations. They are the public relations firm Paws of War uses to promote the services it provides. Bill Corbett, Jr., the firm's president, was immediately behind in promoting my hike.

As my departure date for Georgia neared, my schedule was filled with meetings with the media. I couldn't believe how many TV and radio stations and newspapers were interested in what I was going to attempt. I could easily understand why the Long Island and New York City media markets were interested in what I planned to do. While 9/11 was a national issue, the consequences that day had locally were tremendous. Hearing about a friend or neighbor who survived the attacks or was missing or confirmed dead was a frequent occurrence. What surprised me was how the media in other states were just as interested. I guess part of me felt that, except for one day a year, the country moved on. I'm glad I was wrong. I think that was when I started to get a glimpse into the potential for how inspirational my hike could be, not just for me but for so many others who suffer silently due to the negative stigma associated with mental health.

This underserved shame makes no sense to me. I'm sure we all have a family member or friend with heart issues. Someone can discuss their issues openly, and others will freely share their experiences with them. However, for some reason, it is taboo to speak openly about mental health. I don't understand why that is. The brain is the one organ that controls the entire body. It even controls the heart that everyone talks about. Hopefully, sharing my experiences will help break this senseless branding.

CHAPTER 10
On the AT

I shared with Kathy my need to go on my hike. She understood things inside my head weren't good and told me to do whatever I needed to do to feel better. While she told me to do it, she was concerned for my safety. She only set one condition for me to go. She made me promise to do it with a group. When I told her that I had joined one, she called me a liar. She was right!

I did a lot of research regarding how to approach hiking the AT, even though I'm an experienced hiker with countless rugged miles behind me. After all, this would be more than just a casual Sunday stroll in the woods, and I understood the opportunity for getting hurt or worse was real. It included finding out what gear to use, how to physically train for the hike, and strategies prior AT hikers recommended or didn't recommend.

There is a saying on the trail which is "Hike your own hike." The trail is the trail. It is up to you to decide how you approach completing it. Your approach can, and most likely will change while you are on it. What you are looking to accomplish from attempting to complete the trail may also change.

My original goal was fairly simple. I just wanted to complete the entire trail. However, during the time I spent researching the trail and planning how I was going to approach it, my perspective changed. Completing the trail was no longer my priority. In fact, the trail changed from being my goal to being the tool that I would use to achieve four new ones. My goals became:

- Find happiness

- Raise awareness about suicide within the veteran, active military, and first responder communities

- Make a connection with one person who was emotionally distressed

- Raise funds for Paws of War

Being happy is an inalienable right for any living creature on this planet. I didn't do anything that should have caused me to give up that right. It was time to open the curtains and let the sun shine on my face without feeling guilty.

There needed to be a purpose for every ounce that I carried on my back and how every bit of space in my backpack was filled. Taking anything extra on the AT would have been considered a luxury. Therefore, I had to be very particular about each item I took with me. I brought two items for inspiration during the challenging days that were waiting for me.

One item was a necklace my sister-in-law, Trish, gave me. It had a dog-print pendant with an emergency contact number engraved on the back of it. It was perfect since I was trying to raise funds for Paws of War. The necklace also had an arrow on it. For an arrow to hit its target, it needs to be pulled back against the bowstring before it can be propelled forward. The arrow represented my hike and me since we both knew there were going to be days where I would feel like I was going backward before I was going forwards.

The other item I wore were the dog tags Jim Lasher from my Scout troop made for all of us who hiked together in the Rockies the prior summer. That hike, like this one, was physically and mentally challenging. The dog tags would remind me of what I already accomplished and what I was capable of doing on those challenging days.

Long Island, New York (March 8, 2023)

After spending a year training and testing different camping gear, the day was finally here. It was time to leave my family and my life behind on Long Island and head to Georgia. This included leaving Chip. He already did so much for me. There was no way I could ask him to join me on this epic journey and live in the woods for 6 months, too. That wouldn't be fair to him. Besides, he never saw a bear or rattlesnake before. I could never prepare him for situations like that.

When I got to Long Island's MacArthur Airport, I kissed Kathy goodbye and checked my gear at the desk. On my way to the gate, I saw an American Flag that was used to memorialize September 11. In each of the red stripes, the names of the first responders who were killed that day appeared in white. However, the way the flag was presented on the wall showed the impact that day had, not just on New York City but on Long Island, too. The laminated cards funeral homes provided for those who died were squeezed between the glass covering the flag and the wood frame around it. I recognized numerous pictures including my Suffolk County Fire Academy instructor Pete Martin. He was also an FDNY lieutenant with the prestigious Rescue 2, based in Brooklyn. I'm positive that what he and my other instructors taught me saved my life. I also saw a picture of my friend, Glen Petit. He was an NYPD police officer. Primarily, he would perform stakeouts, photographing illegal activities taking place around the city. Like me, he was also a volunteer firefighter. We first met at a joint-training session. Glen and I used to commute to the city together. I always enjoyed our conversations. One day, he reached into his bag and pulled out an NYPD patch for my collection. I treasure it! In a way, I saw this flag as an omen. It was telling me that my friends were with me on my journey, and I had their support as I searched for the peace I needed. I stood by the flag and took some selfies with the flag behind me. Immediately, someone from the airport came running over, screaming at me. They told me I couldn't take any pictures in the airport. I guess my peace would have to wait!

Georgia (March 8 – 21, 2023)

Preparing for and completing my journey would require a tremendous amount of support from others. As I mentioned earlier, supporters along the trail are known as trail angels, and their support is known as trail magic. When I got to Atlanta, I met my first trail angel, Jackie. She worked at the hotel where I was staying. Even though I didn't meet her on the trail, she helped me get ready for my hike. She gave me my Amazon packages that the hotel was holding for me until I arrived. The packages contained things I couldn't bring with me on the plane, like fuel for my stove. I knew Atlanta was a major city with plenty of places for me to pick up these items, but I didn't want or need the stress of having to run around the city getting them. Jackie also literally showed me where some of the local stores were, just in case I needed to do any last-minute shopping. Jackie's smile and kindness set me at ease when I started to stress out about my upcoming adventure. Such an angel!

Then, I met David Conn from Corbett Public Relations. He drove me everywhere that I needed to go. For example, he arranged meetings for me with the local media and provided me with the opportunity to visit the Boy Scouts of America's Atlanta Area Council office, where I met their incredible staff. As an Eagle Scout, this was a meaningful visit for me. I will always appreciate the love and support they showed me.

Saturday, March 11, was finally here. It was the day I would finally start my hike. However, I first had to keep a promise to my son, Justin. He made me promise that I wouldn't shave after I started my hike and to not shave again until after I returned home. So, just before 7:00 am, I did what I promised him I would do. I shaved one last time and then threw away my razor!

Around 8:00 am, David and I made our way north from Atlanta to Georgia's Amicalola Falls State Park. I registered my hike with the Appalachian Trail Conservancy (ATC) at the visitor's center and went through their required orientation. A local ridge runner (an ATC employee who maintains a section of the trail and looks out for hikers) explained the expected dos and don'ts that hikers should be following to protect the trail. Afterwards, my fellow hikers and I went outside to watch the ridge runner demonstrate how we should hang our food and other "smell-ables" to minimize unwanted aggressive interactions with the trail's wildlife.

Just completed my orientation!

With the paperwork and orientation behind me, it was time to start my hike. But I wasn't just starting my hike. It was so much more than that. I was starting the metamorphosis my life desperately needed. It was time to clear the issues in my head that had been suppressed for over 20 years. It was time to unburden myself from the unnecessary, undeserved baggage that I had been carrying for way too long. It was time to find a place where I could leave behind all the self-imposed guilt and blame that kept pushing me into very dark places mentally.

David and I made our way to the parking lot of the AT's southern terminus, Springer Mountain. This is where I met my next trail angel, Miss Janet. She has been supporting AT hikers for over 30 years and has quite a following on YouTube. She is definitely someone I will never forget. She saw me getting out of David's car, took one look at my pack with rescue rope hanging from it, and asked me if she could help me. Even though she "asked" me if she could help me, I could tell it was actually more of a directive. What she was really saying was, "Hey, dumbass! Let me help you before you kill yourself!!!" How could I say no to that? She told me that she would like to spend 30 minutes with me doing a shakedown. That is where I dump my overstuffed pack, and she inspects each item laid out in front of us to determine what was needed, what was nice to have, and what should be sent home. Let's just say Miss Janet was surprised to see how much rescue gear I had with me. She wasn't surprised when I told her I was a firefighter and wanted to be able to help another hiker in case there was an emergency. This is where she gave me some of the most important advice I received on the entire trail. She told me to "turn it off". She told me it was time to change my mindset and stop thinking like a firefighter. It was time to start thinking like a thru-hiker. If there is an emergency on the trail, it will be dealt with. It wasn't my responsibility to take care of everyone on the trail. It was ok to focus on me. That wasn't being selfish.

I don't think anyone realized how much Miss Janet's advice specifically applied to me. Ultimately, my desire to help others was how I ended up here in the first place. Accepting and implementing it was going to be tough for me. One of the demons I was fighting was survivor's guilt, and I was about to start my dangerous journey without any emergency gear.

My 30-minute shakedown took 2 hours. Miss Janet removed 33 pounds of gear from my backpack! She took my "extra" gear and dropped it off at the Mountain Crossing Outfitters in Neel Gap. That would be a few days hike from Springer Mountain. By then I would have a better idea as to which items weren't needed and could then have the outfitter ship them home for me.

While I was going through my shakedown with Miss Janet, I was caught totally off guard. A Marine veteran from Houston, Texas, who served in Operation Enduring Freedom in Afghanistan and Operation Iraqi Freedom in Iraq, approached us with his PTSD dog, Dot. His name was Rich Sandefer. He was going by the trail name "Strugglebus". He said with a huge smile, "You're Rob! My father told me to look out for you!" I confirmed who I was, and then I asked him how he knew me. He told me his father, who was the Texas State Fire Commission, saw the story FOX News Digital did about my hike. This was the first time I met a total stranger who knew about me and my hike. Strugglebus, Dot, and I became friends. We hiked and camped together numerous times. I loved playing frisbee with Dot while we were on the trail. She was such a good dog and a great shelter companion! We still keep in touch!

I have to share a quick story about some trail magic Strugglebus received. One day, he and Dot needed to get some rest. Strugglebus decided to visit the local VFW post while Dot slept in their motel room. He tried hitchhiking into town when a Georgia State Trooper pulled over. He was immediately concerned that he was about to be arrested for hitchhiking. The trooper asked him what he was doing so he explained to the trooper that he was just trying to get to the VFW. Instead of getting arrested, the trooper told him to hop in and drove him to where he needed to go.

Observing wildlife has been a passion of mine since I was a kid. Before I was a teenager, I used to watch "Mutual of Omaha's Wild Kingdom" on TV every weekend or any other nature show for that matter. I loved anticipating which and how the wildlife on the trail would greet me each day. What I noticed initially were the flocks of turkey vultures flying overhead, searching for the remains of anything that would provide them with a meal. Seeing them made me wonder, "What was I getting myself into? Am I going to be their next meal?"

Mother Nature had no problem reminding me that the weather was the biggest variable on the trail, and I had no control over it. I couldn't control the cold, the heat, the rain, the drought, the humidity, and the smokey atmosphere from the Canada wildfires. Those days with the perfect weather conditions for hiking were slightly more than rare during my time on the trail. These conditions didn't just impact the trail itself. The conditions could have easily entered my head. Those perfect days made it easy to wake up, eat something, and start my day. Those less-perfect days were more arduous, for sure. Getting out of a warm sleeping bag to endure a cold, wet morning or entire day wasn't an attractive choice, but it was the necessary one.

Mother Nature also didn't waste much time introducing me to "the trail's dangers. The SEALs have the saying, "The only easy day was yesterday." While the AT isn't anything compared to what those guys go through, I could understand it a lot better after being on the trail for only 7 days. I was quickly learning that there were no easy days on the trail. There were just days that were less challenging! I have years of hiking experience with several miles behind me and have rarely fallen. With less than a week under my belt, I had already fallen 4 times and was already exposed to boat loads of rain, slippery mud, and hypothermia-causing conditions. But that wasn't the worst of it. I was hiking in the freezing rain along a section of trail that hugged the mountain on the right side and had an 80-degree downward slope on the left side. I placed my left foot down near the trail's wet, muddy edge to avoid some large rocks. The ground beneath my foot broke off and slid over 100 feet down the steep embankment, and I followed along with it! I was already a body length into my slide when I saw a rock by my head protruding out of the dirt. Luckily, I was able to grab it with my left hand to stop heading further down the mountain. I was then able to grab a sapling with my right hand. I wasn't sure if it would hold me. Luckily, it had some strong roots. Next, I dug the toes of my boots into the dirt and started my climb back up to the trail while I was still wearing my backpack and hiking poles. When I was back on the level ground, I noticed my pants were ripped, and my right shin was bleeding. I couldn't complain when I considered something similar happened to another hiker who suffered some pretty significant injuries. I never thought Mother Nature could be such a bitch!

It is important that I give some perspective on the calories I was burning. On a typical day, like there really is a "typical day" on the AT, I was burning between 5,000 and 7,000 calories. Eating enough to cover those calories was nearly impossible for me, and I love to eat. I weighed 235 pounds when I started my hike. In one week, I was down to 216. Before I fell down the embankment, I had already booked a night at the Around the Bend hostel. After my fall, I booked a second night to rest, eat, and give my body a chance to repair itself!

Around the Bend hostel was the first hostel I ever stayed at in my life. It was exactly what I needed. I had my first shower since leaving Atlanta, and I was able to wash my clothes. It also allowed me to eat real food and meet other hikers that I would cross paths with several times further down the trail. The hostel also had an outfitter where I was able to switch out some gear. For example, the pack I started my hike with weighed about 8 pounds empty. I switched to an ultralight pack that was just under two pounds. Dropping 6 pounds from my back was a huge win!

My dog trainer from Paws of War, Rebecca Stromski, uses a phrase that was so applicable to my hike. It is "Slow is smooth. Smooth is fast!" She even has it tattooed on her shoulder. When Chip and I train together, Rebecca makes sure that we aren't rushing through our exercises. Taking things slowly allows us to clearly communicate what we need from each other. It also allows us to pay attention to the details. This way, Chip and I could accomplish our goal the first time. On my hike, I could have rushed through things, but I'm sure that would have meant doing some things twice. The last thing I was looking to do was waste my time and energy. Both were valuable resources, so I needed to use both of them as efficiently and effectively as possible. Such great advice!

I continued getting the kinks out of my hike over the next several days and developing a routine. For example, I made sure to pack my backpack the same way each day. This way, I could easily find what I needed blindfolded. This was important since there would be times when I got into camp after the sun went down and the forest was pitch black. I could have used my flashlight, but I didn't want to wake the sleeping hikers who arrived in camp hours before me. I also needed to develop a rhythm for my days. Each day needed to flow smoothly from beginning to end. I experimented with different techniques to see which ones worked better than others. I was probably psyching myself out a little bit since hiking the AT can be an intimidating, even overwhelming, challenge. Spending time each day trying to figure out what I needed to do was a waste of time. What I really needed to do was trust my experience.

I enjoyed watching other hikers to see what they were doing so I could learn from them. It would have been foolish of me to think I knew everything about hiking. In case you are wondering, yes, old dogs can learn new tricks! For example, the trail is loaded with rhododendron bushes and springs that dribble out of the sides of mountains. There were times when I wouldn't have been able to get the precious water into my water bottle since the water was hugging the mountain. A rhododendron leaf is pretty hearty and can be used to create a spigot. One end of the leaf is placed by my bottle's opening, and the other end of the leaf is placed against the mountain. There is something very satisfying about watching the water flow into my bottle. I love adding new tools to my toolbox!

The early days of my hike were pretty cold, and the nights were even colder. By pretty cold, I mean below freezing. Most nights were in the 20's or lower. I wasn't sleeping well since I kept waking up in the middle of the night shivering. One morning, I woke up and was ready to camel up (drink a lot of water so I was properly hydrated) before I started my hike for the day. I was surprised to see the water in the top half of my water bottle was frozen solid. I couldn't access the remaining liquid that was below the thick layer of ice. Going forward, when I went to sleep, I made sure my water bottle was turned upside down. This way, when I woke up in the morning, I just had to turn it right-side-up so I could drink my water while the ice melted during the day. I spent a lot of time hiking in the rain, which most of the time turned to sleet. I managed to pick up a sleeping bag liner in town, which gave me another 20 degrees of warmth. I should have been good to 0 degrees. I was still cold, but at least I was sleeping better. Not good, but better!

Cooking just one meal a day became a great time saver. I noticed hikers were mixing two Carnation instant breakfast packets with a packet of hot chocolate mix, a packet of instant coffee, and water for breakfast. I'm not a coffee drinker, so I left that part out. It was quick to make and clean up afterwards and was loaded with protein. Best of all, it tasted great. I loved it so much I still make it at home!

I was using a paperback book called "The A.T. Guide: A Handbook for Hiking the Appalachian Trail (2023 Edition)" by David "Awol" Miller and AntiGravityGear to plan several days in advance and get through my daily hikes. It fits perfectly into the pocket of my cargo shorts. Then I saw other hikers using an app called "FarOut". That was a game-changer for me. It allowed me to see where I was on the trail, quickly track my mileage, see elevation changes, locate water sources, and obtain other critical information. While I still used my book for planning purposes when I got to camp, I used FarOut to get the information I needed in real-time while I hiked. More tools for my toolbox!

To give some perspective on how challenging the AT is, the U.S. Army Rangers use a section of the trail in northern Georgia for their training. While I was doing my research, I remember reading that I could run into these guys during my hike. The passage stated that I shouldn't talk to them since they were training and wouldn't talk to me anyway. A Ranger friend of mine from Paws of War told me the same thing. I always had a problem with being told I couldn't talk to someone unless there was a real threat to my safety or to the safety of anyone around me. Well, sure enough, on March 15, I ran into several small groups of Army Rangers. I was climbing Georgia's highest peak, Blood Mountain (4,458 ft), and they were making their way down it. Most of the groups consisted of younger men while there were a couple of the groups that consisted of older men. Even the "older" men were much younger than me. I noticed the rank patches on their shirts as I passed each group. Of course, the younger guys were GIs, and the older guys were officers. Even though I wasn't supposed to, in all cases, I smiled, said hi, and told them to stay safe. It was just my way of saying thank you to them for their service. Surprisingly, almost everybody, including the officers, smiled back at me, wished me a nice day, and thanked me for my concern about their safety. Only one GI told me that he wasn't authorized to talk to me since he was in the middle of a military operation.

So many people and organizations have shown me unconditional love and support after I went public about my struggles with PTSD. Therefore, I dedicated individual hikes or days when I rested during my journey as an expression of how much I appreciated and still appreciate what I received. I know this was a simple gesture, so I can only hope that my words were an adequate "thank you."

For me, 9/11 wasn't just a day. It was an event. For me, numerous days are tied back to that specific day. I made my first dedication on March 15 to my brother, firefighter Chris Raguso, and his family. Besides being a Commack firefighter and FDNY officer, he was also a Master Sergeant with the Air National Guard's 106th Rescue Wing. If you knew Chris, you would agree that he was a hugger. Any time he came into the room, you knew you were getting hugged. Chris and his team were killed on March 15, 2018, in Iraq when their helicopter crashed. I can't adequately express how much I miss him.

Part of my healing process included giving forgiveness. On March 18, I took a zero day (no miles hiked to rest and heal). The way I saw it, that was the perfect day to dedicate to Tiffany Hamilton and New

York City's Legal Department. After being injured on 9/11, I had to go through New York State's Worker's Compensation Board to address my medical expenses, which were over $2,000. After numerous hearings, and the City's appeals to the decisions that were made in my favor, the Board determined the City should reimburse me for my medical expenses. For the City, that amount wasn't anything significant. For me, it was a mortgage payment. I called Tiffany at her office and asked her what was holding up my payment. Instead of responding to my question, she replied very nastily with questions, asking me how I got her number, and then demanded that I never call her again. Needless to say, New York City never reimbursed me. Therefore, I dedicated 0 miles to Tiffany for the 0 support and the $0 I received. While I do forgive Tiffany, I hope she isn't expecting a Christmas card!

The following day, I completed my biggest hike to date, 16.9 miles. I dedicated those miles to my wife, Kathy and my sons, Justin and Shane. As I mentioned previously, I knew living with me and my issues hadn't been easy. I could never thank them enough for their love, support, and understanding.

Even after returning home from the trail, my hope is someday they could somehow understand what things are like for me. Articulating what living with PTSD is like is difficult. My family may hear my words, but they will never grasp what those words are really trying to express. Unfortunately, the only way for them to truly understand me is for them to experience their own traumatic event. Maybe it is better that they don't understand what it is like being me.

North Carolina / Tennessee (March 21 – April 30, 2023)

I combined my time in North Carolina and Tennessee together since the AT crisscrossed their boundaries several times. While it was difficult to determine which state I was in, there was one way to tell when I arrived at camp after completing my hike for that day. In North Carolina, the shelter sites included a privy (outhouse). The ones in Tennessee didn't. While I enjoyed the scenery in Tennessee, I must admit I did my best to camp in North Carolina. I didn't want to find out that I didn't have enough time to dig a hole when nature called!

I dedicated my hike on March 22 to my cousin Mandy. She has ALWAYS been there for me. Unfortunately, I wasn't there for her during her serious illness. Trying to take care of myself had been a challenge and taking care of my immediate family and mother complicated things for me even more. I hiked about 8 miles that day. While it wasn't a high-mileage day, it was very challenging. It rained the entire day, visibility at some points was minimal, and the trail conditions were hazardous. This was my way of thanking her for keeping me company as I hiked that day. I also promised to do a better job of being there for her when I got home!

On March 23, I crossed the 100-mile mark. I hiked about 16 miles that day, finishing up at 109 miles behind me. I dedicated that hike to my friend Tom Kelly. We met in 2000 after we both signed up to ride our bicycles from Bear Mountain in New York to Boston in July 2001. Tom was a very experienced cyclist. He helped me train for a year to get ready for the ride. He also taught me how to do some basic roadside repairs. When we first started riding together, he had me doing 20-mile rides. Then, over time, the mileage increased until we were completing 100-mile rides. I can easily remember one time when we were taking on this very long, very steep hill. My legs were burning! I finally got off my bike and started pushing it up the remaining portion to its crest. Tom circled back to me and said, "The bike works better when you ride it!"

Tom was a member of FDNY's Ladder 105. His firehouse was on Dean Street in Brooklyn, just across the Brooklyn Bridge, and was one of the first units to arrive at the Towers. Tragically, Tom was killed on 9/11 with his 105 brothers. I keep the program from his memorial service in my dress uniform hat to this day. I thanked Tom for his companionship that day. I wish we could have spent that day hiking together for real!

The following day, I hiked 10 miles. I decided to dedicate those miles to myself. I didn't want to come across as selfish, but hopefully, my explanation of why I did this makes sense.

It would have been naive of me to think this hike was going to miraculously cure me of all the demons I had been fighting. The anger, the sorrow, the guilt. I had been experiencing a welling up of emotions each day I spent on the trail. Sometimes, tears were rolling down my face. That particular day was different. It started with being a dad. While staying at the Onward Hostel, I was on two phone calls with my sons' school, planning out next year's courses. After taking care of my gear, I still managed to get my hiking in for the day. The sun felt great, and I only needed to wear a T-shirt. My emotions were in check the entire day. What I experienced on the trail that day was what I had been hoping to find. I found a day where I was just happy being me, enjoying the environment I loved being in!

The Scout motto is "Be Prepared." Even though I didn't hike on March 25, I dedicated that day on the trail to Scouting America's (forming known as Boy Scouts of America) Atlanta Area Council.

While getting some rest at the hostel, I gave my gear the attention it needed. My gear would take care of me as long as I took care of it. Getting rest and taking care of my gear allowed me to "Be Prepared" for the following day's hike!

The Atlanta Area Council graciously hosted my visit to their office the day before I started my hike. The executives, program team, and accounting department collectively make up an amazing team. The support everyone showed me was a living example of southern hospitality!

On March 26, I hiked through Rocky Bald, so it made perfect sense to dedicate the 12 miles I hiked to Sylvester Stallone since he created my favorite movie, "Rocky". Please allow me to explain why. When I was driving to Paws of War with Chip for my send-off, the theme of "Rocky" was playing on the radio. I thought about how fitting this was. As the movie progressed, you saw how his character changed. At first, he wanted to win, but by the end of the movie, he just wanted to be standing when the bell rang at the end of the fight.

For me, I would have loved to complete my hike on September 11. However, having been 2 weeks into my hike, I already learned that I shouldn't have been focusing on completing my hike by a certain day. The trail was too physically and mentally challenging. I just wanted to make it to Maine. If that was on September 30, it would have been a win!

I dedicated my hike on March 27 to my brothers, Brian Smith and Brian Gordon. As I mentioned previously, these are the two EMTs fate paired me with on 9/11. Their shift ended, but with everything going on, they took a spare ambulance from Brooklyn to 10 House. That was the firehouse where I set up the triage center. I want to be very clear. What the three of us accomplished was a team effort. We worked together, we were injured together, and then we continued to work together some more. I met them for the first time that day. Fortunately for all of us, we worked like a team that had been together for years!

This dedication wouldn't have been complete without taking a moment to honor Kevin Smith, Brian's father. He was part of FDNY's Haz-Mat team. Unfortunately, Kevin was one of the 343 FDNY members killed that day.

The following day was another day where 6.9 miles on the AT may not have seemed like much, but they were grueling! It took about five hours to complete them. The elevation change was significant. I started just below the 2,000-foot elevation mark and finished above the 4,000-foot mark. Except for about a half mile, the entire day was spent trudging uphill. The terrain was very rocky, too. There were more downed trees throughout the trail, which added to the day's challenges. I also couldn't forget the surprise hail!

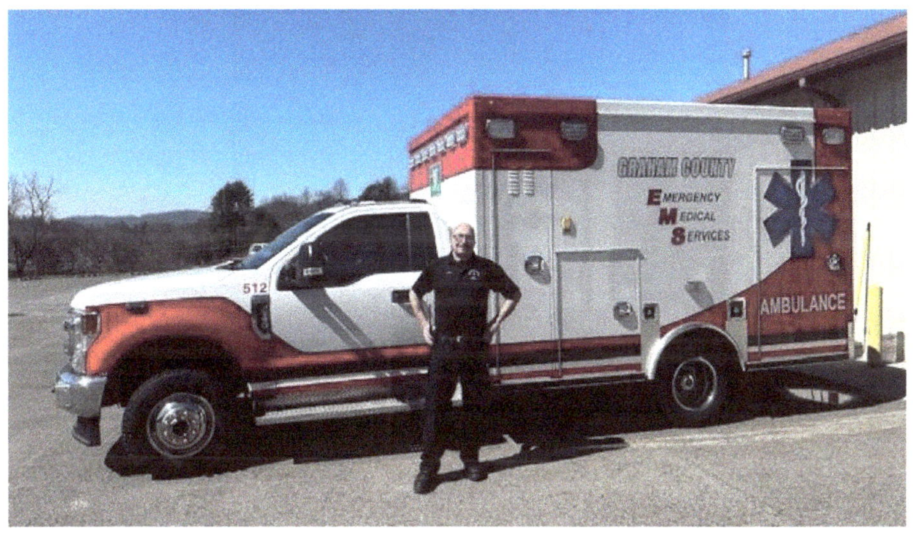

Joshua Rae at his ambulance station.

I dedicated those miles to my brothers and sisters of the Commack Fire Department and the Commack Volunteer Ambulance Corps. These volunteers are simply THE BEST! They spend countless hours away from their families, responding to calls, training, and attending meetings. These are hours spent in addition to work and school schedules and other responsibilities. I'm not sure the public really understands the commitment these people make to their community.

When I first went public about my hike, Joshua Rae, a fellow first responder who I never met before, reached out to me. He offered his home and his EMS station as places where I could take a shower and get some rest. On March 29, Joshua met me on the side of the road and brought me back to his station. I had a chance to get cleaned up and charge my phone. He then brought me to the restaurant where he had lunch earlier that day. He told the restaurant about my journey, and they told him to bring me there for lunch on them. I was amazed. Everyone took such good care of me, a stranger hiking through their "neck of the woods"! Afterwards, Joshua brought me back to the trailhead so I could finish my day's hike.

Obviously, I dedicated that day's hike to Joshua Rae and the caring team at Papa's Pizza!

March 30 was another rough day. The miles were long, and the terrain was challenging, but the Fontana Dam Shelter was perfect. It was spacious and even had a nearby bathroom and shower house. I could understand why it was nicknamed the "Fontana Hilton". The weather matched the shelter's perfection. Unfortunately, we had a nasty storm on the way. This was when I learned to appreciate and enjoy really simple things like a warm sunny day!

The end of March started out great. I came across some trail magic where I enjoyed some homemade cookies and a ginger ale! This was particularly memorable for me since I was craving a ginger ale the day before, but the shop I came across didn't carry it.

I crossed the Fontana Dam and made it into the Great Smoky Mountains National Park. I completed 12 miles, covering an upward elevation change of 2,500 feet. As I neared my finishing point, the sun came out like a light at the end of a tunnel. Unfortunately, that light was Mother Nature's freight train coming at me full speed! Mollies Ridge Shelter was full, so I had to set up my tent. With my tent unrolled on the ground, the skies opened up. My pack, tent and I got soaked! My tent filled with water as the rain passed through its mesh ceiling since I didn't have time to place the rainfly over it. This definitely became an "adapt and overcome" moment. I had to use my hand shovel to bail out my tent. I then wore my socks like mittens to mop up the remaining moisture as best I could. Fortunately, I had a plastic garbage bag lining the inside of my pack, so my other clothes and sleeping gear were still dry. The rain continued through the night, and the wind was intense. Another hiker gave me the heads up that the wind gusts were going to be in the 60-mph range. We checked that box!

The following morning, I woke up, and it was April. I was feeling down since all of my gear was still wet, and I was really tired. I stayed in my sleeping bag for a while, just trying to stay warm. However, just lying there and feeling sorry for myself wasn't an option. I got out of my tent and hung my wet gear on a tree to dry out. The tree looked like a hiker's garage sale. After enjoying a bowl of ramen, I started feeling much better. By around 2 pm, my gear was dry and packed. Instead of taking a zero for the day, I did 6 miles. It wasn't a big day, but I kept moving in the right direction!

I dedicate that hike to my friends, Josh Quarterman and "Rodeo" Rob Chenoweth. They were cadets at the United States Air Force Academy.

I met Josh over at Philmont the previous summer. He was my crew's ranger. He taught us how to live in the New Mexico Rockies wilderness. I had dinner this past October with Josh and his former roommate, Rob, when I was at the academy. Rob wasn't a ranger. He was doing his SERE training instead. In a nutshell, he was training to survive behind enemy lines. His training was based on the U.S. Army's Ranger Handbook. It is a great resource if you are interested in survival techniques. In case you were wondering, Rob was on the Academy's rodeo team, which is why I call him "Rodeo Rob"!

I dedicated those miles to these soon-to-be officers since they, too, will have days when they would rather stay in their bunks but won't have that luxury!

There was no easing into April. The brutality continued. I covered just over 6 miles, and it took almost 6 hours. A lot of the trail was uphill. Some of the incline was at a 70-degree plus angle, and the elevation made it hard to catch my breath. Fortunately, the scenery was stunning. In some areas, the ground was covered with little flowers. I had never seen them before. They were pleasant distractions!

An amazing view in Great Smoky Mountains National Park.

On April 3, I summited Clingmans Dome. It is the highest point in Great Smoky Mountains National Park. It is also the third-highest peak east of the Mississippi. Of course, it was raining. Actually, to say it was raining was an understatement! The winds were holding steady at about 75 mph and gusting up to 100 mph. I didn't go to the observatory, which was slightly off the trail since visibility was very limited, and I was soaked and seriously concerned about hypothermia. By the end of the day, I had completed over 200 miles of the AT!

I dedicated that hike to my friend Branden Kelledy and his parents, Mike and Deanne. This family had been through so much more than I have been through on the trail. Sadly, both Mike and Deanne lost their fathers recently. This, of course, meant Branden lost both of his grandfathers.

Let me tell you about Branden. He was one of my Scouts in my prior troop. He was one of the most respectful young men you could ever meet. About five years ago, we were talking about an issue I was having with my camera, and he told me to look it up on YouTube. I explained to him that he was trying to teach an old dog new tricks since I didn't grow up with YouTube. He said I wasn't old, so I asked him to tell me how old he thought I was. He guessed 35. When I told him I was 51, he didn't believe me, so I showed him my driver's license. He was floored. We had such a good laugh!

Unfortunately, Branden had been very sick for the past several years. He spent way too much time in hospitals for someone his age. While I was doing my hike, Branden was in hospice. Sadly, he passed away in October, shortly after I returned home. I will always treasure our time together, especially when we say goodbye to each other.

The day after the storm on Clingmans Dome, I took a zero day to rest and take care of my gear. I dedicated my zero miles hiked that day to a really big ZERO, Christie Todd Whitman. She was the Administrator of the Environmental Protection Agency on 9/11. After the Towers came down, she announced to the world that the air was safe for us to breathe. I believe in my soul this was a total lie. I don't know if she was told to lie or if she did this on her own. If she was instructed to do so, where was her backbone to push back and do what was right? All I can really say is her action basically said my fellow rescue workers and I were expendable. We worked down there searching for civilians and our brother and sister first responders. We would have done it anyway, regardless of the conditions we faced, but we would have done it differently. We would have used the proper safety equipment to meet the environment we were actually working in. I don't know how many people are aware of this, but we lost more first responders from 9/11-

related illnesses and continue to lose them than we actually lost that day, and those numbers were significant. What I believe is even worse is families had to, and continue to, literally watch their loved ones deteriorate in front of them! SHE COULD HAVE HELPED TO PREVENT THIS!!!

While Whitman finally apologized in 2016 for her blunder, I wonder how sincere her apology truly was. First of all, if she really meant it, why did it take her 15 years to make it? It isn't hard for me to believe she was probably aspiring for another government position, so she needed to get her disastrous decision behind her. Secondly, in her apology, she stated, "We did the very best we could at the time with the knowledge we had."[20] Like the air surrounding Ground Zero, I still find her comment hard to swallow. I couldn't return to my office for several months. One of the reasons was the air surrounding my desk was contaminated with asbestos. How is it that a company with approximately 100 people was able to acquire better testing equipment than our federal government? Just saying…

April 8 was another rainy, freezing cold day on the trail. Fortunately, I was able to complete 13 miles and make it to the Standing Bear Farm hostel for a hot shower.

What made that hike special was when I summited one of the peaks, I was able to FaceTime with my family and wish my sister-in-law, Trish, a happy 60th birthday. I also spoke briefly with other family members and friends. It was hard staying in touch with everyone while I was on the trail. While I did my best, the lack of electricity and connectivity was definitely an issue.

---

[20] https://www.theguardian.com/us-news/2016/sep/10/epa-head-wrong-911-air-safe-new-york-christine-todd-whitman

I dedicated those miles to Trish. She has been a huge supporter of my hike and has been encouraging me throughout my journey and healing process!

Easter Sunday was such an amazing day! It started with an Easter Egg hunt at the hostel where I was staying. Afterwards, I hiked in the inviting sunshine. It was a bit chilly but dry, and the trail was relatively rock and root-free. The scenery was absolutely breathtaking. I knew that night was going to be cold, but I was ok with that. It wasn't going to ruin the experiences I had that day!

The following day was what I would call a "Paws of War" kind of day. It started out freezing cold. The temperature overnight was in the 20s, and the wind was really strong, blowing directly into Walnut Mountain Shelter. With the windchill, it was close to 0. However, the sun came out and warmed my body and soul. The hiking conditions were great. I had to remove a bunch of layers since it was really warming up. The harsh wind became gentle, and I appreciated how it cooled me off. I cranked out 13 miles and then checked into the Sunnybank Inn.[21] It was located in Hot Springs, North Carolina. The AT took me right past it, so it was easy to find. After any long hike, easily finding someplace comfortable to sleep is a godsend. It was also the perfect place to resupply and get some dinner. Interestingly, what is now the hostel was a historic home the Union and Confederate armies used as a hospital during the Civil War.

After dinner, I met up with three of my trail friends, who I nicknamed, with their approval, "The Golden Girls." Two of them, Mighty Mouse and Tinkerbell, met on the AT in 2021. In 2022, they met Hoops on the trail. These women are inspiring. They were out there crushing it. They had their aches and pains at the end of the

---

[21] https://www.sunnybankretreatassociation.org/home

day, but they managed to laugh it off. The following day, they enjoyed some time in the hot springs!

I called that day a "Paws of War" day since I had and still have days that start out rough. But after a training session with Chip, our instructor Rebecca, and our classmates, or if I were to just drop by the Paws office to say hi to whoever may be around, everything seems to just fall into place for me. For this reason, I dedicated my hike that day to everyone at Paws of War. This included the amazing staff, volunteers, and my human and canine classmates. I could never thank everybody enough for providing me with a safe place for me to be me!

I left Hot Springs, NC, the next day. It was such a cool little town. It had a bit of that Mayberry vibe. After I walked over the bridge to cross the river, it was mostly uphill for about 11 miles. These weren't easy miles, but they were at least easier. My hiker legs were kicking in!

April 12 was absolutely amazing! I hiked 15.9 miles and had so many experiences covering them. I ran into my dear friends, the Golden Girls. They couldn't wait to tell me about the trail magic the Cookie Lady was providing. I found her note posted on a tree telling hikers to come by her house. It was worth the trip. Delicious!

After a more than 5-mile incline, the trail really got crazy! I had to literally climb down rock faces. No joke, 90-degree drops, straight down. My words can't fully express how dangerous some of these descents were. This particular section of the hike that day was the most dangerous hiking I ever did to that point in my life! There was one spot where, if I didn't control my momentum, I was headed off a cliff. I really wasn't enjoying this. Little did I know what was waiting for me further along the AT!

Once I got through this area, I saw a really cool sign made out of rocks. It was simply "300". I crossed the 300-mile mark of my hike. It took me 13 days to complete my first 100 miles and only 20 days to complete the next 200 miles. Overall, it was an exhausting but exhilarating day!

Did you ever have a moment where you started craving something really badly? Well, on April 14, I started craving a hamburger. Literally 15 minutes later, I was hiking along, and suddenly, these three very nice ladies stopped me to ask me if I would like a cheeseburger. I was like, "Yeah! Where can I get one?" The next thing I know, they pull a McDonalds cheeseburger out of their backpack. It was like real magic! They could see how much I was enjoying it. Then they asked if I would like another one. I was like, "Are you serious?" The next thing I knew, I was having a second one! They were laughing at me while they watched me devour that one, too. I'm sure they were thinking, "Dude, remember to chew it!" They were telling me "The trail will provide." The next time I have a craving when I'm hiking, I'm going to crave $1,000,000. Wish me luck!

Thanks again, N3MO, Beans, and Fire Fly, for having lifted my spirits! I must mention Fire Fly is a retired army veteran. Thank you for your service!

N3MO (orange and yellow bandana), Beansie (pink hat), and Firefly (blue shirt) coming through with McDonald's cheeseburgers on the trail!

I decided to make the following day a Nero (near zero, very low mileage) day. I hiked just a few miles to get to Uncle Johnny's Nolichucky Hostel & Outfitters since thunder and lightning were expected. I already hiked several miles of the AT in freezing rain, but lightning can be really dangerous and something I could do without.

When I got to my pickup point around 9 am, there was more amazing trail magic waiting for me! Gabby and Lisa asked if I would like a hot dog or a hamburger. I said, "Yes, please!" and enjoyed them both, with a few Pepsis, chips, and some oranges. It was a real breakfast of champions!

After dropping off my gear in the bunkhouse, I spent the day getting some much-needed rest, relaxing by the fire with a fellow hiker's dog, Zeus. It was perfect!

April 15 started out with some wet weather, but it was manageable. Later on, it turned into a lovely day. I could have finished my 13 miles sooner, but I met and talked to so many interesting people.

One very nice couple I met was Warren and Lauren and their goldens Josie and Junie. We just stood there on the trail and had the most pleasant conversation like we knew each other for years. As it turned out, they knew the minister from St. Paul's Chapel in lower Manhattan. That is where I was based during the rescue/recovery effort until May 31, 2002. Of course, petting their pups was also a highlight of my day!

On April 16, I made another new friend. Her name was Amy, and she helped her brother run Nature's Inn Hostel & Cabins. She was a true southerner who knew how to take care of her guests. Amy made me and the other hikers feel like we were visiting with family. We shared so many stories together in the hostel's kitchen / common area. She shared stories about her family during the Civil War and how they had family members fighting on both sides.

Amy was an awesome driver. You had to see how she could take those turns on the mountain roads. I wish I could have gone for a ride with her after getting her Supra restored!

Amy also had a very "no-nonsense" side. One time, a very belligerent man came up to her when she was in her car and started yelling and screaming at her. When he leaned into her car, she calmly unzipped her fanny pouch and told the lunatic that if he came any closer, she was going to pick his nose with her Ruger. Problem solved! I really hope to meet up with her again someday!

April 17 was a sensational day. It started with a ride to my starting point from Miss Janet. In case you forgot, she was my Trail Angel, whom I met the day I started my hike on Springer Mountain in Georgia. She did the 2-hour shakedown for me that removed 33 pounds of emergency/rescue gear from my pack. She also told me I needed to approach my hike as a thru-hiker and not as a firefighter. I was getting much more comfortable with this change in mindset each day.

I slack-packed about 12 miles in the Erwin, TN, area. It was a little cool and windy but dry, with clear skies. The scenery was some of the best I had come across so far.

I headed southbound that day, so I was able to pass and say hi to numerous people who knew me by name as well as others who knew me by sight. Even though it was cool when I started, it did warm up. This meant I needed to keep an eye open for snakes since they would want to catch some of the sun, too. Sure enough, I found one! It wasn't anything dangerous. It was just a 2-foot-long garter snake, and I was just glad that my knowledge of the environment kept me safe!

That evening, I went into town for dinner and some supplies. Dinner included a Big Mac, a basket of fries, and a Sprite from McDonalds, as well as a ham and cheese sandwich, a fruit salad, and some chocolate chip cookies from the local supermarket. As I mentioned, I was burning over 5,000 calories a day. I just had to remember that I couldn't keep eating like this when I got back home!

My plans on April 18 changed rather quickly. Originally, Miss Janet was going to take me to the trail at 8:30 that morning. However, she needed my help. There were seven hikers who were extremely sick with norovirus, which is an illness that destroys the entire GI track. She needed me to help her put together care packages for each of them. Of course, I said I would help, so we went to the supermarket to pick up bottles of water, Gatorade, and ginger ale. We also bought Jello cups, bananas, chicken soup, crackers, and other items that would help these hikers get back on their feet. Once we delivered everything, it was time for me to go hiking. Even with the delayed start, I was still able to complete about 15.6 miles. That day wasn't about the miles or the scenery. It was about taking care of my brother and sister hikers!

The following day, I got my miles in, ate some dinner, and went to sleep. At about 11 pm that night, the nasty norovirus decided to let me know that it got me too (not from helping the sick hikers yesterday). Then, around 1 am the next morning, it decided to let me know that its visit wasn't over. I sent my angel, Miss Janet, a text letting her know that I was in serious trouble. She saw my text later that morning, around 6:30 am, and replied, letting me know that if she didn't hear back from me within the hour, she would be contacting Carter County Emergency Services. I didn't see her text since I was sleeping, so she contacted them. I'm so lucky she did! Before I fell asleep, I was planning on hiking about 3.5 miles to a road where I could catch a ride off the mountain. What was I thinking? I could barely stand up. I received multiple calls from a 911 operator as well as the lead rescue worker. Two EMTs rode ATVs to the shelter where I was. Further back on the trail were more ATVs and a side-by-side. These guys were great, getting me and my gear off the mountain, into an ambulance, and to the hospital. Once I got to the hospital, I was greeted by numerous talented, highly experienced doctors and nurses. Having been an EMT, I knew I was in very capable hands. One of my nurses was Jenn Rowe, RN. She got me squared away with my blood work and an IV since I was pretty dehydrated.

I kept Miss Janet updated with what was going on. She then drove 45 minutes to the hospital to pick me up when I was discharged, took me to Walgreens to get a prescription filled, and then drove me to a motel where I could have some privacy while I recuperated. She even gave me one of the extra care packages we delivered the day before. I was hopeful that I would be back on the trail within a few days. I don't know how I could have expressed how lucky I was to have received all of this support during my journey!

I spent the next few days flat on my back. On April 21, I decided to take a walk around Erwin, TN, to see how I felt. I wanted to confirm my strength was coming back and the dizziness was gone. Overall, I felt pretty good and optimistic I would be back soon!

Even though I didn't do a real hike that day, I thought it was appropriate to dedicate that day to all the care givers, program administrators, and support staff at the World Trade Center Health Monitoring Program. It was appropriate to make that dedication since that day was about taking care of my wellbeing.

As I mentioned earlier, this program was created to track and address the health-related issues of rescue workers and victims of the 9/11 attacks, as well as those New York City residents who lived in the Ground Zero area.

I have been part of this program since its inception. Annually, I go through a thorough physical and psychological evaluation. Then, based on the results of my evaluation, the program provides me with the necessary additional tests, medications, and other services. All the evaluations, tests, medications, and services are provided free of charge. I laugh every year when, during my evaluation, someone sees my ID number, and they are like, "Wow, you are one of our first members!" I also have to admit that I usually start getting really anxious about a month before my annual visit. I can't help but wonder, is this the year I'm going to get the REALLY BAD news?

On 9/11, the loss to the first responder community was catastrophic. New York City alone lost 403 first responders (343 FDNY: 341 firefighters and 2 EMS personnel, 23 NYPD, and 37 Port Authority PD). I know other volunteers like me also responded and were killed, but their deaths weren't included with those the city employed. Most people are probably unaware that we, the first responder community, lost more first responders due to 9/11-related illnesses than we lost on 9/11. This includes two of my brothers from my fire department, Joe Bodamo, and Lou Sollicito. This is why this program is SO IMPORTANT.

I have always enjoyed listening to music. Sometimes, I would come across a song that resonated with me for one reason or another. Maybe its lyrics triggered a memory of someone or someplace, or maybe it was the message the song was trying to convey. The song "Hope You're Happy Now" Carly Pearce, released with Lee Brice, is one of those songs. It became my hike's theme song. I can't tell you how many times I whistled it on the trail. Sometimes, I did it to make noise to keep the bears away. Other times, it just felt right!

While the song is a breakup song, which doesn't apply to me, I appreciated the lyrics from a different perspective. The chorus is:

"I hope you find what you were lookin' for

I hope your heart ain't hurtin' anymore

And you get movin' on, all figured out

And you don't hate me somehow

'Cause I hope you're happy now."

When you lose one friend, it is devastating. When you lose several friends at one time, it is beyond overwhelming. As far as relating to my "… heart ain't hurtin' anymore", I lost numerous friends on 9/11. It became incomprehensible. In my case, I was informed repeatedly about another loss. There was no time to grieve since there was a lot of work to do. All of that grief was suppressed until I made it to the trail.

Additionally, except for the line "And you don't hate me somehow", this song totally applied to my hike. Before leaving for Georgia, I was hoping to find the peace that has been missing in my life and the ability to just be happy. As I was finding out, my time on the trail was allowing me to process so much. I was already able to see how my thinking was changing. For example, when I had to hike a dangerous section of the trail, I noticed that I was extremely concerned for my safety. While most people would have already had this expected reaction to the danger the trail presented, it was the first time in years that I felt that way. Some don't usually think about self-preservation when they are contemplating suicide. This would be a HUGE breakthrough for me!

As my hike progressed, besides wanting to raise money for Paws of War, I also became focused on raising awareness about PTSD and the suicide epidemic within the military and first-responder communities. The funds raised would support Paws of War's mission to aid those veterans, active military, and first responders with PTSD.

I tried to keep politics out of my dedication. However, I felt it was necessary to bend my rule a bit here. I needed to share that it was extremely frustrating for me to hear that when New York's congressional members asked Congress to fund the health monitoring program, getting those funds appropriated was painful. Outside of New York, many politicians weren't behind the program. They saw it as sending their tax dollars to New York. My question to those politicians has always been, "Was New York attacked, or was AMERICA attacked?"

I made it back to the trail on April 22. The closest place to get back on was about 2 miles before the point where I left it. I ended up doing the 2 miles again, plus about ten new ones. Not too bad for a late start and getting my legs back underneath me.

I made it to Roan High Knob Shelter. This shelter is situated at the highest elevation on the entire AT (6,270 feet). Needless to say, it was FREEZING! When I left the following morning, the sun was out, and things started to warm up. The thermometer in the shelter made it up to 36 degrees! I had a very short hike to get to the Mountain Harbour B&B and Hiker Hostel that I lined up before starting the trail. I picked up some boxes that I had sent there, took care of some logistical matters so my next week would hopefully go smoothly, and caught up with some trail friends. I also made a new friend. Her name was Misneach. She was the hostel's resident German Shephard. Such a sweetheart!

The following morning started out a bit disappointingly. The Mountain Harbour was known for its breakfast. It was a total culinary experience. My friends told me all about it, so I was pretty excited to try it. Unfortunately, several people who didn't sign up showed up so there wasn't enough food to go around. To make matters worse, the "extra" people were at the front of the line. They took a lot and threw out a lot. Those of us at the back of the line didn't get much to sample. While I was getting ready to head out, Misneach sat by me and kept me company. Things were starting to turn around!

Then, "The trail will provide" happened again! When I got to the trail, there was trail magic waiting in all its glory! Three kinds of hot soup and grilled cheese sandwiches had been waiting since it had been so cold. There were also fresh fruits and vegetables as well as all kinds of snacks, Gatorade, and water. Fresh fruits and veggies are a big deal for hikers. They are heavy to carry because of their moisture so they are rarely found on the trail and are real treats!

After the trail magic, my day just kept getting better. The scenery I saw that day was the most mind-blowing I had seen so far. The sky was clear, and you could see for miles. I took some pictures, but I'm sure they could never capture how spectacular the views were on top of these balds!

When I made it back to the hostel, I ran into some friends. One friend was Mike. He was a combat medic for 5 years, having served in Iraq with a very busy unit. After returning home, he became a firefighter. He was hiking with his dog, Brody. When Mike went to take his shower, Brody knew his spot was on my lap. It was the perfect ending to a great day!

For some reason, the trail magic I enjoyed that morning brought me back to Wednesday, September 12, 2001. I'm not sure why, but it reminded me of the concern and generosity the elderly ladies on the PATH train and the commuter couple showed me. I was so touched by these thoughtful gestures. How could I not dedicate the

15 miles I traversed that day to these four strangers who provided their own magic when I really needed it!

April 25 was amazing. First of all, I crossed the 400-mile mark. If I didn't get sick, I would have completed the last 100 miles in just 9 days. This would have been my fastest 100 miles so far!

There was something special about the scenery that day. Maybe it was the bench that I came across on the trail. I believe this was the first one I found. I sat down to remove some layers of clothing. The morning was pretty cold, but I was warming up from hiking. While I was sitting there, the bench directed my line of sight to this gorgeous view of a clearing surrounded by trees with a mountain peak in the background. To the side of the clearing, I heard some rustling in the brush. It was a deer following the clearing's edge. It was just perfection!

Later, I came across a gigantic waterfall. It was over 100 feet high. Afterwards, I met up with my friend Michael and his dog Brody. More pup time on the trail. What can I say? It was such a great day!

There were so many spectacular days on the trail, including April 26. There was a steady drizzle that day, and the wet rocks were challenging to navigate, but I got through it. Most of my hike followed a stream with plenty of rapids and a breathtaking waterfall. Just listening to the water flow by while I hiked was extremely relaxing!

Unfortunately, my journey kept me away from my family during holidays, birthdays, and other significant events. I missed another significant event that day. My son Justin, who was 17 at the time, is an extremely talented musician. He loves playing the bass clarinet and bass guitar. He can also play the saxophone. That evening he and his classmates did a concert at Carnegie Hall in New

York City. I wish I could have been there for their performance. I'm sure it was AMAZING! I did get to call him before the show to wish him well and tell him to "break a leg". Fortunately, he didn't tell me to do the same. Of course, I dedicated those 13 miles to him!

Did you ever wake up and say to yourself, "Today is going to be a great day!"? Well, that was how my day started, and the funny thing is, I can't remember the last time I felt that way. The good vibes actually started the evening before when I arrived at Laurel Fork's shelter. It can hold up to 6 people. Two people passed me shortly before getting there, so I figured it would be full. To my surprise, my new friends, Two Shoes and Giggles, were the only ones there, and it would just be the three of us for the night. We had plenty of room, which was great!

Two Shoes and Giggles started talking to each other about their lack of food. Two Shoes decided he was going to walk about a mile and a half to a road, try to get a ride to town, buy some supplies, and then make it back to the shelter before it got dark. I told them that it was already too late in the day to make it back before the sun set, and navigating the rocks in the dark would have been too dangerous. I then took my food supply out of my backpack, laid out everything that I had on the shelter's floor, and told them to take whatever they needed. They gratefully accepted my offer. Problem solved!

Afterwards, Two Shoes noticed I was wearing my scout troop's T-shirt from our Philmont trek. Like both my sons and me, he was also an Eagle Scout. We talked for hours like old friends, sharing our scouting experiences. I made sure to include Giggles, so she didn't feel excluded. It was such a relaxing evening after another challenging hike.

The temperature that night was perfect for sleeping. It was the first time in a while that I didn't need to wear my gloves when I slept outside. When I woke up, I actually felt refreshed.

During a conversation the next morning, I saw Two Shoes and Giggles flashing hand signals to each other. I learned that Two Shoes is hard of hearing and reads lips. I also found out that Giggles was majoring in education and studying American Sign Language (ASL). My younger son, Shane, was taking ASL in high school and was looking to major in it when he went to college in a couple of years. I also studied ASL in an adult education program at night when I was in high school. We said our goodbyes, but I did run into them further along the trail.

During my hike that day, the rhododendrons were blossoming for the first day this season in all their glory. I came across some more scenic views along the river, which were also really pretty. The drizzle returned, but I made it to the Boots Off hostel before the really bad weather showed up. At the hostel, I ran into my friends Mike and his dog Brody, Steam Engine, and Witch Doktor. I also found my friend Fire and her husband Dan, Fruit Snack, and her husband Sgt. Pepper, and my friend Treadhead. This night had "special" written all over it!

The hostel brought us into town to get some real food. We brought our treats back to the hostel and devoured them. Afterwards, it was time for a nice hot shower. On the trail, hot showers are dreamed about, especially since it could have been several days since the last one!

Just before going to the bunkhouse, I stopped by the kitchen for some water. Fire and Dan were cooking a batch of steak fries for whoever wanted some. What a treat. I have to say, even with the rain that afternoon and evening, it was the great day I thought it would be!

April 28 was another day filled with sunshine and perfect trail conditions on the AT. Unfortunately, it wasn't where I was hiking. Mother Nature teased my fellow hikers and me with some sunshine, but the forecast was for more rain, and we got it. It wasn't just a misting. It was POURING!

My initial plan was to trek around 17 miles to the Iron Mountain Shelter. But with the expected storm, I figured it made sense to hike to a closer shelter about 9 miles away. While I was adjusting my plans, I reached out to my favorite Trail Angel, Miss Janet, to let her know I heard about a sick hiker stuck at Iron Mountain Shelter 17. I knew the hiker, and I also knew he was a dear friend of hers. She wasn't in the area, so I tried calling and texting him. I also tried to gather more information from other hikers. Nobody had an update on him, so it was time to put on my big-boy pants and make it to that far-off shelter. I pushed through two separate storms and some challenging trail conditions. The mud and rocks were quite slippery. Luckily, I only fell once! I finally made it to the shelter around 8 pm, totally soaked and very cold. Of course, he wasn't there. I guess that was a good thing. However, I was rewarded with a deer walking by the shelter, so it was worth it!

After making it through that night's storm, it felt good to sleep in a bit. I then dried out some gear as best I could before covering the next 16 miles of the trail. The hike progressed pretty uneventfully until, you guessed it, TRAIL MAGIC! I met Richard, aka "Hydrator." He provided a delicious hot dog and brat! He also had electrolyte drinks called "Electro Max" and assorted snacks! Hydrator section-hiked the prior year and knew what we were going through.

As it turned out, Hydrator was originally from the Bronx. However, you would have never known since he acquired a rather strong southern accent and could pass for a Southern Gentleman. It turns out that after 9/11, he enlisted in the army at the age of 31 and was a member of the 82nd Airborne division. I told him he and his brothers were represented at Paws of War!

The rest of the day was filled with more picturesque scenery, plants, and butterflies. I made it to a shelter for the night, where some friends I had made the day before, as well as some new ones, joined me. Just another day in the AT!

Virginia (April 30 - June 14)

By now, I'm sure everyone could guess that April 30 started out with MORE RAIN! I planned on waiting it out since I only needed to do about 10 miles that day. Eventually, there was a break in the rain, so I went for it. I completed about half my hike when the rain arrived in all its glory. Even though I was completely drenched, I loved knowing that I made it to Virginia!

About 25% of the AT's total milage is in Virginia. Therefore, some hikers may find themselves fighting the "Virginia Blues." It is one of the mental challenges hikers may face because they find themselves hiking for such a long time in the same state that they start to question if they are making any progress. Just like eating an elephant is done one bite at a time, crossing Virginia is done one step at a time!

The sun was finally showing itself when I entered the charming town of Damascus. For such a small town, it had a very impressive memorial for its veterans. I ran into about ten friends while I was crossing town. This included my friend who I went looking for a few days before after hearing that he was sick. As it turned out, he just had a stomach bug, nothing serious.

After securing my gear at the Broken Fiddle hostel, I went to some shops for supplies and dinner. I then returned to the hostel and planned out my next several days. While I was working out my plans, Rosie, the hostel's dog, came by to make sure I was doing a good job. Her owner, Freddie, was stunned because she didn't usually go to strangers. In my case, she jumped up on the couch next to me and snuggled in. It was a great way to wrap up my day!

While I was hiking that day, I had a lot of time to think about how I wished my kids had known me before 9/11 and my PTSD. During that time, I thought about a Maya Angelou quote my friend, Kelli Porti, shared with me. It was, "I can be changed by what happens to me. But I refuse to be reduced by it." I also thought about a conversation I had a few days prior with Mary, who owned the Mountain Harbour B&B and Hiker Hostel. She was a nurse in a hospital's psychiatric ward. Her son was a marine who suffered from PTSD from his deployments. She saw firsthand what her son was going through. She explained to me that I was trying to turn back the clock and it just didn't work that way. She also explained to me that everything I experienced in my life made me who I was. I couldn't pick and choose what impacted my life.

In my case, I was almost killed several times that day. How could literally facing death not have an impact on my life? I guess looking at how I was living my life afterwards was just as important. For example, pushing through two storms, covering 17 miles, to check on a sick hiker is an example of how I had been living my life. Hopefully, my kids saw this side of me more than the negative side of my PTSD.

My hike on May 1 was a great way to kick off the month. It was cold and windy but almost completely DRY! I covered 18 miles and saw a lot of friends on the trail. I could have finished earlier, but it was fun catching up with people I hadn't seen in a while. After I finished hiking for the day, about 10 of us went into town for dinner. The waitress was laughing because some of the guys were ordering multiple entrees to cover the calories we incinerated. I went for the meatloaf sandwich. It really hit the spot!

When we got back to the hostel, Rosie was waiting for me. You may remember my friend Mike and his dog Brody. Well, Brody and I got a chance to catch up as well. As it turned out, it was Mike's birthday. We celebrated with multiple cakes and ice cream. More calories!

Did you ever have a day that just didn't go according to what you planned? Well, May 2 was one of those days for me. I had some boxes that were being held at a local outfitter. The prior day, I called the owner, and he told me that I could come by at 9 am the following morning to get them. I got there at 8:50 am so I could use one of them and take the others to the post office and forward them to the next town that I would be in. To my surprise and disappointment, the owner was known for having unreliable hours, so I waited around. A few HOURS later, I decided this was a complete waste of time. I needed to do something more productive, so I went back to the hostel and arranged a slack pack hike.

Around 1:30 pm, I started a 13-mile hike. I was glad I was only wearing a day pack since a good part of the day was spent trudging uphill on very rocky terrain. Some parts were so challenging that I was only covering about 1 mile in an hour. I was getting concerned that I would be finishing my hike in the dark. After a while, I came across some wide-open meadows where I could start making up time! But then I had some self-imposed delays because I came across some wild ponies! In case you have forgotten, I love being around horses. When I'm home, I volunteer at a stable that runs therapy programs for adults and children with various physical and mental disabilities. When I'm not assisting with the therapy sessions, I help take care of about 25 horses. Besides finding the ponies, I also found several longhorn cattle that were recently introduced to the area. They are such noble creatures as well!

During my hike, I completed another milestone. Over 500 miles of the trail were now behind me. This time, it only took me 7 days to cover the next 100 miles. Granted, I had some really big days that week, and I was looking for a sick hiker, so keeping that pace would be tough!

As luck would have it, I was able to finish my hike before it got dark. Even luckier, Freddie, the hostel owner, was able to contact the shop owner, and he delivered my boxes to the hostel, so they were there when I got back. As I found out, the shop owner never showed up to open his store that day. Talk about turning a lost day into another great day!

May 3rd was a day of extremes. I started my day by hiking in snow and hail! Fortunately, they both melted when they hit the ground. The wind gusts were so strong that when I lifted my foot to take a step, the wind would actually cause me to lose my balance. I really could have used the 45 pounds I lost!

Eventually, the skies cleared, and the sun came out. The warmth on my face was something I have learned to appreciate and not take for granted.

I came to a meadow with some pretty thorny brush and thought I found a few more ponies. What I actually found was a small herd. I even had the opportunity to watch a mother pony nurse its foal. What a special moment that was!

When I got to the Old Orchard Shelter, which I had to myself, I had a quick dinner and, at 6:30 pm, settled in for a really cold night. I wore five layers, used a sleeping bag liner and my sleeping bag, which is rated for 20 degrees, and I still froze! It was around 35 degrees, but the windchill brought it down to the '20s. It was May!

The following day started out really cold. That was no surprise, considering how I froze the night before. You can tell it is cold when you see birds fluffing up their feathers to warm the air trapped between them. I didn't have a big mileage day planned so I was able to stay in my sleeping bag a bit longer and hope the temperature would go up just a little more.

Overall, the scenery didn't disappoint me. I saw some beautiful streams, another impressive waterfall, and a deer crossing the trail to feed in the brush. I quickly learned that I didn't have to have to be a big day to have a great day!

I felt like May 5 was a day that I earned. The weather was absolutely perfect. It was in the high 60s to low 70s and dry, with a gentle breeze to cool me off during some of the big uphills in the sun. I covered 15.5 miles in about six hours.

For the most part, the scenery was similar to what I had seen before. But that was ok. I was still outside enjoying the moment, and it gave me a chance to think, process, and unload some more of the baggage I had been carrying inside my head.

The best part of my day was when I arrived at the Long Neck Lair, which was an alpaca farm with a bunkhouse. Cyndie, the owner, took me and some other hikers into their enclosures. We had a blast hand-feeding them! She and her husband also had goats and chickens on the farm. Depending on the type of chicken, the eggs were different colors. Apparently, the chickens really like the alpaca feed. They would actually push the alpacas away from the trough so they could eat, too!

I dedicated the miles I covered that day to my dad. He was the one who turned me on to nature when I was a kid. He would tell me that what we saw didn't have to be spectacular. What counted was the fact that we got out there in the first place. I can never express how much I miss him. He wasn't just a great dad; he was my best friend.

In case you were wondering, I did my best to do my therapy sessions while I was on the trail. This was important since I typically hiked by myself so I could let my mind wander and think through different issues. Depending on the issue, I may have talked about it with my therapist to try to make sense out of it or develop a strategy to deal with it. Usually, the sessions were on Thursday evenings, so I tried to be in a hostel then to eliminate any problems regarding lack of electricity or connectivity.

The following day was phenomenal. The weather was perfect for taking on the challenges the AT threw my way. I completed 11.5 miles which included some pretty steep, rocky inclines. The reward was totally worth it. Hiking through a green tunnel, protected from the strong sun, with a smooth trail surface was almost magical.

Then, I found the perfect place for lunch. Honestly, I can't remember when a simple tuna sandwich tasted so good!

The scenery was incredible as well. I even came across a historic, one-room school house. Towards the end of my hike, I crossed some railroad tracks that were pretty busy with freight trains, walked along a boardwalk, and saw a really pretty butterfly. The best part had to be listening to so many different birds singing simultaneously. Then I made it into town to buy some bread and grape jelly for PB&Js!

After taking care of my gear, I just chilled out and relaxed as I watched the sun set behind the mountains. An absolutely amazing day! Right?!

The next day, I said goodbye to my alpaca friends and hit the trail. I came across a birdhouse at the edge of a meadow. It was such a simple but touching tribute to someone who really embraced the AT. As I completed my miles for the day, I crossed the 25% completion point for the AT. I just had to do everything over again three more times!

After enjoying some more incredible scenery, I thought I heard a Buick crashing through the brush. I knew that could only mean one thing since I didn't hear a car engine. BEAR(S)! I saw a bear climb up a tree, so I stepped to the side of another tree to take its picture. When I did that, I saw Momma about 15 yards closer to me. She watched me like a hawk or more like a momma bear! It was remarkable watching her instruct her cub to come down from the tree and cross the ravine so it would be in a safer place. After her cub crossed the ravine, Momma turned around and followed behind it. I was in such an adrenaline rush for the rest of the afternoon. After crossing a meadow, I found some cows. They were nice, but compared to the bears, they came up a bit short!

Momma Bear keeping a close eye on me!

Baby Bear climbing down the tree

May 8 was absolutely grueling! I trudged along for about 9.5 miles and was so grateful when I made it to the Chestnut Knob Shelter. One uphill stretch went on for miles. The burn in my legs was so intense I felt like I was just learning how to hike!

At one point, I was supposed to cross a stream using a bridge. Of course, the bridge was destroyed, so I had to cross the stream on foot. I used this as an opportunity to rest while I swapped my boots for crocs, devoured my remaining PB&Js, and enjoyed the cold water on my feet and legs! For those not familiar with crossing a stream, this can be quite dangerous, especially when hiking solo like I was doing. To minimize the risk of drowning, it is important to remember to unbuckle your hip belt and chest strap and loosen your shoulder straps. This way, you can quickly ditch your pack if you fall. Fortunately, my stream crossing was uneventful!

There was also rain in the forecast. I was able to complete my hike and resupply my water before it arrived. I considered that good fortune my participation trophy!

I arrived nice and dry at the shelter before the rain started, and the view was stunning. However, these gifts weren't free. I paid for both of them the following morning. Visibility into the valley was minimal at best. I checked the weather and saw I had a short window to get some of my hike in before the rain started spraying down on me. I got a few miles down the trail when the rain returned, BIG TIME. Even with my rain gear, I was SOAKED!

There are several expressions on the AT. One of which is "No rain, no Maine". If there is lightning, you need to find a safe place to wait out the storm. Otherwise, you need to get your miles in, even if it means hiking through the showers. Not hiking just because it is raining can bring other problems. For example, taking an unplanned zero could mean running out of food on the trail. I don't know about you, but I don't like being hungry!

I knew the rain was supposed to end in a few hours. Then, it was almost like Mother Nature spent enough time laughing at me. She seemed to have snapped her fingers, and the rain stopped. The sun was shining, and the birds were chirping in full force. If I had to guess what the birds were saying, my guess would probably have been something like:

"What a storm! The nest is destroyed! Call Jake from State Farm!"

"I tried, but he isn't answering. He's probably making another commercial, so I will try again later!"

When I got to the Jenkins Shelter, I laid out my gear in the sun to dry out and made some dinner. Around 6:30 pm, I started getting ready for bed since I had no cell service. Shortly before falling asleep, about six friends showed up. It was great catching up with them. We talked about a deli that we would be passing the following day. I would need to get up early since it closed around 4 pm. The idea of enjoying one of its famous hamburgers was enough motivation for an early start the next day!

May 10 started out really cold. While I was sleeping, the temperature dropped into the 40's. I just wanted to stay in my sleeping bag, but that wasn't an option. An incredible hamburger was waiting for me. I was out of my bag, cooked some oatmeal to warm up, packed my gear and was on the trail about an hour earlier than normal for me. The sun warmed me up quickly and I was sweating in no time. The trail was tough at times, but overall, it was a great hike. The scenery was unforgettable, of course, and I met up with my friends from the night before. I made it to the deli just before 2 pm and enjoyed my reward. The bacon cheeseburger, fries, Dr. Pepper, ginger ale, and Fritos corn chips were the best meal I had in a while!

Countless people during my hike asked me my trail name, so I told them it was "Sleepwalker," and then I explained the story behind it. I was blown away by how many veterans and civilians thanked me for my service. This situation happened again the same day I savored my burger. The thanks I received along with the burger reminded me of something that happened a few years ago.

When I was going to physical therapy after an injury, I met a veteran named Dana Gutierrez. We quickly became friends and still keep in touch. During one of our sessions, he was telling me what it was like coming home from Vietnam. Finally, on American soil, while in uniform, he went into a restaurant to get a burger and a beer. Basically, the owner threw him out, telling him there was no way he was going to be served. Needless to say, he never got his burger and beer. I was crushed when I heard what my friend experienced. I needed to do something about this. I needed to correct this wrong. On the way to our next session, I stopped by Wendy's at 10 am. I made a special request for them to make a burger and fries since it was still breakfast time. Then I stopped by a beer distributor to get a cold 6-pack. At 10:30 am, I gave Dana the burger and beer he waited almost 40 years for and welcomed him home. Many people in the PT office were crying!

I dedicated the 11.4 miles I covered on May 10 to Dana and all of our Vietnam veterans and welcomed them home!

May 11 was probably my favorite day on the trail to that point. The weather was pretty much perfect. Except for a couple of challenging uphills, I spent most of the day slack-packing the ridge line of a series of peaks for just over 18 miles. This allowed me to reach another milestone. Over 600 miles completed!

While I was hiking, I came across my friends Tom, 505, and Boss at different times. Boss and I met earlier on the trail. We hiked for a bit together today and shared some very personal aspects of our past. I'm not disclosing what he shared since that wouldn't be appropriate. However, I can say there is mutual respect between us. Later, Tom, 505, Boss, and I all ended up at the Weary Feet hostel and enjoyed a hearty pasta dinner together!

The following day was also a great trail day. It started with a quick drizzle, but it stopped shortly after it started, and the clouds helped keep the heat off of me for most of the day. About a mile into my hike, I came across a suspension bridge. I was worried since I didn't have my E-ZPass. Fortunately, the duck near the bridge told the toll booth attendant to put my charge on his bill. Sorry, I couldn't pass up the opportunity for a dad joke!

Overall, the trail conditions were pretty good. I liked how someone left a marker at one point, clearly letting hikers know which way to go. Every little bit of help was appreciated!

During my hike, I came across a flower I didn't recall seeing previously. If peace had a scent, this would have been it. It made me feel so relaxed. That was pretty cool since fragrant flowers usually trigger my PTSD. If the plant could have smelled me, it would have shriveled up and died. Too bad I couldn't return the favor!

One part of the trail was pretty much straight uphill for a mile. Gratefully, the view from the top was worth it. As the saying goes, "If you want to dance, you gotta pay the band!"

My hike wrapped up by spotting a deer nearby. It was a simple interaction with nature, but still really enjoyable!

That evening, I stayed at Woods Hole Hostel and B&B. It was an OASIS near the AT. As it turned out, I stayed there with several friends. It was such a different hostel experience. At dinner and then at breakfast the following morning, the staff rang the bell, letting everyone know it was time to assemble on the property's front lawn. Before our meals, we all stood in a circle, and everyone was asked to share what they were grateful for during the day or what they were looking forward to, depending on which meal we were about to enjoy. I shared why I was on the trail and what I was hoping to accomplish. When I went to settle my tab after breakfast, I spoke to the owner, and she said she was giving me trail magic. I was really confused. She told me she listened to what I shared the night before and that morning and then told me that my bunk, dinner, and breakfast were on her. I was caught so off guard my eyes immediately teared up. I couldn't have thanked her enough!

Sharing our thoughts at Woods Hole Hostel.

But this wasn't the only thing that happened to me that day. When I got to the hostel the day before, I noticed my hand shovel, which hung from my pack, had fallen off. As it turned out, my friend 505 saw it on the trail about half a mile from the road, but he didn't know it was mine. I went back to the trail that morning, hoping to find it, but it was gone. I hiked a mile for nothing. About an hour into that day's hike, I met up with my friends. They were resting at a shelter where a mother and son were also taking a break. The mother and son heard them talking about how I went to look for my shovel and would be meeting up with them soon. They told my friends that THEY FOUND IT AND HAD IT! I showed up at the shelter about 5 minutes later, and they gave it back to me. What were the chances that everyone would have been in the right place at the right time for me to get it back?!

Something else very special also happened. The night before, my friend Early Bird (82nd Airborne/police officer retired) asked me if I wanted to hike with him, SnailsIt (volunteer firefighter/EMS), and Beepers (Air Force retired) since we are always leapfrogging each other. I thought about it a lot during the night and some more that morning. I then told him that I usually hiked alone so I could process things. However, if everyone was ok with me having some alone time, when necessary, I would love to join their tramily (trail family). Of course, they were! That day, we trudged 11.5 miles together, and it was really nice talking and laughing. The scenery was pretty; I saw some different flowers and found a photogenic garter snake! After our hike, we met up with SnailsIt's husband, Willie (aka Radioactive since he was a ham radio operator). He drove a van to support SnailsIt. He also took some of our extra gear and drove us around town for supplies and dinner, which was very much appreciated. That evening, we hit the local Dairy Queen for some ice cream, checked in at the Angels Rest Hiker's Haven, which was a hostel in Pearisburg, and then set up camp at a nearby Chinese buffet for dinner!

When I think of May 14, the only word that comes to mind is exhaustion! After hiking a section of highway, the trail threw two major uphill, very rocky sections at us that literally went on for miles. They were demoralizing! After several hours of battling the mountain, we made it to the top, where the views were again magnificent!

Nearby was a shelter where we could take a break and have some lunch. Afterwards, we walked the ridge line, tripped over more rocks, and slipped on more mud. Water was scarce, and we were getting concerned since we were almost out. When we were about a mile from our campsite, one last insanely steep uphill battle remained. Once we got to the campsite, Beepers and I dropped our packs and just looked at each other. We both asked if that last uphill section was really necessary.

Totally exhausted from hiking 15.6 miles, it was time to address the water situation. From what we could tell, we might be able to find water about .2 miles away. We eventually found the stream off the trail. We collected and purified our water so we could hydrate and make dinner. While we ate, more friends showed up to camp with us. We all just relaxed together, sharing funny stories from the trail and back home. It was exactly how we needed to wrap up our day!

May 17 was, without a doubt, the most emotional day on the trail so far. Three days prior, SnailsIt told our tramily that she wasn't feeling right and needed to leave the trail, so our day started with saying goodbye to her and her husband, Willy. There were plenty of tears to go around.

The 16.4 miles of trail that day took me past a memorial for Congressional Medal of Honor recipient Audie Murphy. He died in a plane crash not far from the memorial's location. Seeing all the trinkets veterans left to honor him was both touching and impressive. I was disappointed when I listened to a 20-something talking about how she walked past the memorial honoring the most decorated World War II veteran[22] without stopping because she had no idea who he was. One would think that seeing all of those American flags in the middle of nowhere would have at least piqued her interest to walk the 100-foot side trail.

My day also included summiting a peak called "Dragon's Tooth." Climbing to the peak was tough enough, but the descent was nearly impossible and definitely death-defying. The ominous trail

---

[22] https://en.wikipedia.org/wiki/Audie_Murphy

sign didn't adequately warn me about my pending doom. It didn't mention anything about scaling a sky-scraping rock face on two to three-inch ledges without any ropes. My hiking poles were useless. I placed them in grooves along the rock, shimmied myself across the face, and slid my poles along with me so they weren't left behind. All the while, I was wearing my pack. To make matters even more hazardous, while I was hanging onto the rock face with just my fingertips, bees appeared, and I needed to swat them away. I really didn't need that. On a positive note, I crossed the 700-mile mark!

As I hiked through the woods, there was always a possibility that I would come across a bear. On May 18, while covering 10.7 miles, I heard a commotion and knew I was coming upon something HUGE. What I found was a heard of cows. They were cool, but honestly, I prefer bears. I continued along my way to the trail's iconic McAfee Knob. While its view was breathtaking, one slip can be fatal, and it has happened in the past.

Besides enjoying the trail's beauty, I thoroughly enjoyed another rat snake encounter. This handsome specimen was sunning itself on the trail. It was only about 4½ feet long (the first one I found was over 5 feet long). It had no interest in moving when some fearful hikers, a dog, and I wanted to get by. I used one of my hiking poles to gently encourage it to move off the trail. After we made our way past it, it immediately returned to the trail so it could enjoy the afternoon sun. It found its happy place!

The next day I hiked 15.4 miles with most of my clothes strapped outside my pack. I had been trying to dry things out for almost a week without much luck. My day included hiking an almost 1,900-foot elevation gain to Tinker Cliffs. Looking deep into the valley created a National Geographic experience for me. I watched a turkey vulture soaring 100's of feet above the ground pass right by me. It was only about 20 feet away. In nature, sometimes you can capture the moment. Other times, you can't. In those cases, you just have to enjoy them. This was one of those moments. I finished my hike in Daleville, Virginia. I used the following day to rest, take care of my gear, and EAT since I'm now down over 55 pounds!

May 21 was an enjoyable day on the trail. For a change, the weather was perfect! The 11.2 miles included some big uphills, but they were manageable. The scenery was pretty, and I found another rat snake in camp. They are probably a good starter snake if you want one for a pet!

After hiking all day and getting into camp, using a privy (outhouse) is a gift that the trail provides. I was thrilled to see a note posted on the door warning users about a copperhead nest inside it. I guess if you are going to be scared, the privy is the perfect place!

I dedicated the miles I hiked that day to my mom. She passed away a year and a day ago. I love her and miss her.

What a wonderful day May 22 turned out to be! The 13.8 miles started with gorgeous weather and a short 2-mile hike to trail magic that Bear Claw hosted. Those of us who stayed at the Wilson Creek Shelter the night before knew about it since he stayed there, too. For breakfast I dined on a grilled hotdog, a fried bologna sandwich, an apple, and some water. The water wasn't only refreshing but key since it was pretty scarce the night before, and it was going to be difficult to find for the next several miles. I was also able to charge my phone!

The night before, I met a gentleman named Slow Poke, and we met up again at the trail magic. He had to be the kindest, gentlest soul I met on the trail to date. He was a Virginia native who loved hiking and trout fishing. He grew up hiking sections of the trail and continues to do so with his sister when she is available. His wife passed away from cancer. It was so clear to me how terribly he missed her.

The 11.9 miles on May 23 started out with a visit with a gentle deer. I had just finished breakfast and was on the trail for only 10 minutes when we met up. Later, I came across a "No Bicycle" sign on the trail. Silly me, I figured it was pretty obvious, given all the rocks, roots, and ledges. I would let Darwin work his magic if someone was stupid enough to even think about biking there!

The day included two substantial uphill battles. The first one was just the warm-up. The second one was a 2,500-foot ascent over 4.5 miles. I was grateful to have my hiker legs!

I dedicated that day's miles to Kathy's cousin Geri. I believe she is the first of the cousins, and Kathy is the last for that generation so there is an age gap of about 20 years. Geri is also the family's historian. If anyone ever has a question about the family, she is the expert!

When Kathy's mom passed away, Geri was always there helping with our kids or Kathy's sister's kids. In fact, when my son Shane was born and placed in the NICU, Geri would tell the nurses that she was his grandmother so she could stay with him. As I mentioned, she is the family's historian but not necessarily the family rule follower!

When Geri first heard about my hike, I didn't think she thought it was a good idea. Mainly because she was worried about my safety. I totally understood and appreciated her concern for me. However, I knew she was following my hike and had her total support and blessing!

Billy Joel's "Say Goodbye to Hollywood" includes a stanza where the lyrics are:

"Life is a series of hellos and goodbyes. I'm afraid it's time for goodbye again."

On the AT, I learned the trail was a series of ascents and descents, and it was time for ascents and descents again!

For the most part, the 12.4 miles I covered on May 24, like most other days, were either heading uphill or downhill with very few flat areas to hike comfortably. Fortunately, the scenery was a great distraction. I came across a government communications facility. Interestingly, I heard there was an outlet on the property where I could charge my phone. I couldn't believe nobody stopped this "hiker trash" as I walked all around the property looking for it. Sadly, I never found it, so I left. By the way, "hiker trash" is how thru-hikers refer to themselves since we haven't showered, worn clean clothes, or combed our hair in several days. The term is used affectionately, although some towns people may not use it that way!

My day included walking through a section referred to as the "Guillotine." It looked like the boulder scene from "Raiders of the Lost Ark." I also saw two more rat snakes and took pictures of their faces that only their mothers could love. When I found the first one, I tried moving to the other side of it so I could get the perfect shot. That was where I found the second one. They were about 4 and 5 feet long, respectively. Amazing! Part of my day included a nice walk through a rhododendron tunnel. The flowers in full bloom were stunning!

The "Guillotine!"

My friend One Lung.

When I made it to camp, I set up my tent and enjoyed my dinner. Everything tasted great after a long hike. I wondered if I would have liked it back home in my kitchen. Early Bird already had his dinner, so I was joined by One Lung and Craw Dad. One Lung has been hiking with us for the past few days. His appearance was a cross between my father-in-law and Willie Nelson. Talk about two worlds colliding! He was a Vietnam veteran and a lot of fun to hang out with. When he wasn't looking, I took a picture of him with his trademark scowl. I captured his personality perfectly. Someone tried to rename him "Happy Camper" purely for sarcastic purposes, but it didn't stick! Craw's Dad was a marine biologist. He was about 24 years old and recently completed his Masters. I can't forget to mention he was also a fellow Eagle Scout!

May 25 was a much-needed relaxing day. Early Bird, One Lung, and I only needed to hike 7.6 miles to get to our pickup point for Glasgow, Virginia. The trail treated us kindly. There were almost no ascents, the descents were gradual, and there were a lot of flat sections. I also found another variety of Mountain Laurel and some other pretty flowers!

We made it to Stanimal's 328 Hostel and Shuttle Service. The plan was to rest the following day and then slack pack about 22 miles the day after that. Our stay included meeting up with Treadhead, who was able to return to the trail and hike with Early Bird and me for the next two weeks.

Arriving at a hostel was always interesting since I really had no idea who I would find there. I was surprised to see so many friends, including 505, Nacho and his dog Dahlia, and Frozen Belt.

Near the hostel was an Italian restaurant with a delicious menu, and I'm not just saying that because of what I had been eating from my pack. A bunch of us went there for lunch AND dinner! Hiker hunger was really kicking in. The quantity of food I was consuming would typically be considered disgusting. I even amazed myself by ordering more food after I finished my initial order. Under normal circumstances, the waitress would have been asking if I was serious. I could tell she was used to dealing with hiker trash!

As I mentioned previously, the following day was a rest day. Even though I didn't hike, I was busy. Early Bird, Treadhead, and I planned out our hikes for the next few days and picked up supplies to survive them!

Stanimal's put out an incredible spread that night to kick off the Memorial Day weekend. It was insane! There were beef nachos, Polish kielbasa, burgers, pork tenderloin, chicken thighs, coleslaw, mashed potatoes, sweet potato fries, and corn on the cob. It was your own fault if you left hungry! It was great sharing this meal with so many friends. We caught up on our hikes and gave each other advice. During our conversations, the sky was suddenly filled with about two dozen turkey vultures. I never saw so many at one time in my life!

While we sat around the fire, I had the opportunity to meet Sir Stops A Lot (aka Stops). He is a Trail Angel from Vermont. He came by to wish us well on our hikes. We spoke for a while, getting to know each other and I was able to glean some advice. For example, eat as much ice cream as I can. The fat in ice cream will help me slow down my weight loss. He also mentioned hiking a number of hours a day and not a number of miles a day. This would take the pressure off being 10 miles away from camp at 4 pm. He gave me his contact information and told me to reach out to him when I'm in the Bennington, VT, area. It was reassuring to know I had another angel looking out for me!

A very special moment occurred that evening that I must share. I won't disclose the other party to respect their privacy. I know I made myself vulnerable by disclosing a lot of personal information that I literally kept secret for over two decades. These revelations were made to hopefully inspire or connect with others. I can honestly say that I started seeing the positive impact of what I was attempting to accomplish. A veteran who was following my journey came up to me with outstretched arms, wrapped me in a hug, and sobbed into my left shoulder. While we hugged, through his sobs, he told me, "Finally, someone who understands me." He then told me that if I ever headed down that dark path again, he was there for me.

Countless times, I had people tell me they couldn't imagine what I went through. It isn't their fault that they can't relate to what I experienced. For so many people, the hardest thing can be just having someone to talk to who really understands them. Our experiences weren't normal ones. Finding that connection is invaluable!

After my day of rest, I had an absolutely unbelievable day! First of all, I hiked 21.9 miles. The was my biggest mileage day on the trail so far. I didn't want my ride back to the hostel to wait for me, so I actually jogged about half of the last mile, where the trail conditions allowed me to do so. By the way, the miles I hiked that day represented approximately 1% of the AT's entire mileage. During those miles, I reached another milestone. I crossed the 800-mile mark. I only had 1,400 miles to go!

Another aspect that made that day memorable was how many friends I came across on the trail and how many new people I met. I found Sir Stops A Lot doing trail magic at the trail head first thing that morning. I just had a huge breakfast, but I did stop by for a short visit! I also had a chance to talk with 505, Plum and One Lung, Nacho and Dahlia, and Cruise Control, to name a few.

At one point, I came across a 12-pack of root beer left for hikers. Honestly, root beer wasn't my favorite, but it was that day!

Additionally, the scenery that day was beyond astonishing. I also saw two deer, a garter snake, and a rabbit. I never got tired of finding forest creatures!

On May 28, the weather was gloomy, and the trail was more difficult than expected. It felt like the entire 14 miles were uphill. I was grateful that I was able to complete 10 of those miles before the rain came in hard! The weather forecast was pretty sketchy, and the day itself hinted at what Memorial Day would be like. For such a solemn holiday, it would have been inappropriate to have enjoyed a sunny day.

When I got to the Seeley-Woodsworth Shelter, I was thrilled to have run into some friends, and there was space available for me. After putting on some dry clothes and having something to eat, my sleeping bag was the perfect place to relax while catching up and making some tentative hiking plans with them!

On May 29, Memorial Day, I hoped everyone took a moment to reflect and appreciate our fallen and Gold Star families for their sacrifices. I hiked 14.2 miles, mostly in Mother Nature's liquid sunshine. I felt the weather appropriately matched the holiday. It was fun, however, finding little messages along the trail. On that somber day, I found a heart made from rhododendron flowers. It was a lovely tribute to honor those we lost while serving our country!

When I arrived at the Harpers Creek Shelter, I was surprised to see that Early Bird and Treadhead weren't there. I was concerned since they left camp that morning before I did, and I didn't pass them during the day. Later that evening, another hiker notified me that Treadhead got hurt so he and Early Bird went into town to get Treadhead squared away. That was another nice thing about the trail. Even when our phones didn't work, other hikers helped get critical messages out!

The next day, I enjoyed a 7.9-mile stroll to a road crossing, where I hitchhiked to our meeting place. It was a local brewery that welcomed AT hikers and allowed them to camp and use their bathroom and shower facilities for free. I used that opportunity to dry out my gear after three straight days of rain and eat a crazy amount of food in their restaurant!

May 31 was such a relaxing day. I spent it camping at the brewery. After setting up a clothes line in an open field to dry out my gear, I had a chance to enjoy a shower that Mother Nature didn't provide!

Early Bird and Treadhead caught up to me around lunchtime. We ate a TON of food at the brewery's restaurant while celebrating Early Bird's retirement from the police department and then went back to the campsite. Early Bird decided he would work on his tan, and Treadhead went to his tent for a nap. About 20 minutes later, Beeps and Link arrived at the brewery, so we went right back to the restaurant. We sat outside and continued consuming anything that wasn't nailed down. After so much rain, we savored the relaxing sunny day!

I would label June 1 as absolutely spectacular! I completed 19.1 miles while seeing some amazing scenery. The sunshine made the lighting perfect for taking pictures.

My tramily, Early Bird, Treadhead, Beepers, and Link.

I came across John Elwood (US Army / Air Force retired) and his husky, Fenrir, providing trail magic. As it turned out, we had a lot in common. We both turned to the AT to deal with issues from our past that had been suppressed for many years. Besides our conversation, I thoroughly enjoyed a couple of burgers, a hot dog, and a Pepsi. It was nice running into Beeps and Link there, too.

Creature-wise, I saw a deer and a snake briefly. This was a new type of snake for me. I met Earl Swift on the trail. He was a writer for Outside magazine. He helped me to identify it as a Ringneck. I wished I could have taken a picture of it, but the little guy made its way into the brush after I almost stepped on it! I also saw a rabbit and a frog. With all the rain and cold weather we had been having, the warm, dry weather brought out the rattlesnakes that I had heard about. Unfortunately, I didn't see any. I was hopeful that I would find some the following day after I entered Shenandoah National Park!

On June 2, Early Bird, Treadhead, and I covered 21.7 miles, finishing our day in the park. In case you were wondering, "Shenandoah" comes from the Algonquin word "Schind-Han-Do-Wi", which means "Beautiful Daughter of the Stars". How pretty is that?

We had a great conversation with our Trail Angel Ring Ding, from Deer Park, Long Island, accompanied by his dog Elvis, as we headed to our drop-off point. As it turned out, Ring Ding, like me, was very involved with a Scout troop in his community!

As we approached our destination, we saw several deer, a hawk, and a wild turkey. During our hike, we also found a garter snake. The scenery along the trail was simply marvelous. Most of the pictures I took that day had a bit of a haze in them. That was actually smoke from the Canadian wildfires that made its way to Virginia! For the majority of the miles we covered that day, the trail itself seemed to be groomed and waiting for us. There were only a couple of technical areas that required specific foot and hiking pole placements. Fortunately, there were only a few stumbles, and nobody got hurt!

Access to water was very limited and was definitely a concern since dehydration could be life-threatening. Some of the streams listed as viable sources were either barely flowing or nonexistent. Gratefully, we came across jugs of water Ring Ding placed along the trail so hikers could refill their bottles. We informed the hikers we passed going in the opposite direction about the scarce supply of water they would be facing. We made sure to tell them about the one stream where they could access water since the next spot was more than 10 miles away!

On June 3, Early Bird, Treadhead, and I started out as planned. Ring Ding and Elvis picked us up and brought us to Shenandoah National Park. The ranger at the park's entrance gave Elvis his treat (Ring Ding left a bag of treats with the rangers). You had to see how excited Elvis got as we approached the ranger's station. He knew what was coming!

We hiked 5.2 miles and came across trail magic in the Loft Mountain Campground. We really enjoyed how welcomed Tom, Holly, Bonnie, and Steve made us feel. We had so much fun eating and talking with our hosts. Like a football team walking up to the line of scrimmage, we decided to call an audible. We decided to take the rest of the day off and set up our tents at their campsite. We spent the rest of the day eating, talking, and laughing some more with our new friends. When they told us what they had planned for the next day, we were immediately looking forward to enjoying breakfast with them in the morning too. While we enjoyed our day with them, another hiker, Chris, was there with his dog Biscuit. What a great dog!

Shenandoah is famous for its blackberry milkshakes, so Early Bird, Treadhead, and I excused ourselves so we could give them a shot. AMAZING! The walk to the shop was about a mile downhill. I wasn't motivated to walk back to the campsite afterwards, so I talked the guys into getting another round. We then hitched a ride back to the campsite from a retired army veteran. Honestly, it was so much better than walking!

By the way, as a numbers guy, I did math problems in my head to distract myself while hiking. Every 110 miles hiked represents 5% of the trail. I crossed the 40% completed mark that day!

The rain continued dribbling from the sky throughout the night until about noon the following day. I lay in my sleeping bag for hours, listening to it bounce off the tarp over my tent. However, I couldn't miss the breakfast trail magic I had dreamed about. I completely enjoyed two ham, egg, and cheese sandwiches, a banana, and a cup of hot chocolate. There were so many other treats there, too, but I still needed to hike!

The clouds hid most of the views along the 15.1 miles covered that day. However, I was still able to enjoy some of the wildlife, including a deer and an American Goldfinch. The most amazing part about my day was when I crossed the 900-miles completed mark!

June 5 was a blast. Early Bird, Treadhead, and I headed out that morning in the sun! The morning was actually pretty cool, but it did warm up. Watching the rays stretch through the trees was absolutely breathtaking!

About an hour into our 11.7-mile hike, we came across more trail magic! Caveman, an army veteran, gave us chili, soda, and various treats for our second breakfast. His son had hiked the AT a few years prior, so he wanted to help those who followed in his footsteps.

We met up with Beeps and Link at a campground in the park. We raided the camp store, took showers, and did some laundry. The best part was just enjoying each other's company!

When I woke up on June 6, I acknowledged that it was the anniversary of D-Day. While I was in my "happy place" dealing with my issues, others were going through hell 79 years before.

I covered 12.2 miles of gorgeous scenery that day. The smoke from Canada's wildfires still blanketed the mountains, but it was still easy to enjoy Shenandoah's beauty. My friends and I enjoyed lunch at a wayside restaurant, where we were able to delight in more blackberry milkshakes. They were delicious, of course!

The perfect spot to take a break!

During my hike, I came across a cemetery. I thought it was strange since there were headstones that were pretty old, but others were placed recently. I wondered what it took to get buried in a national park. I also came across a "No Horses" sign. Anyone who knows me knows how much I love being around them. I had to give the sign a big thumbs down!

My favorite part of the day was the time I spent relaxing at the Rock Spring Hut (Shenandoah calls their shelters "huts"), talking with old and new friends. Numerous deer and their fawns walked through our site without any care about us. Wildlife viewing has always been my favorite part of being outdoors!

The following day was a totally enjoyable one. About a quarter of the way through my day's 10.9 miles, Early Bird, Treadhead, and I stopped by a park lodge for a real breakfast: a western omelet, hash browns, and a toasted English muffin!

Later, we met up with Hiking for Charlie, his wife Lin, who follows him in their pickup truck, and their dog Ziggy, an Australian shepherd/cattle dog mix. They provided us with fresh grapes, homemade cookies, Snickers bars, and Dr. Pepper. Their treats were so refreshing and appreciated. Once we got to our campsite, we did some logistical planning. I really loved Shenandoah National Park. It was the perfect place for crushing miles and relaxing!

When I came out of my tent on June 8, I started coughing. The smoke from the Canadian fires blanketed the park, and my eyes started to burn. Luckily, I was still able to hike 11.8 miles.

The next morning provided me with a memorable sunrise. Shortly after I started hiking, I saw a fawn hiding in the brush less than 5 feet off the trail. It was only about 18 inches tall and was easily the youngest deer I ever saw in a natural setting. What a special moment for me. The scenery in Shenandoah continued to impress me. Just watching a butterfly on some flowers felt like Mother Nature was sharing one of her secrets with me!

On the trail, I started a game. As I hiked north, I would tell people hiking south to give Early Bird a message since he was about 5 minutes behind me. For example, I would have them tell him that they were from his old folks' home and that they wanted to confirm he had taken his medications. The other hikers were totally on board and wanted to participate. My favorite exchange was when I had hikers tell him that they were from the clinic. His test results came back negative for syphilis, but he still needed to get himself checked out. He got all my messages!

My friends and I met up in the evening to camp. We shared stories about our day as well as jokes and funny stories from back home. As we unwound from our day, deer continued to visit us. While I have done some long-distance hiking before, life on the AT has been like no other experience I ever had!

If I had to match a song to how I was feeling on June 9, it would be Bruce Springsteen's "Born to Run"! Leaving camp that morning, I felt great and was ready to embrace my last day in Shenandoah National Park. I crushed the 19.1 miles that were waiting for me!

I took my time enjoying the stunning scenery and met a Ridgerunner named Bushman. He retired from the Air Force and volunteered to help hikers along his assigned section of the AT. The funny part about meeting him was Early Bird was ahead of me, so he decided to play my game. He gave Bushman a message for me! We had a good laugh as I explained the game's brief history.

Along the trail, I came across a rabbit, several chipmunks and squirrels, a small butterfly, and another deer. It was funny how seeing even the small animals could make me smile!

After getting to The Stumble Inn hostel, I did some laundry, and Early Bird and I laid out the next few days of hiking. Early Bird and I planned on meeting up with his family in Harpers Ferry in a few days. I couldn't wait to meet them. In the evening, my friends and I had dinner together, shared some more stories, and picked up some supplies. I was also able to speak with my family. I really missed them.

June 10 was bittersweet. Treadhead headed back home to his family in upstate New York. He was SO missed on the trail as we shared a ton of laughs together. We crossed our fingers that we would meet up again when the trail crossed New York.

Breakfast that morning was incredible! Our hostel host, David, made biscuits and gravy, a delicious egg entree, and a savory potato side. He also baked a banana bread that was out of this world. I didn't eat again until dinner time. I couldn't wait to see what his wife, Danielle, had planned for our next breakfast!

Early Bird and I were meeting up with his family in a few days in Harpers Ferry, West Virginia, so we didn't need to complete a lot of miles over the next 5 days. We only did 8.4 miles that day, but that was ok. We enjoyed a very leisurely pace and enjoyed the scenery. We passed by the most amazing shelter I had seen so far. The Jim and Molly Denton Shelter wasn't only magnificent to look at; it had a deck with Adirondack chairs, a separate pavilion for cooking and eating, and a horseshoe pit where you could play a few rounds after hiking! The trail crossed another set of railroad tracks. Shortly after crossing it, a train went by, but by that time, I was already too far away to see it.

My favorite part of the day was after dinner when I hung out with the hostel's dog, Josephine. Jo was a border collie and, as expected, extremely smart! I threw a ball countless times for her to fetch. Actually, it was all her idea. We played for a bit the night before, and she let me know she was ready to continue that night, too. What a great way to wrap up my day!

Before covering 15.2 miles on June 11, it was Danielle's turn to make our hearty breakfast. Again, it was fantastic. David and Danielle were evenly matched in the kitchen. There was no way someone could leave the Stumble Inn hungry!

Originally, we planned on having a low-mileage day. However, the weather forecast changed, and we were looking at rain later that night through the following day. We figured it was better to cover more miles that day, so fewer miles needed to be done on wet rocks.

But that was ok. It allowed me to reach another milestone. By then, I had completed more than 45% of the trail!

The trail knew how to address things in my personal life. That day, my family met at my mother's grave for a special service. While I couldn't be there, I FaceTimed with everyone afterwards, which was very nice. While I hiked those extra miles, I came across a bench of a family dedicated to their mother, Helen. I stopped for a while, rested, and made an entry in the book they wanted hikers to use while enjoying it. I just had this feeling that coming across a memorial bench on the same day as my mother's service was more than a coincidence!

June 12 was another milestone day. The 9.8 miles took me more than halfway through Virginia's Rollercoaster section of the trail. It was a challenging section of the trail with strenuous ascents, descents, and rock scrambles. It was particularly challenging since the rain made everything very slippery. I fell once backward onto my pack. Luckily, my five-pack of ramen cushioned my fall!

That night, I stayed at the Bears Den hostel. I was able to get out of the rain, dry out my gear, take a hot shower, do laundry, eat some hot food, and catch up with friends. While all that sounds busy, it was actually pretty relaxing.

But what was more exciting for me was I crossed the 1,000-mile mark. I had been giving this hike my best effort and learned so much along the way. I learned it was ok to make changes. These changes could be to my hiking plan, nutrition, gear, and pretty much anything else. Flexibility was so important to my journey since there were so many variables that were outside of my control!

After a great night's sleep, I started my day by making pancakes! The 11.3 miles I cranked out brought ANOTHER milestone. I made it through the remaining portion of the

Rollercoaster. This section of the trail could easily get inside your head causing you to doubt your abilities if you allowed it to. However, hikers needed to realize that everything we had done to that point had trained us for it. We got our hiker legs, and our eyes allow us to quickly identify the best spots to place our feet and hiking poles!

The weather that day was perfect. Not only was I able to enjoy some breathtaking views, but I was also able to enjoy some fresh black raspberries. I would have to fight the bears for them as they continued to ripen!

I enjoyed more wildlife too. I made several attempts throughout my hike to get a decent picture of a bird so I could identify it, and I finally got one. It was an Eastern Towhee. While I stayed at the David Lesser Shelter that evening, I also came across a lizard that I hadn't seen before as well as several deer passing through to enjoy their dinner!

An Eastern Towhee

West Virginia (June 14 – 16, 2023)

June 14's 9 miles brought yet ANOTHER milestone. I completed Virginia's miles and made it to Harpers Ferry, West Virginia! Admittedly, leaving northern Virginia was a bit sad since the shelters in this area were really nice! Also, the environments I hiked through were so diverse. You could see how the vegetation changed over the miles covered. Each was remarkable in its own way!

After exiting the woods, I crossed Storer College reading historical placards, visited the Appalachian Trail Conservancy, and briefly explored Harpers Ferry's historic district.

Early Bird and I then met up with his wife, Michele, and his daughter, Christina, who came down from Pennsylvania. I was looking forward to getting some rest and seeing more of Harpers Ferry with them the following day!

June 15 was a much-needed zero day. While I didn't complete any trail miles, I did a short hike with Early Bird, Michele, Christina, and their dogs, Sadie and Heidi. We walked along the river, where the pups were able to enjoy a swim!

Harpers Ferry has a rich history. If you are interested in the Civil War and the impact John Brown had on it, you must visit there! Seeing the old buildings and visiting the John Brown Museum were highlights for me. I must admit I also enjoyed visiting as many of the ice cream shops as I could!

Maryland (June 16 – 18, 2023)

If you were thinking June 16 was another milestone day, then you would be RIGHT! The 16-mile hike that day brought me to Maryland! I also started using my third pair of boots!

About two miles into my hike the skies opened up. Getting soaked was ok, but the temperature dropped just enough to make me cold. Stopping to put on my rain jacket to warm up was always a bit of a production since I had to take off my pack and I didn't want to place it in a puddle. Fortunately, I found a bench where I could get myself squared away without any issues!

After a couple of hours, the refreshing rain stopped, the sun came out, and I came across my Trail Angel Sir Stops A Lot at Gathland State Park. It was great catching up with him while I enjoyed the treats that he provided at his trail magic. Like Harpers Ferry, this park had a lot of Civil War history too. As it turned out, Stops did Civil War reenactments and the unit he was in did them at that park!

Before hitting the trail on June 17 to cover 15.7 miles, a little rat snake, about two feet long, greeted me on the steps of the privy. I thought this was perfect for those who don't like snakes because first they say it, then they do it. Think about that one for a minute and you will get my joke. While staying at the Ensign Cowall Shelter, I came across the biggest spider I had ever seen. This thing was enormous. On the trail I found another rat snake. This one was over 5 feet long!

I hiked by some more Civil War monuments and a battlefield. I couldn't help but think about what a terrible time this was for our country. When you think about it, every soldier that died was American.

I met so many people on the trail that day. One person was a man named Don. He gave me a handmade Maryland AT keychain. I also met Nicki and Keith doing trail magic. They were newbies at providing trail magic and they crushed it! The food was delicious, and it was so much fun answering their questions about trail life. I enjoyed their company for about an hour. Then I went about 100 yards and enjoyed trail magic with Cub Scout Pack 278! I enjoyed their offerings and conversation too. My Scout troop had its annual BBQ and awards ceremony that day so spending time with the Cubs was the perfect place for me to be. I spent about an hour with them too, so I was really behind schedule.

After making it to the local Washington Monument, I cranked out the miles, battling some seriously rocky terrain, and finally made it to camp around 6:30pm. That is pretty late considering hiker midnight is around 7:30pm!

Pennsylvania (June 18 – July 7, 2023)

On June 18, Father's Day, I spent most of my day covering 14.8 miles. It wasn't due to the rocky terrain or the steep ascents or descents or because I was able to call home and talk to Kathy and my boys. It was because Early Bird and I had the opportunity to meet Cragg, the cousin of one of Early Bird's 82nd Airborne buddies. Craig met us at Pen Mar County Park. Early Bird got to the park before I did since he always woke up early and started hiking before I was even out of my sleeping bag. Early Bird knew Cragg and I would hit it off immediately when they first met since he was wearing an FDNY 10 House T-shirt. That was the firehouse I was working at on 9/11. He bought it when he visited Ground Zero.

Cragg took us into town where he treated us to lunch. Afterwards, he took us to pick up some supplies before returning to the park so we could finish our miles for the day. We all had a great time getting to know each other. It was more like we knew each other forever and knew exactly how to make each other laugh! We hoped Cragg would have been able to join us for some miles on the trail. Unfortunately, we never met up again.

Once back on the trail, I had another milestone moment. I crossed the state line between Maryland to Pennsylvania. I was curious to see how The Keystone State's 230 miles were going to challenge me, but I had a pretty good idea. I already knew the last third of the state was going to be pretty tough, especially since hikers nicknamed the state "Rocksylvania"!

Mother Nature provided me with a Father's Day present on the trail. It was a 5-foot rat snake. Even though it was getting late, I spent about 15 - 20 minutes watching it climb over and under the surrounding brush. I really do find snakes fascinating and enjoyed my gift!

June 19 started with me waking up to a beautiful sunrise that I could enjoy from my sleeping bag. For mid-June, I couldn't believe how cold I had been at night. I was actually shivering at times. I wondered if part of it had to do with all of the weight I lost.

Fortunately, about two miles into my 13.2-mile hike I met Tycoon doing trail magic. There wasn't anything better than a second breakfast around 9:30am consisting of grilled hot dogs, Pepsi, clementines, and assorted pastries. For a while, I was Tycoon's only guest, so we were really able to get to know each other. A little while later, other hikers arrived, including Bear Claw who provided trail magic to me about a month before. It was great catching up with him and meeting the other hikers!

The rest of the miles included a spectacular view, a butterfly that found my dirty backpack interesting, and some serious boulder scrambles. Early Bird and I planned on meeting up at the Thru It All hostel, which a local church ran. It was located about a mile off of the trail. As I walked along a highway to get there, one of the locals saw me with my gear, pulled over, and gave me a ride. It was heartwarming to see how these small towns supported the hikers!

One of the people running the hostel showed us a refrigerator whose contents were available to its guests. That was a big mistake on their part. We were more than delighted to help ourselves. It WAS stocked with fried chicken. It WAS delicious! Actually, we didn't finish it since we decided to do a 20-mile hike the following day and return there for another night. Just thinking about that chicken was going to be enough to motivate us to finish as soon as possible!

I loved the hostel's coffee cups. Inscribed on them was, "We care more about your future than your past!" Everyone has a past that can't be changed. The ministry focused on supporting everyone's future. What a great purpose!

June 20 was such an exciting day since the 19.9 miles covered a few milestones. One was I finally found a Timber Rattlesnake. It was a thrilling encounter! It was lying next to the trail and Early Bird walked right past it. I called him back to show him what he missed. Afterwards, I decided to pick some wild huckleberries about 20 feet away from it. I figured it was safe to do so since snakes don't typically live in groups when they aren't mating. By the way, I don't think the snake noticed the "foot traffic only" signs posted along the trail. Think about that one for a minute and you will get my dad joke!

A Timber Rattlesnake

Another milestone I reached was crossing the trail's halfway point. In 2023, the trail covered approximately 2,198 miles. I knew the worst was yet to come, but every day I was getting stronger physically and mentally. I loved the trail's tradition of doing a half-gallon ice cream challenge at a general store at the trail's midpoint.

Needless to say, I crushed it in about 24 minutes. One hiker puked. Rookie!

The third milestone that day also included crossing the 1,100-mile mark. When I wasn't completing milestones, I just enjoyed the trail and everything it offered me!

On June 21, I covered 19.2 miles which was more than what was originally planned. Some bad weather was heading my way, so I wanted to cover more miles in better conditions. The extra miles were grueling. They included boulder scrambles, climbing over and squeezing between them. My hiking poles were totally useless during this section of the trail!

After walking across a farmer's pasture where all I saw were enormous crops of corn and wheat, I made my way into the town of Boiling Springs. It greeted me with a first-day-of-summer celebration. The town was giving out free ice cream. I had two sundaes. Of course, they were delicious. Boiling Springs was very veteran friendly. The monument in town showed how much its veterans and their service were appreciated!

4 of my friends and I were able to able stay at the only "hostel" in town, Lisa's Shed. It was literally a shed in Lisa's backyard. Her husband built some wooden bunks in the shed, ran an electrical line to it for power, and added a couple of creature-comforts so we could heat our food and watch a movie on the combo TV / VCR unit. We were allowed to go inside their house to use the bathroom and take a shower and Lisa did our laundry.

Early Bird asked Lisa if she was a hiker and how she got the idea of allowing hikers to sleep in her shed. The expected response was she was a hiker and thought it would be cool to help fellow hikers since there were no other hostels in the area. Lisa's response was something like, "Oh God no!" What actually happened was she and her husband were drinking rather heavily around the fire one night and the idea just came to them!

That night my friends and I arranged for a pizza delivery. After a long hike in the cold rain, hot cheesy pizza was the edible form of heaven. We told them the address and made sure they understood that our order needed to be delivered to the shed in the backyard!

As I expected, it RAINED on June 22! It was a real soaker. Throughout the day, the rain bounced off the hood of my rain jacket. But that was ok. Rain was just part of the fun. I still managed to get 16.5 miles behind me!

Along the way, I came across a stone bench. It was actually pretty comfortable. I also hiked through a tunnel that went underneath a highway. That was so much better than one of my other road crossings when I almost got hit by a car!

Except for a couple of manageable hills and some mud, the trail was pretty good. I came across a toad almost as big as my fist and a plant I had never seen before. My favorite part was foraging for blackberries and mulberries. They were so delicious!

My friends and I spent another night in Lisa's shed since the rain was relentless. Lisa had three horses on her property. I spent part of my afternoon chilling out with Buster who was quite friendly. For me, horse-time makes a bad day better and a good day perfect!

The following day I slogged across 8.7 miles. The weather was horrible, and the trail conditions were even worse. The trail was wet. The rocks, leaves on the ground, and the leaves on the rocks were all wet and slippery. Luckily, I stuck the landing after each slip and stumble! I loved seeing a sign on the trail for a breathtaking view. I guess I will have to come back another time to see what was hiding in the fog!

I made it into the town of Duncannon where I stayed at the Kind of Outdoorsy hostel with Early Bird, Pork Chop, and some other friends. We met up for dinner and had a few laughs. The restaurant had some live music, which was quite a treat. They played 70's rock, which sounded awesome. Usually, I don't play music on the trail since I really enjoy listening to whatever nature wants to share with me and I need to save my phone's battery!

Before hitting the trail on June 24 to cover 18.1 miles, I had to give Scraps some belly rubs. She was a canine guest who was also staying at the hostel with her owners. Like all the other hikers, she was looking for a reason to not go out into the rainy mist!

The first few hours on the trail were very damp and the conditions continued to be pretty slick. As the day progressed, the sky cleared, and the sun came out. That helped tremendously when I needed to navigate the rock scrambles. I guess the one good thing about the wet trail was I found a newt. I came across several of them along the way. There was something about these little guys that just made me happy. The rat snake I came across was just a bonus!

When I made it back to the hostel, I sat on a bench outside to catch up with my family and friends. It started to drizzle and then it POURED! I was so happy that I could just walk inside, sit on a comfortable chair, put my feet up, and relax!

Trying to get my 16 miles completed on June 25 was a bit like playing the game "Beat the Clock." I wanted to get my hike in before the rain arrived as there was a mist already in the air. I appreciated it when the sun came out, cleared the air, and gave me an opportunity to complete a bunch of miles in more enjoyable conditions.

I found another ring-necked snake on the trail. The one I saw about a month before was such a brief encounter. This time I was able to get lots of pictures. I also found another newt. I loved the way they always appeared to be smiling. Then I found a puddle filled with tadpoles. It was so strange since the rain created the puddle in the middle of the trail!

And then the rain came. It lasted for about an hour. That was enough time to soak the trail and me. I spent the last hour of my hike drying out before getting into town where I was able to address my hiker hunger with a turkey club sandwich, a BLT, fries, lemonade, and a chocolate milkshake. I loved visiting the towns along the trail!

The following day was another round of "Beat the Clock". Not only did I lose, I lost badly. My hike started out in a soupy, humid mess. About 10 miles into my 22-mile day, I enjoyed some trail magic with Tin Man, who served in the navy, Ranger, and their dog Moose. Tin Man and I had a lot in common. We were both from Long Island, we are both Eagle Scouts, and we both went to the same Scout camp. We also went to college in Colorado. He went to CU - Boulder and I went to the University of Denver!

Shortly after leaving the trail magic, I experienced the worst rainstorm on the trail for me by far. Within minutes, the trail was under 3 inches of water. I even saw a toad who looked totally confused by all the rain. Then, the hail came. I was getting pelted by pieces of ice, 1/4 inch in diameter, by the hundreds per minute. If you have never experienced this before, I must tell you it really stings!

After about an hour of getting completely drenched, the rain finally stopped, and the sun came out. It gave me a chance to dry out before reaching another milestone. I crossed the 1,200-mile mark. I had just under 1,000 miles left!

I dedicated those 22 miles to my sons, Justin and Shane. They just completed their school year. Justin became a high school senior, and Shane became a junior. They both had amazing years academically and with their extracurricular activities. I couldn't have been prouder of them!

On June 28, Early Bird and I won "Beat the Clock". We completed the 14.8 miles before the rain came. And it poured. Again!

Our destination was Port Clinton, PA. If I ever had to pick a town to skip, this would have been it. Early Bird and I were hungry and looking for a place to eat. The only place in town was a hotel with a restaurant and bar. Apparently, their business model included being closed on Mondays and Tuesday. I guess it made sense to someone so I must have missed something!

I saw a woman by the local firehouse and asked if she could help an out-of-town firefighter. When she asked what I needed, I told her my friend and I could really use a ride to the local Cabela's a couple of miles down the road. She gave me the nastiest look and 3 very emphatic "No! No! No!" This would never have happened at my firehouse. As it turned out, there was an AT hiker pavilion in town and Cabela's ran a free shuttle from it to their store. The next one would be in a few hours. Since we had time, Early Bird and I went to a candy store that sold piece candy and nice chocolates. I picked up some treats until the next shuttle arrived.

After checking out the Cabela's, Early Bird and I were allowed to leave our gear in their vestibule while we went to a Wendy's across the street. We again consumed a disgusting amount of food. We then returned to Cabela's to get our gear and meet up with Early Bird's friends, Joe and Michele, their young son Joe and their Belgian Malinois pup, Dakota. Early Bird used to work with Joe in the police department. They brought us back to their home, gratefully, not in Port Clinton. It was the perfect place for me to get to know them and catch a great night's sleep!

Early Bird and I took a zero the following day to get some much-needed rest. Joe and Michele were such gracious hosts. They provided us with a comfortable place to sleep for two nights, lunch, and dinner, let us do our laundry, and gave us full access to their refrigerator!

I loved playing baseball in their backyard with Joey. Afterwards, Early Bird and I borrowed their car to go into town for some supplies and planned out our hiking schedule for the next 5 days. Fingers-crossed, we would cross over from Pennsylvania to New Jersey in just a few days!

During our down time, Dakota got lots of attention. As I mentioned, he was a Belgian Malinois, which is the breed the Navy SEALs like to use. They are such smart dogs. Once I passed his inspection, which did take some time, he was my buddy!

I hope Joe doesn't mind my sharing this story. Joe went to work and the guys at the police station were asking him who was staying at his house. He told them Early Bird was there as well as "Sleepwalker". Then he told them that he didn't know my real name. The other officers were like you have a guy staying at your house, your wife and kid are there, and you don't even know the guy's name? They were involved with numerous calls in the past where they were arresting people in a house where the home owner said they didn't know the people staying there and the officers were like "yeah, right". Joe realized he was now one of "those guys"!

On June 29, after getting some rest, I covered 15 miles without any threats of rain. The trail started out with a pretty challenging 1.5-mile climb, which had a brief plateau about half way up. I was proud of myself since I found it much easier than I expected it to be.

I was totally digging my hiker legs. Overall, the rest of the terrain was fairly flat, but there were some pretty challenging rock scrambles. Considering northern Pennsylvania's reputation, there weren't many surprises.

I did manage to have a few nature encounters. They included a rat snake, fawn, butterfly, and a rabbit. Overall, it was a nice day on the trail!

June 30 didn't go exactly to plan. Originally, my goal was to complete about 17 miles. However, I needed to reduce the mileage to 11.5 miles due to the terrain. My hike started with a pretty drastic two-mile incline. It was then followed by rock and boulder scrambles. The hours were flying by, but the miles weren't!

My day did have a few highlights. One was when I came across a porcupine. It was the first one I saw on the AT. I spent about 10 minutes watching it. Another was when I got some nice pictures of a butterfly. I was able to capture the details in its wings. A third highlight was when I did an interview for Allentown, PA's newspaper The Morning Call. I thought it went well and looked forward to seeing it when it is available.

I have been asked numerous times, "When was the best day on the trail?" People were astonished by how quickly I could provide them with my response. It was July 1. Surprisingly, it had nothing to do with the fact that I hiked 14.4 miles that day. It had nothing to do with the scenery that surrounded me or the wildlife encounters that I experienced. It also had nothing to do with the great dinner I enjoyed with Early Bird and my new friends Anthony and his lovely wife Debbie. It was because I met a young man who was out on the trail hiking for the day. He was curious about my hike. He wanted to know why I was on the trail. I openly and honestly told him about my issues with PTSD and how I wanted to kill myself. While I was sharing with him what I had been dealing with, I could see him getting upset. I saw the tears forming in his eyes and his bottom lip starting to quiver. I asked him if he was ok, and he told me he wasn't. I told him he didn't have to hold back his tears, and it was ok to let them out. I then told him to forget me so we could focus on him. He told me that he hadn't been happy. We talked some more, and then I asked him if he had health insurance. He confirmed that he did, so I told him to check out his coverage. I told him that it most likely covered therapy to address his mental health and recommended that he seek help. I also mentioned that if he didn't feel like he was making a good connection with the first therapist he tried, it was ok to try a different one. After talking for about half an hour, we went our separate ways but ended up meeting again further down the trail. He stopped me to let me know how much he appreciated our talk. I told him that if I could stop one person from heading down the path I was on, then mission accomplished. He told me to "Go find person number two"! I made the connection I was striving to make IN PERSON! I put out numerous posts on social media hoping they would reach that one person. For it to happen in person, face-to-face, it couldn't have been better!

That evening, Early Bird and I made it to Danielsville, where we stayed at the Country Side Deluxe Suite. Rooster was a terrific host as well as her canine companion, Apollo. Rooster understood hikers. When she met us at our meeting point, she greeted us with perfectly chilled Cokes!

Sometimes the weather decides for you if you will hike that day or not. July 2 was one of those days. My next hike was going to cover more rocky terrain and include some pretty steep inclines and declines. The forecast included thunderstorms which would have made hiking too dangerous. Therefore, Early Bird and I decided to postpone hiking for a couple of days. Early Bird went home to see his family and I rented a car so I could see my family who I hadn't seen since March 8, since they were renting a cabin by a lake just over an hour away. They were there with my sister-in-law, Trish, my niece, Colleen, and her boyfriend, Mike. I told Kathy not to say anything to the kids since I wanted to surprise them. As it turned out, the cabin's owner wanted to stop by to check something, so Kathy told the kids to expect a visitor. When I arrived, I called Kathy on her phone since I didn't see her car and I wanted to confirm I was in the right place. She and Trish were on their way back from running an errand, so I waited outside. When they got back to the cabin, I walked inside with them. I then walked right past my kids. My younger son didn't recognize me at first because I lost so much weight and grew a totally legit mountain-man beard. It was great seeing them. Too bad my dogs couldn't make the trip too!

The following day I said goodbye to my family and met up with Early Bird and his daughter, Caitlin. After enjoying some pizza in town, we returned to the Country Side Deluxe and shared stories about our family visits with Rooster and Apollo!

I figured this is a good place to share something funny about being on the trail. To be completely honest, thru-hikers smell! It could be days before we have the opportunity to take a shower or wash our clothes. This is probably no surprise to you. One hostel even gave out a rubber bracelet which stated, "I stink therefore I am!" When we were hiking on the trail, we could actually SMELL day hikers. These are hikers that are out on the trail for the day and then return home in the evening. They stood out from the rest of us since the body wash they used that morning and the fragrant fabric softener in their clothes delighted our noses. We loved walking past them so we could smell anything that wasn't US! We could even detect a day hiker that we couldn't see. They either left behind a pleasant vapor trail where they already hiked, or the wind was sending their scent ahead to us. If anyone is ever interested in making a thru-hiker happy, please come hike a section of the trail for just a day!

As expected, July 4's 20.9 miles went down as one of the top 3 most difficult days on the trail. The hike started with a severe, uphill challenge. However, everything I had done so far trained me to get through it. Afterwards, most of the day was relatively flat. There were some rocky sections along the way which were still wet and slippery from the prior night's rain. Then, with about .75 miles left to my day, I started my descent down a boulder-covered, rock-faced mountain peak. I had to put my poles into my pack along with my fanny pack. This way I could lay flush against the rock wall and lower myself down onto the ledge below without getting hung up. I had to do this numerous times. I was constantly looking for hand and foot holds that I could use so I wouldn't fall 20 to 50 feet! What was worse was I was placing my hands and feet into crevices not knowing if there was a rattlesnake or copperhead hiding in them to escape the hot sun. Gratefully, I made it to the end of the hike without any injuries. I have to admit, I was pretty exhausted afterwards. I met up with Early Bird shortly after getting off the mountain and we both agreed that we left everything we had on the mountain that day. If there was a silver lining to this grueling experience, it would have to be the time I got to spend with Apollo when Rooster picked us up!

Staying on the trail was preferable logistically and cost wise. However, even with all the rain, there was such a water shortage on the trail. I felt it was safer to stay somewhere where I knew I would have access to water before and after my hike. Just as an example, with only about 3.5 miles remaining that day, I ran into some friends who needed water. I gave them a liter since they still had a long way to go, and I was almost done for the day.

Before starting my hike on July 5, I had to say goodbye to my friends Rooster and Apollo. Rooster was camera shy, but I will never forget her. What a helpful and caring soul!

I covered 15.3 miles over more rocks and boulders. I wasn't disappointed that the trail didn't have more rock faces to scale. I had some nice wildlife encounters which included a giant toad, and a deer. I also came across a gigantic footprint. I noticed there were claw markings, so I was very relieved. Dog prints typically include claw markings. Mountain lions, which have similar footprints to dogs, typically don't include them. I knew some other hikers had a mountain lion encounter, so anything was possible!

During my hike, I met the caretaker for one of the shelters. He asked if I was a thru-hiker, and I told him I was. He then gave me a large Peanut Chews candy bar. These were my mother's favorite. I thanked him not only for the treat, but for the nice memory too!

One of the hostels that Early Bird and I stayed at the week before sent him a text. It included a copy of the article that The Morning Call ran about my hike. However, after taking a closer look at it, we realized the Reading Eagle ran it. I could never express how much I appreciated everyone's support for my hike!

That night I stayed at the Live Life hostel. Not Today was such a gracious host and his team was extremely helpful. They provided a delicious BBQ dinner and a relaxing campfire where Early Bird and I were able to get to know the staff and the other guests!

New Jersey (July 6 – 11, 2023)

My hike on July 6 included a few milestones. Even though I was tormented by severe heat tand humidity that coated my skin with its moisture, the 11.1 miles I completed allowed me to cross the border from Pennsylvania into New Jersey. Another state finished!

These miles also got me past the 1,300-mile mark. Less than 900 miles to go!

The scenery was very diverse. Walking across the bridge over the Delaware River was beautiful. Walking along a stream was beautiful too. I had to climb over some boulders that surrounded a gorgeous pond, but they were more than manageable with the training the trail already provided!

Speaking of the trail providing, near the end of my hike, I came across a cooler chest that a local church placed on the trail. It provided me with a refreshing Sprite and a peach fruit cup. It may sound like no big deal to you, but to thru-hikers like me, it meant EVERYTHING!

I was so grateful that I could do my 17.9-mile hike on July 7 while avoiding the expected thunderstorms. I could hear them in the distance and felt the lightest sprinkle for about a minute. Who knows, maybe a brief storm would have been nice to lower the very uncomfortable humidity!

Overall, I enjoyed my day on the trail. It started with one of the best trail magics I ever saw. Moose was an expert trail angel. Not only did he provide all types of supplies hikers needed and food hikers enjoy, HE HAD ICE CREAM! He actually packed a portable refrigerator / freezer. When I arrived at his generous spread, I felt like Norm from Cheers. Everyone who saw me started screaming out my name. It was a terrific welcoming, and such a nice surprise seeing so many friends. Moose was probably like, who is this guy?!

The trail itself was pretty nice. You could easily see how the rocks were lessening, and the scenery was diverse which helped the miles pass by quickly. I did have some nice wildlife encounters. I saw two more rat snakes. One was over 5 feet long. I also saw a rabbit and a turkey. The turkey was a surprise considering I came across it on a mountain peak. That is the cool thing about being out in nature. You never know what you are going to find or where!

Even before starting my 14.1-mile hike on July 8, my day was pretty exciting. I saw several deer, a vulture, and a momma bear with three cubs! In Yellowstone I saw a momma bear with two cubs, and I was thrilled. Three cubs, SO MUCH COOLER!

The weather made the hike more challenging than it needed to be. My friend Tater summed it up best when she said, "The humidity made the air so thick, you had to chew it before you could breathe it!" I first met Tater back in Tennessee at the Mountain Harbour in Tennessee. Our paths crossed a few times since then and she has been hiking with Early Bird and me for the past few days.

Meeting so many cool and interesting people along the trail was one of my favorite parts about my entire AT experience. I met some hikers several times along the way. Sometimes those meetings were brief and other times the friendships formed quickly and deeply, and we would spend several days or weeks hiking together!

The terrain included more up and downhills with lots of rocks. It was nice when terrain like that, which had once been considered challenging, had mostly become just a nuisance. The weather for the next few days was most likely going to include thunderstorms so I used part of that evening to come up with a few alternatives so we could hike safely. I was hopeful that at least one option was going to work. As I have mentioned before, flexibility on the trail was key!

A low-mileage day was planned for July 9 since thunderstorms were predicted for the late afternoon. My 8.8-mile hike started out with more of the thick, soupy humidity. I noticed that I could hear birds singing when the weather was nice, and the trail got really quiet when a storm was coming. I knew the storm was close by how eerily silent my surroundings were. With about 3 miles to go, the rain started much earlier than expected. I was soaked within minutes. The trail was submerged and what wasn't submerged became a muddy, slippery mess.

I stayed at the Sola Appalachian Christian Retreat that night with Early Bird, Tater, and Hungry Bird. The local pastor and his family hosted the hostel in the basement of their home. Typically, Pastor Doug would accommodate up to 4 hikers. However, there was already a hiker there, so we were concerned that our group was going to be turned away. I will never forget hearing Pastor Doug telling us how he took pity on me specifically when he saw how the day's storm had me completely drenched and how it would have been inhumane to turn us away.

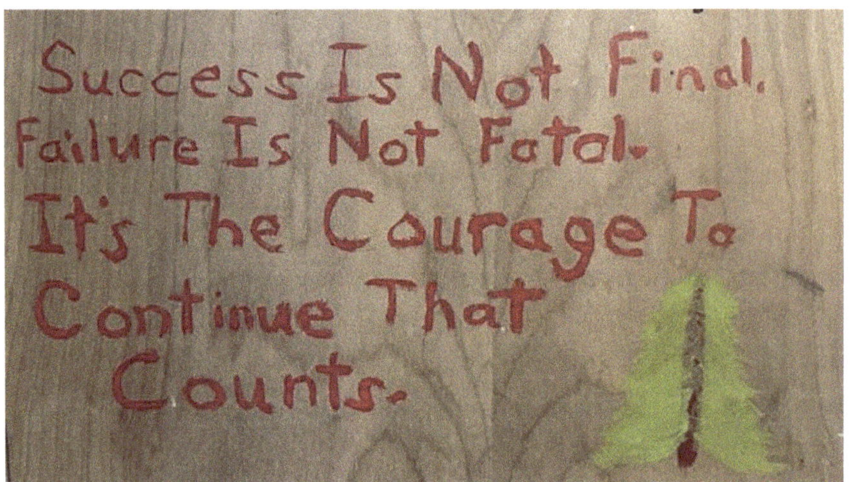

An inspirational message at Sola Appalachian Christian Retreat.

Sola was decorated with inspirational messages hikers painted. Some of them really resonated with me. They inspired me to acknowledge the challenges in front of me, but they also inspired me to crush them!

That evening, we went to Pastor Doug's service at his parish down the street. It was so inspirational. After having warmed our souls, my tramily went to the local pizza place to warm our bellies with some cheesy delights. We ran into some other friends there who were enjoying their own good fortune. A local hosted 9 of them in his barn. The deal was they had to let him buy dinner for everyone or they had to leave his property. That was a true no brainer!

Luck was on my side when I covered the 11.8 miles on July 10. It didn't rain for most of the day. There was a quick sprinkle; maybe 2 minutes. The rest of the day was pretty clear. The trail itself was a mixed bag. Most of the country's northeast was hit by significant storms the day before and parts of the trail were still underwater. Other sections were just muddy. My boots were still soaked from the storm, so I tried using a dry pair of sneakers left in a hostel's hiker box[23]. They weren't waterproof, so my feet got wet pretty quickly. I ended up ditching them and wearing my wet boots.

My favorite part of the day was hiking along the Pochuck Boardwalk in Vernon, NJ. I saw an amazing variety of plants, birds, amphibians, and insects. I never saw so many types of dragonflies!

The hike ended at Heaven Hill Farm. There, I met up with Early Bird, Tater, and Hungry Bird for some fresh fruit, soda, and ice cream. Ice cream was a great post-hike treat since it was refreshing and had a lot of calories. While enjoying our treats, I had the opportunity to meet a very nice man named John Maguire. John had been following my hike since March. He showed up with real bagels!

---

[23] A hiker box is a box that thru-hikers can find at most hostels. They are usually filled with extra food and gear that hikers who previously stayed at the hostel left behind for other hikers to rummage through. The earlier hikers may have upgraded their gear or simply decided they wanted to reduce the weight of their pack didn't want to carry the extra gear.

My friends and I shared a motel room that night since the forecast included even more rain. The nearby motels were full for some event, so John graciously made himself available to help us get to our motel which was pretty far, by foot, off the trail. He couldn't take all of us and our gear in his truck, so he reached out to the local police department. The chief was aware of my hike and wanted to support my effort and help a fellow first responder. He sent some unmarked cars to assist us with rides. This was how the brother / sisterhood worked!

New York (July 11 – 19, 2023)

July 11 included 15.1 beyond-treacherous miles. It started with a section called Stairway to Heaven. This section was pretty steep, but manageable. I kept thinking of Led Zeppelin as I hiked. Then I thought I would have preferred giving belly rubs to a Black Dog instead! After summiting this section, I hiked sections that were dry and enjoyable or still underwater from the storm a couple of days before. Sometimes it was difficult to tell if where I was hiking was the trail or the nearby stream!

Then things got really dangerous. The trail changed from hiking to serious rock climbing without ropes. I had to scale numerous rock faces, either up or down, while wearing my pack and looking for hand and footholds. If I slipped the fall would have easily ended my hike or worse. One section did show some mercy. Steel rebar was inserted into one rock face allowing me to climb quickly to the top of the rock. If I had a choice, I would have preferred to have had the rebar in a number of other locations instead!

I did achieve another milestone that day. I finished New Jersey and made it into New York. The best part of the hike was when I came off the trail. Not because I was out of danger, but because I was a short stroll away from Bellvale Farms Creamery. I heard a lot about this place from other hikers. Their ice cream was supposed to be amazing. I went for their banana split. IT DIDN'T DISAPPOINT ME!

The 12 miles I covered on June 12 were tough, but not as dangerous as the day before. Sections of the trail were still underwater or muddy, but overall, the conditions were improving. The rock and boulder scrambles were still there, but thankfully there were fewer of them and most of them weren't as precarious!

I came to a river crossing which required me to take my boots and socks off. The cold running water felt invigorating on my feet as I carefully took each step. Drying off my feet and getting them ready to hike some more actually made for a nice break. I was always looking for that silver lining. I enjoyed my lunch by a waterfall. It was the perfect place to take another break and just listen to the water flow by. Before this last storm came through, the stream and the waterfall were both dry!

I saw something that day that I had never seen before. I came across another rat snake that was over 5 feet long. The way I found it is what was so interesting. At first, I thought I heard a rattlesnake, so I told Early Bird and Tater to stop since they were a few feet behind me, and I wanted to keep them safe. Then Early Bird and I were able to see where the rattle sound was coming from. Right away I knew we were ok. The rat snake was imitating a rattlesnake by slapping its tail on the leaves. I knew some animals mimicked dangerous ones as a defense mechanism. This was the first time I ever saw this happen in a natural setting. It was such an incredible experience!

I only hiked 9.9 miles on July 13. I thought it made sense to take things slowly a bit longer since several trails thru-hikers were using were still closed to the public due to the prior storm.

After the trail had me cross over the NYS Thruway, it was off to the Lemon Squeezer. This was a very tight passageway where you had to take off your pack and squeeze your way through two rock walls. Overall, it wasn't too bad. I went through this section with Early Bird and Tater which worked out well. Once I went through, we were able to pass our gear through without any issues. Teamwork made this area so much easier!

The rest of the hike was very enjoyable. The trail overall was relatively tame and scenic. I saw a handsome buck with velvet on its antlers, some toads, and of course, another snake. This time it was a garter snake.

I made it to the William Brien Memorial Shelter pretty early. This gave me a chance to dry out my clothes before the expected rain the following day, take care of my gear, catch up with my family, and do an interview with the LoHud Journal News newspaper. The reporter was writing a story about how the recent severe weather closed numerous nature parks. My understanding was they were also going to work my fundraising effort for Paws of War into their story!

July 14 included another 9.9-mile hike. The plan was to go to bed early the night before and get up extra early that day to beat the rain. That WAS the plan. What actually happened was around 11 pm the night before, an insane thunderstorm arrived and lasted most of the night. Early Bird, who preferred using his tent instead of the shelters, quickly packed up his gear and moved into the shelter where Tater and I were sleeping. Then, around 2:30am, I felt something substantial grab my leg. At first, I thought it was a bear since I knew there was one in the area. I yelled and kicked to free myself from whatever it was. I then grabbed my phone and turned on the flashlight. It was just a raccoon that climbed onto my sleeping bag while I was asleep. I had forgotten there was a nearby raccoon that liked to snuggle with hikers in this particular shelter. After everyone settled down and fell back to sleep, it returned a second time. Now it was Early Bird's turn to get rid of the raccoon after it sat on his head. When we woke up in the morning, we found Early Bird's gear scattered around the shelter. Our friend came back a third time to see if we had anything of interest. Surprisingly, being the shelter's slob, my gear was untouched. Needless to say, our hike started a bit later than expected since nobody got much rest!

Rain was anticipated in the mid to late afternoon. However, it arrived in full force in the mid-morning. The thunder and lightning were spectacular. I would have enjoyed watching it if I were sitting in a chair on a porch protected from the elements. Instead, it was pretty nerve-wracking since I was on a mountain peak. The one good thing was I achieved another milestone. I crossed the 1,400-mile mark!

After getting off the mountain, the trail led to a road crossing where a sign stated the trail that crossed Bear Mountain was closed. Hikers were instructed to follow a road around the mountain. What I saw was unbelievable. There was so much destruction the storms from the last few days left behind. Huge rocks were washed off the mountain and deposited onto the road. Sections of the road itself were washed away. New streams were running down the mountain. The one good thing about doing the road walk was having access to all the raspberry bushes. The berries were totally clean from all the rain and were really nice treats. When I first started hiking the AT, I thought Mother Nature wasn't happy. I now thought she had shifted from unhappy to very angry!

I cherished the moments when I got to see my family during my hike. Later that day, my cousins Marion, Wayne, and Liz came to see me. I couldn't thank them enough for the trail magic they did for Early Bird, Tater, and me. Any time I could see my family while I was away was so special. These were definitely absence makes a heart grow fonder moments!

Enjoying trail magic with my cousins, Wayne, Liz, and Marion!

I wanted to cover a lot of miles on July 16 since I didn't hike the day before and I wouldn't be hiking the following day. Another storm was expected, and it looked like it was going to be another big one!

The 18.4 miles covered were beyond exhausting. It took almost 12 hours to complete them. The miles weren't the tough part. It was the storm-altered terrain. So much of the trail was a swampy mess. Twice, I had to take my boots off to cross new streams that were now part of the trail. Other times, the trail hid the water below the tall grass. I didn't know the water was even there until it was filling up my boot! At one point, I was standing next to a stream trying to find the best way to cross it. The ground underneath my feet washed away and I fell backwards. Fortunately, the thorn bushes behind me broke my fall. Once I pulled the thorns out of my hand, I crossed the stream without any issues!

The best part of the hike was the break I took with Early Bird and Tater at the Appalachian Market. It is a joint gas station and convenience shop at an AT road crossing. The sandwich, fresh fruit, and cold drinks gave me the energy to push through the last 5 miles!

I liked seeing some of the historical points along the trail. One spot was where General George Washington had his troops inoculated for smallpox during the revolution. Hiking the same terrain Washington and his men hiked made me appreciate even more what they went through to form our country!

Nature-wise, I saw a few cool things. They included a frog, a couple of toads, a rat snake with cool markings, and a beehive!

I was curious to see what the trail conditions were going to be like in the next few days. Until then, I just wanted to see the inside of my eyelids!

On July 17, the 12.1 miles I covered were pretty enjoyable. The weather was hot and humid, but it was manageable since the trail's canopy kept me out of the direct sunlight most of the time. The trail conditions also improved. While some sections were still submerged or muddy, they weren't as bad as what I had been getting used to.

I came across some interesting sites on the trail. One was an American flag painted on a mountain peak as a memorial for September 11. I appreciated seeing this as a reminder that nobody should forget that day.

I also came across my favorite butterfly. Not only did I get a chance to see and enjoy it, but I also had the opportunity to get some nice pictures of it too.

I met many interesting people on and off the trail during my journey. When I was done hiking for the day, I met up with Early Bird at a local pizza place while we waited for Tater to finish her hike. A woman, Bethany, came up to us and asked us if the packs outside were ours. We said they were, and she offered us a ride to where we needed to go. We told her we were good, so we hung out and had a nice conversation. It turned out she placed some of the water jugs on the trail for hikers like me. It also turned out she was a therapist who specialized in PTSD. We talked about my situation for a bit and then she shared something very interesting. Her cousin was one of the pilots for one of the American Airlines flights that was hijacked on 9/11. It seemed like my day came full circle. I was hiking because of my PTSD from 9/11, I found a 9/11 memorial on a mountain peak, and I met someone else with very personal ties to 9/11. I just never knew what the trail had in store for me!

The 14.8 miles I completed on July 18 were a bit more challenging than expected. There wasn't anything about the terrain that I couldn't handle, and, for the most part, the trail conditions continued to improve. Unfortunately, the humidity was very high, even early in the morning. Just trying to catch my breath was tough. The hike itself was mostly enjoyable. I came across several hikers that I knew which was always nice. I crossed a few different natural settings, too. The changing scenery kept my hike interesting.

With about 3 miles left in my hike, my enjoyable hike became challenging for another reason. I was caught in the worst thunderstorm I experienced so far on the trail. The amount of rain that came down was astounding and the threat of a flash flood was very real. I couldn't see the trail underneath all the water. I had one more stream crossing to do before completing my hike. Gratefully, I made it to the other side without any issues!

Connecticut (July 19 – 24, 2023)

The 9.7 miles I completed on July 19 made for such a pleasant day. It started by crossing some farm pastures before spending most of my time in the woods. Except for a handful of muddy sections and patches of excess rain runoff covering the trail, the trail itself was dry. The humidity was also lower than what it has been recently.

There were some cool moments on the trail. For example, I met Magic Jack. He was doing trail magic, providing hikers with bacon, cheeseburgers, beer, soda, and chips. That morning, he made breakfast sandwiches. He never hiked the trail, but his son did it in 2013.

I also came across a free library on the trail. Hikers could take a book to read or leave one that they finished. Honestly, I couldn't justify the extra weight in my pack. Another cool moment was when I escaped from New York and entered Connecticut. 9 states done; 5 states left to complete!

The 16.1 miles I hiked on July 20 were TOUGH! I summited so many mountain peaks that I lost count of them. The descents were equally challenging. Luckily, the scenery made my effort worth it. Part of the trail followed a river. It was still ROARING from all the recent rainfall. Some parts of the trail were difficult to navigate due to the downed trees laying across it. One part of the trail was being detoured. This meant I had to do a road walk for a few miles. Even that was nice. I walked through the Kent School campus, which was gorgeous. I hope the kids who attended that school appreciated the opportunity they were given.

The road walk actually provided me with an opportunity too. I saw a scarlet tanager. It was one of the most eye-catching birds I had ever seen. Its colors were stunning. While I was able to get a picture of it, I wish it could have better captured its beauty!

July 21 was a nero day. I only hiked 4.1 miles so I could take care of things while I was in town.

My journey took me to Cornwall Bridge, Connecticut. It was such a charming little town. First, Early Bird, Tater, and I stopped by the local bakery for some treats. Then I picked up my package that was waiting for me. It included new boots since the pair I was wearing were completely trashed, and some snacks to keep me going while hiking. Then Early Bird needed to get his "supplies" at the local liquor store. The counter person was very nice. They keep a logbook of all the hikers that come through. If you signed their book, you got a free beer, soda, or Gatorade. I went for a Sprite.

There was an apartment over the shop. I got to meet Polaris, who lived there. Another great canine connection!

That night, some friends and I stayed with a local dairy farmer named Tommy. He picked us up in his pickup truck. We rode in the truck bed back to his place. He used to live in Italy and made a flavorful Italian dinner for us. Afterwards, he showed us around his property. You really need to spend time with a farmer to see how hard these people work. They are so underappreciated!

On July 22, I hiked 11.2 miles. I could have done more, but I couldn't find a safe place further down the trail to set up camp. But that was ok. I found a flat, root, and rock-free place to pitch my tent, and there was an adequate water supply nearby.

The weather was terrific. With my early start, I was hiking in temperatures in the mid 60's to low 70's. The humidity was also very low. This made doing all the inclines much more tolerable. Let me ask you, do you think they were ever really enjoyable?

I came across an adorable fawn, which always made my day. I liked them more than snakes, and I think by now you know how much I enjoyed them!

I had to make my way through another lemon squeezer. Luckily, I was able to squeeze through while leaving my pack at that time. Near the end of my hike, I could swear I heard race cars. They have a pretty distinct sound, so I was sure I was right. As it turned out, on the other side of the mountain where I was hiking was the Lime Rock Park race track. There was a race that day and I was able to watch part of it from the trail. It was such an unexpected treat!

I covered 10 miles on July 23. It may not have been a big mileage day, but it did include some milestones. For example, I single-handedly fed thousands of mosquitoes! I also completed over 1,500 miles of the trail. I now had less than 700 miles to go!

My hike took me through Falls Village, CT. I got to see a spectacular waterfall where the water that passed over it was used to generate electricity. It was nice seeing Mother Nature being put to work!

After spending some more time in the forest, the trail took me to Salisbury, CT. It was such a charming little town. So many people were walking around enjoying their Sunday. Local restaurants provided outside dining since the weather was perfect, and I already fed the mosquitoes!

Salisbury had a solemn monument honoring its townspeople who served in our country's military campaigns. It was nice that their service won't be forgotten!

Massachusetts (July 24 – July 31, 2023)

My 10-mile hike on July 24 included some of the most enjoyable and scenic miles I experienced on the entire trail. The trail covered a combination of forests, mountain peak clearings, streams, road walks, and boulders. I even had the opportunity to watch a garter snake eat a frog. I could have helped the frog escape, but it wouldn't have been the ethical thing to do. Nature has the hunter and the hunted. It wasn't my place to determine which animal goes free and which one goes hungry. The weather cooperated for the most part, too. There were threats of thunderstorms, but it never materialized to anything more than a few refreshing sprinkles.

I did reach another milestone that day. I completed Connecticut and started making my way across Massachusetts. 10 states done, 4 more to go!

My day ended with a very special evening. My friends, SnailsIt and her husband Radioactive, drove 3 hours, one way, to meet up with Early Bird, Tater, and me for dinner. We caught up on our trail lives and our lives back home. While we were sitting around the table, we were sitting with family!

While I logged 8.4 trail miles on July 25, I actually hiked a few more miles since I needed to get to the trailhead. The miles were again enjoyable and scenic, and I again crossed various environments. I really liked hiking through one forest where the ground was blanketed with pine needles. Each step felt like my foot was landing on a cushion. My knees and ankles really benefited from this!

One section of the hike was pretty technical. Climbing up and down the rock walls was time-consuming. Again, my hiking poles were useless. I wish I could have shared pictures of this area. Unfortunately, I couldn't take any since I was holding onto the rocks with both hands!

I came upon trail magic near the end of my hike. Several hikers enjoyed burgers, dogs, homemade chocolate chip cookies and other snacks, lemonade, iced tea, and water. I had just under a mile left to cover for the day. After some food and rest, I left my gear at the trail magic, finished my hike, and returned to the trail magic for more enjoyable conversations. I was so glad I did this since a friend of mine, who I hadn't seen since April, showed up. At first, he didn't recognize me because I lost so much weight and grew my beard. It was great catching up with him!

The 13.5 miles I logged on July 26 were, for the most part, pretty miserable. Hey, at least I'm being honest! Besides the intense humidity, for the first 8 miles, the mosquitoes were swarming me. They literally sucked the life out of me. Bug spray was useless. I had to remember to breathe through my nose. When I forgot to do so, I swallowed 4 or 5 of them at a time!

The last few miles were more enjoyable. The humidity dropped, and for some reason, the mosquitoes took pity on me and left me alone. I was actually able to enjoy the scenery and take some pictures. However, once I got to camp, it was game on again. The swarming mosquitoes were back! I set up my tent, secured my gear and me inside it, and zipped everything up. The mosquitoes were so bad I decided to skip getting out of my tent to cook dinner and just went to bed. Even after hiking all those miles, I knew going to bed without dinner was the right decision!

On July 27, the 15.8 miles I hiked were so much better than the miles I hiked the day before. After leaving my mosquito-filled campsite as fast as possible, I made my breakfast while I hiked. It felt good to eat after skipping dinner the night before!

The hike included some pretty steep inclines. But that was ok. They were a good tune-up for what was waiting for me further north. With about 6 miles to go, I was able to take a break and enjoy some trail magic. Running Water was a great host. His family owned a lot of land in the area. That land is now part of the Appalachian Trail. You can tell how proud he was to be sharing that land. He even thanked me for coming out to hike the trail!

I was excited to get into town that day to get a package. I replaced some heavy gear with lighter gear. I wanted to give myself the best opportunity for a strong finish!

My favorite part of the day was when my brother and his sons took me into town for dinner. I can't believe I forgot to get a picture of us together. Ugh! At least we had a great time catching up!

On July 28, I hiked 19 miles which were very enjoyable, except for a pretty violent fall I had early on in my day. I would easily put it in the top 5 worst falls I had on the entire trail! My shoulder took the worst of it. Luckily, the mud I landed in absorbed most of the impact. I guess that is why you never wish a hiker a nice "trip"! Sorry, I couldn't resist another dad joke!

The mosquito encounters continued to decrease, and my arms and legs felt less like braille. I came across a cooler chest with lemonade, iced tea, PB&Js, and an assortment of other delicious snacks. I was very thankful for them. Then I met another "Cookie Lady". She had a pick-your-own blueberries farm and invited hikers to her place for cookies and lemonade. Hikers were also welcome to pick as many berries as they wanted. I just enjoyed getting some rest while sitting on a rocking chair on her front porch and talking with the other hikers. After my hike, I picked up some glue. My new boots already needed to be repaired!

On July 29, I got to play "Beat the Clock" again during my 13.7-mile hike, and I won! I made it to camp, got water from the stream, put on dry clothes, had something to eat, and secured my smell-ables in the bear box before the storm arrived. The expected rain was going to last for several hours, but it was going to be worth it. The humidity would break, and the temperature would go down a bit. The following day, the weather was going to be delightful!

Overall, the trail was pretty, and the mosquitoes were barely noticeable. I was hopeful that they wouldn't be an issue anymore. I have no problem stating I didn't miss them!

The trail took me past a gorgeous pond. Hearing the frogs was so soothing. Seeing the lily pad reminded me of my son's play "Once Upon a Lily Pad" when he was in kindergartner or first grade. Such a nice memory!

At the Mark Noepel Shelter that night, I got to see Dynamo. The last time I saw him was when I did the half-gallon ice cream challenge. Such a good dog. Also, someone was hiking with a backpacking guitar. Everyone enjoyed some live music with the rain falling in the background!

The 9.6 miles I hiked on July 30 were filled with beauty and enjoyment, except for when I fell again. It was my third fall in three days. My fall the day before wasn't too bad, so I didn't mention it. This spill wasn't as bad as the one a few days before, but it was definitely worse than the one the day before. I was hiking down a steep descent when my foot landed on small, round rocks. It was like stepping on marbles. The next thing I knew I completely lost my balance and was lying face down in the trail. Except for some bloody legs and a bruised ego, I was ok!

My hike took me past a gorgeous pond, where I watched a mist wafting over it. It was a very peaceful setting. Afterwards, my hike took me over Mt. Greylock. It is the highest point in Massachusetts. From the War Memorial set on top of it, you can see Vermont and New York. Peeking into Vermont was pretty cool. I knew I would be there the following day!

That night, I had a chance to meet four great guys from the North Adams Fire Department. I asked them if they had a patch I could buy. Since they were locked up, one of the guys took out a knife and cut up his shirt so I could have the patches that were on it. You gotta love the brotherhood/sisterhood!

Vermont (July 31 – August 12, 2023)

The 14.1 miles I covered on July 31 included some milestones. One related to my mileage. I crossed the 1,600-mile mark. The other was I completed Massachusetts and made it into Vermont. 11 states were behind me, and I just had three more to go!

Let me tell you about my introduction to Vermont. The state should have been called "Vermud"! The mud was ridiculous. I was used to the mountainous ups and downs, the roots, and the rocks, but the mud really slowed me down. I had to do a lot of side stepping, which wasted a lot of time and energy. However, it was necessary so I could keep my feet dry, which was imperative. Also, it wasn't just the amount of mud ALONG the trail; it was the amount of mud ON the trail. It was more than ankle-deep in a lot of spots, so the insides of my boots were getting just as nasty! I guess the good thing was I didn't fall. My falling streak ended at three days in a row!

While I started August with a nero day, covering only 4.3 miles, my day was pretty full. After my hike, I met with reporters from the TV station, ABC 10 Albany, and the Bennington Banner newspaper. Meetings with the press became an important part of my hike. They allowed me to share with more people than I could ever meet what it was like living with PTSD and let people know it was totally acceptable to get help. I became totally committed to crushing the unnecessary negative stigma around mental health!

Afterwards, Billy Clark from the Bennington Fire Department took me from the trail to his firehouse. He gave me a tour of his station and then took me to where I was staying. Another opportunity to meet more of my brothers!

The 14.4 miles I completed on August 2 were challenging but still very enjoyable. The magnificent scenery was my prize for pushing through the steep inclines, declines, and mud!

Usually, when I hiked, I had a high-protein breakfast, snacks during the day, and then dinner when I got into camp. My friends were surprised that I didn't take a lunch break during the day. I tried something different on the trail that day. I took a lunch break. I took off my pack, sat on a log, made myself comfortable, and stuffed my face. I broke a very important rule that day as I didn't "Hike your own hike". I made a change to my approach almost 5 months into my hike. While I wasn't feeling pressured to take a lunch break, I was curious to see why everyone thought it was almost mandatory to do so. Honestly, I just wanted to take a nap after I finished eating. The following day, I went back to snacking during the day!

I dedicated the miles I hiked on August 3 to Rebecca Stromski. As I mentioned earlier, she trains my dog Chip and me at Paws of War, and her mantra is "Slow is smooth. Smooth is fast!" With the trail conditions being what they were, I could hear her whispering those valuable words in my ear as I hiked the 15 miles I covered that day. Her saying made so much sense since I needed to concentrate on each foot and pole placement to minimize the number of times I fell and keep my feet as dry as possible. Before making it to Vermont, I was typically covering about 2.5 - 3 miles an hour. It was a nice pace since it allowed me to cover miles and enjoy the scenery. After entering Vermont, I was only covering about 1.5 miles an hour. Besides taking longer to cover the miles, I was finding myself mentally exhausted because I had to stay focused for so long. It made me appreciate how Chip feels after class. Usually, when we get home, he takes a nap!

The 10.7 miles I hiked on August 4 were pretty challenging. The terrain wasn't bad at all. It was pretty much everything else. The rain started the evening before and continued through the night and into the morning. The forecast showed that the rain would end around 8 am and start again around 2 pm. However, I was meeting with Auburn Sendra, a reporter from GNAT-TV, a cable TV station for southern Vermont, at 2:30 pm, and I didn't want to be late. Therefore, I hiked through the balance of the morning storm. A lot of the trail was either thick, deep mud, or just deep water. My feet were soaked, even with my waterproof socks and boots. At one point, I took a step into a mud pit that went over my entire boot and halfway up my shin. The rocks and roots were just as slippery as previous days, allowing my new fall streak to reach its second day.

Mother Nature wanted to ensure I was totally soaked, so she unexpectedly sent me a late-morning thunder and lightning storm. I'm sure she was laughing when she realized I was near a mountain peak, holding my metal hiking poles. I needed to get off the mountain as soon as possible for safety reasons. However, the worst part for me about hiking through the two storms that day was I couldn't really take the time to enjoy much of the wet scenery and take pictures.

I made it to the inn where I would stay for the night and meet Auburn with plenty of time to take a hot shower and make myself presentable. As it turned out, Auburn was more than a reporter. She was also a First Lieutenant with the U.S. Army Reserves. She was part of the 302nd Maneuver Enhancement Brigade / 368th Engineer Battalion / 424th Engineer Vertical Construction Company / Equipment Support Platoon (2nd Platoon). Her unit's motto is "War Hammers!"

We continued talking off-camera after the interview was completed. She told me that when she heard that the station was looking to assign my story to a reporter, she made sure that she got it. As it turned out, my story was important to her on a personal level. When her unit was preparing for a deployment, one of their soldiers committed suicide just two days before they were supposed to ship out. Deployments require a tremendous amount of planning. Therefore, there was no time to assign this tour to another unit, so her unit was deployed with heavy hearts.

During our conversation, I told Auburn that I collect fire department, police department, and military unit patches. A few days later, Auburn wrote me a touching letter and included her unit's patch. It wasn't just any patch. It was a patch that first belonged to her sponsor and was then given to her on her first day with her unit. Between her sponsor's time and her time with the unit, this patch has been to Iraq, Afghanistan, Kuwait, Qatar, Germany, Guatemala, Missouri, Texas, Kentucky, and New Jersey. Now, it is with me in New York. I will treasure her letter and the patch forever!

My day ended on a very special note. I had the chance to meet Forest Service Firefighter Karen Krieg Smith, who had been following my hike, and her friend Kevin Wolfende. We had a very nice dinner in Manchester, VT, and she provided me with some supplies I needed for my hike. As I mentioned before, you gotta love the brotherhood/sisterhood!

My hike on August 5 covered 16.5 exquisite miles. The terrain was tough, but the scenery was worth it. My hike included Bromley Mountain. When I got to the summit, I saw this spaceship-looking structure. Then I realized I was at the top of a mountain at a ski resort, and I was looking at the ski lift. I guess I was confused because I never saw a ski lift without any snow around it!

My hike also brought me to a gorgeous lake. It was absolutely stunning. I noticed newts swimming in the water. The orange ones I saw throughout my hike were immature ones. The ones I saw this time were green. I thought this was pretty cool since I never saw mature newts before. This is just one reason why I love exploring the outdoors!

My 16.9-mile hike on August 6 was mostly enjoyable, but it did include some technical areas and another nasty fall!

I was a bit concerned that my energy level might have been a bit low since I was too tired to eat dinner the night before. Fortunately, the trail knew how I was feeling, and it provided. I met Spineless Cougar, who provided trail magic. The two hot dogs, multiple sodas, watermelon, and cookies were exactly what I needed, both physically and mentally. Hikers often say, if you aren't going as fast as you should be or if you are feeling sluggish, eat something. I checked that box!

August 7 was another milestone day. The 16.7 miles I hiked took me across the 1,700-mile mark, leaving less than 500 miles to go!

The weather was going to be terrible in the late morning and again in the afternoon so I couldn't play "Beat the Clock". It was more a matter of minimizing how much time I was going to spend hiking in the rain. Therefore, I got up around 4:30 am and started my hike, which included climbing Mt. Killington, as soon as I could. I saw sections of the forest that were destroyed by the storms a few weeks before. I completed about 25% of my hike when the rain started. Then, the trail conditions rapidly deteriorated. I lost count of the number of times I tripped, slipped, stumbled, and fell. By the time I finished for the day, I was such a mess!

My friends and I decided to not go hiking the following day since the weather looked like even more rain. Getting some much-needed rest and giving our bodies a chance to heal was the better option!

On August 8, my friends and I stayed between Rutland and Killington, Vermont. Besides getting some rest, I used that time to reflect on my hike. I enjoyed seeing who was following my hike. What I found so interesting was I had over 500 people following my hike, and I would say over 75% of them were people I had never met. This was just staggering to me. The comments that I received about what I was experiencing touched my soul and continue to do so today. The love, support, and encouragement from strangers motivated me to keep pushing through what the trail was throwing at me, as well as what I have been processing, to help me manage my PTSD. As I mentioned before, there was a good chance I wasn't going to be around anymore. I was so glad that I was still here fighting the fight within me!

I noticed someone new was following my hike. She was from Mexico City, Mexico. I had no idea how she found out about my hike, but it is pretty cool knowing my hike is being followed across the U.S. as well as in Canada and Mexico!

Here is something that may make you laugh. I lost about 55 pounds since starting my hike. My pack weighed just over 40 pounds, and a lot of people will say that it was a heavy pack for hiking the AT. I laughed when I realized I lost about 15 pounds more than my pack weighed. Except for my sore knees, ankles, and muscles, and the bumps, scrapes, and bruises from my falls, I felt great!

I covered 17.4 miles on August 9. Some sections were challenging, but overall, they were stunning. I will admit, after the first 15 miles, my knees and ankles were letting me know they were done!

The weather was pretty cool that day, but I had sweat dripping off my head when I was taking on some of the steep inclines. At times, there was a gentle breeze, which was really refreshing. It almost seemed like Mother Nature was trying to apologize for all of her prior nasty tricks!

That night I stayed in a privately-owned cabin that was on the trail. The owner lets hikers use it for free. There were about 12 of us staying in it and there were about another five who set up their tents on the property. There was a ladder that you could climb to a loft on the cabin's roof. It had the best views I had seen all day!

August 10 started really early. Around 2 am, I really needed to go to the bathroom. The silver lining was seeing the moon and the stars. I never really saw the star-filled skies during my hike since I usually went to sleep before the sun set. I wish I had a real camera to capture the late-night sky's beauty!

My hike covered 14.8 miles, which was definitely on the tougher side. While I wondered the evening before what Mother Nature was planning next for me, I quickly found out. I started hiking just after 7 am. By 7:30 am, I fell in the mud and broke my hiking pole. She was HOWLING!

For the most part, the sun was shining, and the trail conditions were enjoyable. I stopped at a local market just off the trail, where I had lunch around 10:30 am. I treated myself to a chicken salad sandwich, a hard-boiled egg, a black cherry lemonade, an orange soda, and a pint of Moose Tracks ice cream. I loved being able to eat like this and not think twice about it. I made it into camp before the rain arrived. Maybe Mother Nature took pity on me after all!

I started my day on August 11 by meeting Early Riser's husband, Eric, at a road crossing. He had a new set of titanium hiking poles for me. I really hoped I could get 441 miles out of them!

The 13.1 miles I hiked that day were fantastic. I was able to leave my gear in Eric's van and just carry some basic items while I covered the miles. Of course, there was plenty of mud from the wicked, awesome storm that blew through during the night. Can you tell I was in New England? The views were stunning. When I was on one mountain peak, I could hear a bear walking through a meadow and then head back into the woods. When I came down the other side of the mountain, I crossed a bridge and found a family sitting on their porch. They called out to me and invited me over for some trail magic. Linda, Randy, and their dog, Max, were such gracious hosts. I ran into my friend Sunshine, who was there too, which was also nice. After some refreshments and rest, I returned to the forest. I came upon a river crossing where I had to swap out my boots and socks for my crocs (second time in two days) and eventually made it into Norwich, Vermont. I picked up a package with some supplies for the colder, northern weather and made it to the post office to send some warm-weather items home. I loved it when the plans I made played out smoothly!

New Hampshire (August 12 – 21, 2023)

I dedicated the miles I completed on August 12 to my son, Shane. He had just completed 3 weeks of work at a sleepaway Scout camp. He had never been away from home for this amount of time before. He did an amazing job, and I couldn't have been more proud of him!

Those 18.1 miles brought another milestone. Vermont was behind me, and I started working on New Hampshire and its muddy trails. I would be there for the next 160 miles. They were going to be tough as New Hampshire has some of the steepest climbs along the entire trail. My understanding was some sections may take about 12 hours to cover only 7 miles. The way I saw it, everything I had done so far had been preparing me for what was ahead!

My hike that day included a serious adrenaline rush. I made it from the forest to a swampy marsh area with a boardwalk. I was surrounded by a dense crop of cattails. As I stepped onto the boardwalk, I could clearly hear a bear puffing at me, warning me that I was too close to it. It couldn't have been more than 5 yards away from me. However, the cattails were so thick I couldn't see where the bear actually was. However, I could see where cattails were crushed, so I knew where they entered the marsh. When my friend Tater arrived a few minutes later, I warned her about what was going on. While I love seeing bears, fortunately, this was one eye-to-eye encounter that didn't happen!

On August 13, I hiked 17 miles. I made a second dedication to my dad since it would have been his 85th birthday. We spent countless hours together in different environments, watching birds. As I mentioned earlier, that was how I got my passion for the outdoors. I could never thank him enough for that!

My hike started by hiking from the Trapper John Shelter to a road where I met up with Early Riser's husband, Eric, to drop off my gear so I could slack pack. As I was about to continue my hike, he handed me a two-pack of Devil Dogs. Early Riser bought them for me the night before. This simple gift touched me deeply. Thanking her that evening made everybody laugh because they saw the biggest smile on my face. They all know how much I enjoy them!

After doing what bears and hikers do in the woods, the day got serious. The terrain covered was some of the most challenging I faced over the past 1,700+ miles. We had another wicked storm the night before and then two more showers during the day, so the trail was mostly underwater or covered with mud. The inclines and declines were very steep. The rocks and roots were very slick as well as the wooden foot bridges placed along areas of the trail that were prone to flooding.

I was very attentive and hiked slowly when the conditions were that bad. It took me about 11 hours to complete my hike that day. The conditions were so treacherous I had four bone-jarring falls. One fall was so bad I thought I broke one of my new poles. Surprisingly, it was still good. Another fall occurred when I slipped off a slimy footbridge and landed on my back in the marshy soup. It took me hours to dry off. I had fallen so much in the past couple of weeks, my friends wanted to get me a Life Alert!

I came across someone's shoeless footprints in the mud. As it turned out, they belonged to my friend Sunshine. She got tired of trying to keep her boots dry, so she just took them off. All I can say is the views were absolutely stunning so I couldn't complain too much!

I love recycling since it can be great for the environment. That night, I slept in a recycled school bus. It was converted into sleeping quarters. When I was on the trail, I really never knew where I was going to bed down at night!

August 14 was another milestone day. First of all, I didn't fall once during the 10.7 miles I covered. Believe me when I say I couldn't thank myself enough. As I mentioned earlier, I used two resources to manage my hike. One was a book, and the other was the FarOut app. There was a slight mileage discrepancy between them since the trail was adjusted after the book was published. That being said, I crossed the 1,800-mile mark using the app. I figured for three miles, let me celebrate now!

My hike that day, which brought me to the base of my next day's challenge, Mt. Moosilauke, had a few steep inclines and plenty of mud, but I was still able to enjoy the scenery. The sun reflected off of a huge spider web which made the creepy site look lovely. I also came across another frog chilling out in a huge puddle in the middle of the trail. There was so much water on the trail I could probably have found a fish or two as well. My hike included another stream crossing. I figured since I hadn't fallen yet that day, it was going to happen then. Believe me when I say I wasn't disappointed that I stayed upright the entire day!

On August 15, I battled the most physically grueling and mentally draining 8.4 miles I had experienced on the AT. It took me over 8 hours to complete them. I knew the climb up Mt. Moosilauke was going to be tough. Honestly, my hiker legs performed well going up the mountain in the rain. It was the descent where I had numerous issues. The mud and rain totally soaked my feet and made the boulder scrambles extremely treacherous. There were times where my poles were useless, and I needed to hold onto tree trunks, branches, or roots to lower myself down to the next obstacle. Some sections of the trail were on ledges where if you slipped, you could have easily died. I was so drained mentally since I needed to plan out 3 or 4 steps at a time. It became very tedious and time consuming. To clear my head, I took numerous peeks at the waterfall that followed the trail back down the mountain. The good news was when those miles were behind me, I could prepare for the next day's adventure!

On August 16, I hiked 16.1 miles over 13 LONG hours. Like the day before, it was grueling. Like the day before, it rained most of the day so all of the views everyone was telling me to enjoy were hidden behind the clouds. Like the day before, I hiked along a waterfall.

However, there was one thing that made that day very unique for me. I had to cross a river at night. I crossed several rivers before, but the added element of darkness made it interesting and a bit unsettling. Fortunately, I always had my headlamp with me just in case I got caught on the trail longer than expected. I was slack packing, so I didn't have all of my gear with me. Therefore, just stopping for the night where I was wasn't an option. Especially since I was soaked and desperately needed to get into dry clothes. You never knew what the trail was going to throw at you to make each day special!

August 17 was bittersweet. It was Ground Hog Day, day 3, covering 10.5 miles. It consisted of more rain and tough terrain, but had some sadness thrown in there. My friend Tater left the trail. While the shuttle driver brought me from the Notch hostel to the trailhead, I could feel my tears rolling down my cheeks. Lucky for me, my beard hid them. I didn't want anyone asking me what was wrong so I could focus on the tough hike in front of me!

My tramily, Early Riser, me, Tater, and Early Bird saying goodbye to Tater.

I also found out my friend Struggle Bus left the trail. He was the first friend I made on the trail. He fell in New Hampshire and broke his ankle. I wished him a speedy recovery!

My hike on August 18 covered 14.5 miles. My knees had been taking a beating over the past several days and I was really feeling it during my recent hikes. It took me over 13 hours to get to my campsite. I was so beaten up and tired, I passed on dinner for the second night in a row. Fortunately, I met Momma Bear. We both stayed at the Garfield Ridge Shelter the night before. We hiked together so we could keep each other company and help each other throughout the challenging hiking, climbing, and bouldering!

At one point, the sun came out. It gave me the opportunity to catch a glimpse of the spectacular scenery the clouds were hiding throughout the week!

Sadly, on August 19 I needed to end my hike. My knees were shot. When I woke up the past couple of mornings, they were so swollen I couldn't bend them without doing some serious, slow, methodical stretching. Even walking on flat surfaces was extremely painful. I knew I made the right decision. I couldn't put myself or rescuers in a dangerous situation if I required assistance getting off a mountain peak further down the trail. I spent the rest of my day, and the following day, making arrangements to get home, resting, and eating!

My last day on the trail.

I believe the toughest part of my hike wasn't on the trail. It was in my motel room when I called Paws of War co-founder Rob Misseri to tell him that my body was badly beaten up and I couldn't continue with my hike. I will never forget apologizing to him on the phone that my body couldn't cover the remaining 350 miles. Hearing his support in my ear, telling me there was no reason for me to apologize was tremendously comforting. Hearing him tell me that hiking those miles through the storms, sharing with others what living with PTSD had been like made a difference.

As I mentioned earlier, my goals were to:

- Find happiness

- Raise awareness about suicide within the veteran, active military, and first responder communities

- Make a connection with one person who was emotionally distressed

- Raise funds for Paws of War

The way I see it, I accomplished all of these goals. I couldn't have done it without the love and support I received from my family, friends, and total strangers along the way. I was and am so humbled by what I received and continue to receive.

In the end, I was on the trail for about 5½ months covering 1,852.5 miles, making it to 13 of the 14 states. While I was disappointed that I didn't complete the trail, I had and still have no regrets. Even though I didn't make it to Maine, I'm very proud of everything I achieved!

Long Island, New York (August 21, 2023)

I landed back on Long Island late in the evening on August 21. My family had plans that night that couldn't be changed since they weren't expecting my return so they couldn't meet me at the airport. However, the welcoming I received at the airport was still overwhelming. First, I saw my brother firefighter and co-Assistant Scoutmaster Michael "Ace" Wichtendahl, his son James, and my troop's Committee Chairman Jim Lasher inside the terminal. They thought I was going to come down a different hallway so we kind of surprised each other. Then I saw Rob Misseri, and army veteran Derek Cartwright. Everyone helped me grab my gear so we could leave the terminal. When we got outside, I was totally blown away. There were even more Paws of War friends, a rig from my firehouse, and so many of my brothers from my firehouse and the other stations from my department, as well as numerous chiefs. Bill Corbett from Paws of War's public relations firm was also there. He and his team were instrumental in arranging the numerous interviews I had with the press before and during my hike. People in their cars trying to leave the airport were wondering what was going on. Fortunately, our guys were good at directing traffic around our mob blocking the road!

Returning to Long Island, Ray Meyer, Rob Misseri, and Derek Cartwright from Paws of War, me, and Jim Lasher, James and Michael "Ace" Wichtendahl from Scout Troop 349.

Returning to Long Island, members of the Commack Fire Department and Dawn Amato from Paws of War.

Returning to Long Island, Tanya Martin, Alexa Gianfalla, Linda Riopel, Melissa Erickson, Heather DeLuise Duryee, Robert Emprimo, and Bertie Dennington, members of Paws of War.

There were so many different aspects to my days on the trail that made my hike a life-changing experience. One aspect I truly enjoyed was meeting new people. Early on in my hike I realized that I would be meeting new people each day. I literally met hundreds of people throughout my hike. Some of these people I would have never met, not because we lived in different places, but because we just went through our lives in different circles. To explain what I mean, just think about what life in high school was like. There were the studious kids, the jocks, the musicians, and the theater kids. While each kid was most likely a nice person, they may not have interacted with the kids outside their self-assigned circle. The opportunity for me to meet people outside of my circle was a genuine gift. Out of all the people I met, there were only 4 people that I would have been fine with not meeting. If I were to say that everyone was terrific, you would be thinking, "Yeah right, that isn't possible." I mention them here so you can see I'm providing an honest assessment of those who I met along the way.

Our country has the phrase "E Pluribus Unum". It means "Out of many, one". It refers to the 13 colonies coming together to form one nation. In a way, it applies to the Appalachian Trail. My hiker number was 1,019. This meant I was the 1,019[th] registered northbound hiker to attempt to hike the trail from Georgia to Maine during the 2023 hiking season. However, I didn't feel like an individual hiker. While everyone "hikes their hike", WE were all in this together. Even though WE may have been strangers, WE were all supporting and encouraging each other so WE could all make it to Maine. If someone came up short on their food, WE took care of it. If someone got hurt, WE took care of it. If someone was struggling and needed some encouragement or just a friendly smile, WE took care of that too. This atmosphere on the trail is something I wish non-hikers could somehow experience. It is one of those things where just hearing about it isn't enough to fully appreciate it. What I experienced is such a gift. I wish there was a way I could share it in its entirety!

CHAPTER 11
Returning to the Real World

When I started hiking the AT, I was hoping to get my life back to the way it was before 9/11 and my PTSD. My time on the trail taught me that I could never go back. However, it has helped me to manage it better. I looked forward to getting home to my family. I was sure they would see how the trail has changed me for the better.

To my complete surprise, transitioning back to the "normal" world was much harder than I expected it to be. In fact, I had no idea how difficult it would be and didn't prepare for it at all. I had just spent 5½ months focused on my hike and literally my survival. I hiked, ate, hunted for water, slept, planned detours into town for supplies, and followed the weather just so I could make it to the next day. It is no wonder when Kathy told me the gutters needed to be cleaned out, I couldn't think of anything less important!

For weeks after returning home, my dreams were still about my trail life. When I woke up, I had these adrenaline rushes since I thought that I had overslept and needed to get my miles in. Then I would realize that I was in my own bed.

I also realized my life had become a series of segments. As I noted earlier, there was my life before and after 9/11. The time had come to identify new ones. These additional segments represent the time I spent hiking the Appalachian Trail and coming home from it. I believe this makes sense since each of them are such distinct time periods in my life and each brought such a significant change in me. For example, as I transitioned through them, I found happiness and wanted to live each day. These were such unusual but refreshing feelings for me, especially since they had been lost for over 2 decades.

I spoke with my therapist, Ernie, about this and he pointed out something very interesting. As he described my life to me, it sounded like he was describing a Gantt chart. He explained to me that I didn't move linearly from one segment to the next. In some cases, there were gaps between them since the transitions weren't immediately accomplished. These were times where I was lost so going directly from one segment to the next wasn't possible. This made total sense to me. For example, after coming home from my hike, I didn't know where my life was headed. I didn't know my reason was for waking up in the morning. It took me some time to figure out where my place was in this world.

To celebrate my effort and my successes, I got an earring. I wanted to get one for a long time. However, they were frowned upon in the conservative corporate world. After spending 30 years working as an accountant, it was time to do something that I'm sure others saw as a bit out of character for me. I saw it as the perfect way for me to break the mold I was trapped in. I was ready to enjoy my life my way and couldn't worry about what others thought. And yes, I got a haircut and my first hot-towel shave too!

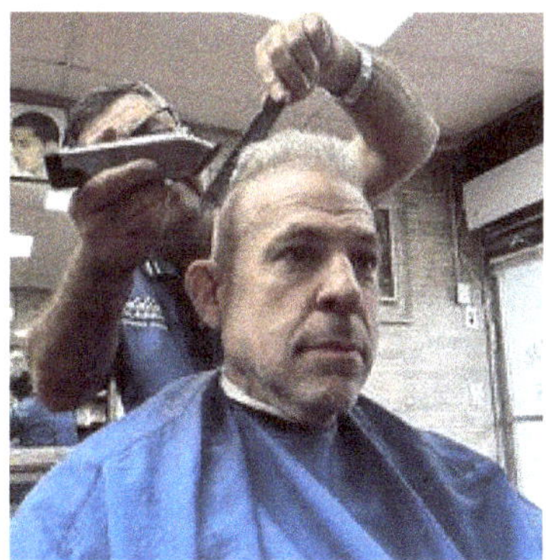

Besides sleeping and eating a lot, I saw the doctor and got some good news. The ligaments and tendons in my knees were ok.

However, the cartilage was severely inflamed. I was ecstatic to hear I didn't need surgery and just needed to take some medicine to address what was going on. I was supposed to feel better after a few weeks. To my disappointment, it took several months. I guess I shouldn't have been surprised since I knew my knees were in pretty bad shape!

I met with numerous media outlets to share my story and continue spreading awareness about suicide within the military and first-responder communities today. For example, I met with reporters from the Long Island / New York City newspaper Newsday, the Smithtown Messenger, The Smithtown News, and USA Today. USA Today ran their story about my hike close to 2023's 9/11 anniversary. I hate calling it an "anniversary" since there is no joy in it. TV reporters from CBS (National), ABC, FOX, PIX and News 12 Long Island were also interested in hearing about my hike. The support they have all shown me was incredibly humbling.

Emmy-award winning camera man Pete Cinnante from FOX covered my story with reporter Jodi Goldberg. He is an old friend of mine. We were firefighters together. It was such a cool surprise to see him behind the camera during my interview at Paws of War. I loved hearing him tell me that he told the station that he was taking my story. By the way, I can't forget to mention Pete is a very proud father of a United States Marine!

September 11, 2023, provided more proof that the trail worked its magic on me. I started my day by watching New York City's memorial service on TV. While I was sad as the names of those killed, including my friends, were read and their pictures appeared on the screen, I wasn't depressed. I don't want this to sound insensitive, but for me, there is a difference between sadness and depression. I think it is healthy to feel sadness. It is a natural emotion, but it should be temporary. Depression is much more serious, can be long-lasting, and can prevent someone from functioning normally. That was my everyday life before my hike. To be clear, my hike didn't cure me. However, it did allow me to calm my mind enough to handle stress more appropriately and minimize my angry outbursts.

That evening, I attended a memorial service at my firehouse. I mentioned earlier that being in crowded places, including places where I should feel safe, was very stressful for me. While I wasn't stress-free, I didn't have that totally stressed out feeling that night. I was much more relaxed being surrounded by so many people. I didn't know how I was going to do that day. I can honestly say, without being disrespectful, that was the "easiest" 9/11 anniversary for me to get through. I'm very proud of the progress I made.

As the pain in my knees continued to decrease, the pain in my elbows and shoulders from my numerous falls on the trail became more noticeable. This meant another trip to the orthopedist and more physical therapy. It was lovely seeing my friends Jim, Heather, and Tim at Costa Physical Therapy. Fortunately, I was able to get this behind me quickly!

It was nice getting back to the things I enjoy. For example, Chip and I returned to Paws of War to continue our training. Chip was phenomenal. It was like we didn't take a break for almost 6 months. Of course, it was also great seeing our trainer Rebecca and our classmates, human and canine!

Of course, I returned to my firehouse once I was feeling better physically. One evening in early October, the guys and I responded to a house fire. Even though we arrived on scene within minutes of receiving the alarm, the flames had already engulfed the entire second floor. We were immediately informed that a young man was trapped upstairs. We did everything we could to save him, but the fire load was just too great. Naturally I felt terrible. I'm sharing this because this was my first bad call after coming home. The trail allowed me to process the baggage I had been carrying. It also allowed me to understand some situations are out of my control. I neither own nor am I responsible for the negative outcomes. While these should be easy concepts to comprehend, it took me over 20 years to learn them.

Besides responding to fires and car accidents, some of my fellow firefighters and I taught fire prevention classes at Wood Park Elementary School. About 100 students learned how to protect themselves and their families from potential fire-related accidents. These kids were very engaged and asked great questions!

As I mentioned earlier, I wanted to join my county's Critical Incident Stress Management Team when I got home. In December 2023, I had my interview with 4 of the county's team leaders. During my interview they asked me, "If we have 100 applicants, but only have 10 spots, why should we choose you for one of those spots?" I just smiled and told them I figured most people on the team would master the "book" training. Then I told them that I could bring something to the team that hopefully nobody else could. I could bring actual experience of what it is like living with PTSD and what it is like facing the decision to commit suicide or not. The rest of my interview changed. It went from me telling them why I should be selected to them telling me why I should join them. Usually, after an interview concluded, the team leaders would discuss the applicant and get back to them letting them know if they made the team. In my case, they were impressed by my answers and experience. Before I left, they issued me my uniform. I made the team. Helping my brother and sister first responders process the bad call or other negative experience they recently dealt with has been particularly rewarding!

Earlier I shared my experience on 9/11. Now, fast forward 22 years, 3 months, and 16 days. When I was talking with Ernie, he told me he had to tell me something before my session ended. I was so curious, wondering what it could be. He never said anything like that to me before. Our session was about to wrap up and then he shared his secret with me. He reminded me that his entire practice is comprised of 9/11 responders and survivors. What he told me maintained my privacy as well as the privacy of the other person. As it turned out, the other person is a civilian who was by the WTC on 9/11. They were by the firehouse across the street from the Towers around the time of the collapses, so they went there. They proceeded to share how much they appreciated the care they received at the firehouse. The entire time they were telling our shared therapist what they went through and how grateful they were, our therapist was thinking something like, "I know more about this story than you realize."

When I shared my experiences with PTSD and survivor guilt, I mentioned I was so focused on the one person who was killed in the firehouse instead of all the lives Smith, Gordon, and I saved that day under near-impossible conditions. I blamed myself for their death for over 20 years. I appreciated hearing what Ernie could share. Do I know if I was the person who provided the care to that specific person? No, this was a team effort. To me, the importance of what was shared is it was another confirmation that we did our jobs to the best of our abilities that day. We couldn't have done anything more.

CHAPTER 12
The Mission Continues

After returning home, I realized the idea of returning to my career as an accountant was beyond unattractive. Just the thought of sitting behind a desk, worrying about corporate profits and shareholder equity made me want to puke. This was especially true since my mission wasn't over. Next to 9/11, I had just had the most intense experience of my life. I had also just gone through another metamorphosis. I loved the idea of helping members of the military and first-responder communities understand there was hope. They didn't need to take the permanent solution for a temporary problem!

I asked Gary Baumann, Paws of War co-founder, what the application process was to volunteer as an ambassador for Paws of War. His reaction was like, "Are you kidding me? You already are one.", so I didn't need to go through their formal process. I love this opportunity. Besides representing an exceptional organization at countless community outreach events, as a Paws of War Ambassador, Chip and I attend various fund-raising activities so Paws can continue to provide its programs that support our veterans, active military, and first responders who are in the PTSD fight. Chip and I have already met with several organizations promoting Paws of War and sharing our story. Together, I share what Chip and I have done for each other and we look forward to meeting with more groups and individuals in the future.

During my hike, I added a goal which was to prevent one person from heading down the dark path that I had been on. I'm confident in stating I met that challenge. However, seeing the impact Chip and I are having tells me we need to continue working on it, so I tweaked that goal. We won't limit ourselves to just one person!

While it is impossible to share each event Chip and I have attended spreading the word, I will share some of them here. One such event was a casino night called "Uncle G's Crew Fundraiser" to honor the memory of a gentleman named Gary Gunning who passed away from a 9/11-related illness. As it turned out, Gary and I had a lot in common. He was also an accountant and a volunteer firefighter. I loved hearing stories about him. I'm positive we would have been great friends!

Gary's family gave me an opportunity to address the audience so they could understand why Paws of War was selected as their event's beneficiary. I explained how Paws supports veterans, active military, and first responders as well as rescues dogs around the world. I also spoke candidly about what it has been like for me living with PTSD and the impact Paws and Chip have had on my life. Afterwards, Chip and I enjoyed meeting numerous family members and friends. Everyone made us feel so welcome. I hope nobody minds me revealing I had several tear-filled conversations. So many people told me about their difficult experiences and thanked me for sharing my very personal situation so candidly in front of such a large audience.

Without a doubt, Chip was the star of the afternoon. Several people came by just to meet him. During some of the other speeches, the audience applauded, and Chip howled. Everyone laughed. Some people asked how I made him do that. I told them it was all him!

Chip and I met Gary's family again when they came to the Paws of War office to present their check to the Paws team. I was blown away when they told me they raised over $27,000. I was quite humbled when they told me that their fundraiser was so successful because of what I shared about my life with everyone.

By the way, anyone interested in donating to Paws of War can go to my Facebook page, "Rob Weisberg Appalachian Trail Hike" and click on the link to make one. I also included the link below.[24] To be clear, all funds donated go directly to Paws of War.

Chip and I are still out there trying to make a difference. We received and continue to receive a slew of invitations to speak at civic organizations, and schools. For example, Chip and I represented Paws of War at Syosset High School and Massapequa High School where we met students from the schools' respective Dog Rescue Clubs. I talked about the various programs Paws of War provides, and my experiences on 9/11 and the Appalachian Trail. Then I talked about how Chip and I are a team and what he does for me. The students loved petting Chip at the end of my presentations, and he loved the attention!

Chip and I also had the opportunity to meet with Shoreham-Wading River High School's entire 11th grade. The school created a double period for me to talk about the great things Paws of War does. I also talked about my involvement at Ground Zero during and after 9/11, PTSD and mental health, and my time on the Appalachian Trail. What made this particular presentation memorable for me was what happened after Chip and I got home. One of the teachers reached out to me asking if it was ok to share my personal contact information with the students. I told them they could, and one of the students e-mailed me. They had PTSD and shared some concerns they thought I could help them address. I provided them with some advice based on my experiences, and they appreciated it. I never know who I'm going to reach or the difference I can possibly make. This is why my mission is so important!

---

[24] https://pawsofwar.networkforgood.com/projects/185340-robs-hike

I also accepted an invitation from retired Captain Christy Warren, Berkeley Fire Department in California, to be on her podcast "The Firefighter Deconstructed: The Human Behind the Uniform." She is also a PTSD survivor. Christy created a podcast that explores the impact "the job" has on first responders' mental health. Originally, the plan was to chat for an hour. However, after an hour, we still had so much more to cover, so we met again to continue our conversation. Included below is a link to the episode we did. I hope you check it out![25]

I will never forget the time I was asked to receive a donation for Paws of War at St. Jude Church in Wantagh. Towards the end of their service, I was asked to come in front of the congregation to receive their donation. As I always do, I made sure everyone knew I was a first responder and not a veteran. I quickly shared my story about my involvement during 9/11 and how Paws of War and Chip have helped me deal with my PTSD. When I was finished speaking to the parishioners, Chip and I walked down the center aisle of the sanctuary. Many people thanked me for my service as I passed them. What really moved me was when I reached the final pews, there was an older veteran standing there at attention saluting me. This may sound like a simple gesture, but the respect that veteran showed me was something I will always remember.

An enormous event Chip and I participated in took place at the Seaford Harbor School and the Seaford Manor Elementary School. These elementary schools hosted a Bring a Veteran to School Day. Between both schools, Chip and I did 5 presentations to all the students and their veteran guests. In all, there were probably about 750 participants. When Chip and I were in front of each group

---

[25] https://podcasts.apple.com/us/podcast/vol-ff-rob-weisberg-hikes-the-appalachian-trail-for/id1500483348?i=1000634791232

talking about the services Paws of War provides and my time hiking the AT, I could easily see everyone's faces. It was cute seeing the children pointing at Chip. Of course, he loved meeting with the kids and receiving their love. What I appreciated most of all was the feedback the veterans provided me during my presentations with their heads nodding to acknowledge my message about mental health and the comments they shared with me afterwards!

Chip and I were also honored to represent Paws of War at the Medford Square Club's holiday party. They are a Freemason lodge. Everyone welcomed us so warmly. During the party, I received a generous donation on behalf of Paws of War. As usually happens, I was given the opportunity to thank everyone and then speak about Paws of War and my challenges with PTSD, the impact Paws has had on my life, and my time on the Appalachian Trail. Afterwards, an individual came up to me and provided me with additional funds. More importantly, I met someone who was hiding their membership in the PTSD club and also had their own plan to leave it. At this point in my journey, I'm becoming less surprised by how many of us have been or are in hiding. The thing with PTSD is it is invisible. There are no casts or bandages indicating to others that you are hurting. It is moments like this that confirm how important my mission really is!

Chip and I also had the pleasure meeting with Girls Scout Troop 1343 of Setauket, Long Island. There was no way I could pass on this invitation. After all, I'm an Eagle Scout and wanted to support my Scouting sisters. I did an age-appropriate presentation for these young ladies about the services Paws of War provides, the impact Paws of War and Chip have had on my life, and my experience hiking the Appalachian Trail. Before we left, the girls gave me a toy they made for Chip and a bag filled with even more toys for the dogs back at the kennel. I'm sure they enjoyed them as I know how much

Chip enjoyed his. Chip, of course, totally absorbed all the love he received from the Scouts!

Numbers often remind me of 9/11. For example, I would often drive along a particular road and see building number 105. That reminds me of my friend, Tom Kelly. As I mentioned earlier, he was killed on 9/11 with his firefighter brothers in Ladder 105. In this case, the girls' troop number is 1343. The number of FDNY firefighters and EMS personnel who were killed on 9/11 is 343. This is just another reason why I had to meet these young ladies!

August 21, 2024, marked my first anniversary of returning home from my hike. I was amazed at how fast the year went by. I'm sure it was because of how busy I had been. Yes, part of the year had been spent recuperating from the injuries I endured, which ended my hike. But the majority of my time has been spent focusing on my mission. I did my best to continue spreading the word that a permanent solution doesn't have to be chosen for a temporary problem. I also did my best to spread the word about the amazing work Paws of War does. The numerous opportunities Chip and I had to meet with countless groups and individuals have been a gift, and the love and support I have received have been humbling, to say the very least.

I noticed something since I returned home from the trail. I have become keenly aware of all the events I would have missed if I weren't around anymore. For example, Justin's French class was planning a trip to Canada in 2020 to practice speaking French. I volunteered to be a chaperone for it. Covid came, and the trip was canceled. The following year, we tried again, and again it was canceled. After all the disappointments and postponements, in April 2024, we spent a fabulous week in Montreal and Quebec. I'm sharing this because, during those 4 years, my mental health deteriorated severely. I was ready to check out. Had I gone through with my plan, I wouldn't have had the chance to push through what I was dealing with, and I would have missed out on such a great trip with my son and his teachers and classmates. Hopefully, those who are currently going through what I went through will see this and re-think what they may be planning to do.

As I often reflect on the positive feedback I have received, I also reflect on losing a friend to suicide in early 2024. While I know what happened wasn't my fault, it tells me my mission is still far from over. I look forward to seeing what the future has in store for Chip

and me. My four-legged teammate and I will continue to fight the fight and do our best to inspire anyone feeling hopeless and alone to seek the help they deserve!

CHAPTER 13
Why I Wrote This Book

I realized during my hike that there were so many of us out there suffering in silence. Regardless of our personal experiences, we ended up in the same place. How we decide to handle our situations is what sets us apart. Writing a book was never part of my plan. Numerous people told me it was something I needed to do. After thinking about it, I agreed. I saw this book as a tool to let those who are secretly hurting know there is help and there is hope. I hope this book allows us to honor those who decided to stay in the fight and remember those who had no more fight left in them. I can only wish that those who have lost a loved one to suicide will see what I have shared. Maybe they will better understand what their loved ones were experiencing and find some comfort in knowing they shouldn't hold themselves responsible for the permanent decisions that were made.

For over 20 years, my life was one of suppression. I suppressed the emotions I felt and the images I saw. I had to live like this because I had responsibilities. These responsibilities started with the victims in 10 House on September 11, and they continued with my family until I left for Georgia. After all, my family was counting on me to provide for them.

When I left my home on March 8, 2023, the time was finally right where I could deal with the undealt. I was finally able to process what was haunting me inside my head. I was finally able to start my mental and emotional decontamination, where my absence would be the least impactful. My hike provided me with the opportunity to leave my baggage along the side of the trail. It was the opportunity I needed to transform myself from the highly stressed, highly suicidal individual that I had secretly become to the relaxed, calm individual I needed to be.

The trail has given me the opportunity to process and reflect upon the suppressed thoughts, the underserved blame, and the guilt. It gave me time to think about what my life was like, what it has been like, and what I would like it to be. It gave me the opportunity for personal and spiritual growth. I met total strangers who cared about me even though they never met me before. One of the biggest takeaways for me was learning that as someone who has always been a helper, it is ok to be on the receiving side of help.

My hike was an affirmational experience. I left home as someone who was seriously considering suicide. It was planned out. I just needed to do it. Then, as I was able to appreciate what the trail and nature made available to me, I began to value my life again. A person doesn't need to be or shouldn't be aware of the fact that they value their life. When I was deliberately considering where to place each step, I was keenly aware of this change I was going through. Recognizing that I wanted to live was a strange feeling. Most people will never have that realization, and they should never need to have it.

As I hiked, some of my other values changed, too. I went from being extrinsically motivated to being intrinsically motivated. Growing up in the 1980s, during a time of excess, society taught us that the big house and the Italian sports cars were the rewards we wanted. These materialistic prizes were no longer important to me. While I had already believed in community service, helping others became my primary focus. For example, I attended a career day with my firehouse at the local high school. I noticed a group of autistic students with their aides, and nobody was interacting with them. I went over to the group and engaged with them directly. I didn't speak to them through their aides. I could easily see that I made them feel included. Seeing their smiles and hearing their laughter was very rewarding for me.

I knew how bad things were for me before I started my journey. I also recognized how my family and Chip, friends, Paws of War, the World Trade Center Health Monitoring Program staff, my therapist Ernie Leuci, my brothers and sisters of the Commack Fire Department, and complete strangers rallied around me to turn things around while I was away. As I mentioned earlier, the mission of my hike changed. When I first started thinking about my Appalachian Trail hike, I focused on the trail and everything Mother Nature would throw at me along the way. Then, it changed to include making my struggles with PTSD public. I realized it was necessary to take one for the team at the risk of making myself vulnerable. I wanted others to know they should feel safe talking about what they were experiencing. I believed, and still do that the negative stigma around mental health should be erased from the world. I wanted others to know that it was ok to seek help. I wanted others to know that they didn't need to hide behind a fake smile, trying to make others think that everything was perfect.

My hike was more than just a 1,852.5-mile stroll through the woods. It was a transformative journey that allowed me to reset my mind. It gave me the opportunity to manage my PTSD. It is important that I say "manage" my PTSD because there is no cure for it. I still have some bad days. However, they have been much less intense, and the durations have been significantly shorter.

Besides addressing my own issues, I was able to share what my life has been like living with PTSD. I hope that I was able to at least reduce the stigma behind addressing mental health issues. I hope I was also able to inspire those who need help to get it.

Lastly, I was able to raise funds for Paws of War. The work this incredible organization does to support members of the veteran, active military, and first responder communities in addressing their service-related mental health issues is desperately needed. It is important that the members of these communities know they aren't forgotten.

In May 2016, I was working for a Japanese company. One of my friends from Japan asked me if I would like to join the company's baseball team. It sounded like fun, so I joined the team. We played against other Japanese companies in New York City. As it turned out, the league was very competitive. In fact, we played against one team called Team Matsui. "Matsui" was actually Hideki Matsui. This name may sound familiar to baseball fans. He played for the New York Yankees, was the 2009 World Series MVP, and was the pitcher I was facing as I took my place in the batter's box. I remember yelling to him in Japanese as he stood out there on the pitcher's mound that I was an old man. He laughed and replied that he was an old man too!

Then, it was time to get down to business as my teammates and family watched. His first pitch came in so fast, and I swung at it. I tipped the ball foul over the catcher's head. I made contact so I knew I could get a hit if I made an adjustment. The next pitch came in just as fast, and I fouled the ball down the first base side. I needed to tweak my adjustment, feeling more confident. Then, the smoking third pitch came my way. I took a nice cut at it and watched the ball sail over the shortstop's head landing in left field as I ran to first base. Standing on first base, I could hear my team cheering for me!

I am sharing this story because it actually ties into my mission. Just like I didn't give up against Matsui, I didn't give up against my battle with PTSD. I'm so thankful that I didn't. I honestly have no idea where my life is headed or where I will ultimately end up. But

I'm ok with that. What I do know is I will be around to find out. I hope those in my shoes continue to fight. DON'T QUIT!

CONCLUSION

There are clear lines drawn in my life that separate who I was as a person before September 11, 2001, who I became on September 11, 2001, and then how I changed again after returning home from the Appalachian Trail on August 21, 2023. Both of my sons, Justin and Shane, were born after that historic September 11. I told them countless times that I wished they could know who I was until that morning. I wish they could know the old me, the fun me, the ridiculous me, the calm me. I searched for the old me, trying to find myself for over 22 years. It wasn't until I was on the trail that a dear friend explained to me that what I was chasing, what I was trying to retrieve, was impossible. She explained to me that all of us are made up of our life experiences. Each experience we have will have a positive or negative influence on what makes us us. We can't accept the positive experiences and carve out the bad ones. What a relief it is knowing the chase was over!

In my case, I had an experience that was so horrific few can really comprehend what I went through. On top of that, I tried to bat 1,000, where the odds of doing so were impossible. While I held myself responsible for so many things that happened that day and on so many subsequent days, I can finally accept that I'm not responsible for one of the deaths attributed to that day. I did my best, my training didn't fail me, and I can be proud of what I accomplished under such unimaginable conditions.

MEDIA LINKS

Below is a list of internet links to various media outlets that followed my hike.

DOCUMENTARY/PODCASTS:

9/11 An American Requiem:

https://www.youtube.com/watch?v=28DZUUAOx68

Everyday Odysseys (Episode 1):

https://podcasts.apple.com/us/podcast/season-1-episode 1-robs-story/id1589782807?i=1000540264078

Everyday Odysseys (Episode 2):

https://podcasts.apple.com/us/podcast/season-1-episode-1-robs-story/id1589782807?i=1000540264078

The Firefighter Deconstructed:

https://podcasts.apple.com/us/podcast/the-firefighter-deconstructed/id1500483348?i=1000634791232

NEWSPAPER and ON-LINE:

Bennington Banner (Bennington, VT):

https://www.benningtonbanner.com/local-news/vermont-voices-a-lot-of-people-out-there-theyre-hurting/article_9d983366-30a6-11ee-8360-6b72e900c435.html

EMS1 (On-line):

https://www.youtube.com/watch?v=ckLkzKn5ddQ

FOX News (Digital):

https://www.foxnews.com/lifestyle/new-york-firefighter-911-first-responder-hike-appalachian-trail-raise-money-awareness-ptsd

Morning Call:

https://www.mcall.com/2023/07/01/volunteer-firefighter-9-11-survivor-is-hiking-appalachian-trail-to-raise-money-for-those-with-mental-health-illnesses-its-saved-his-life-along-the-way/

https://www.mcall.com/2023/06/30/volunteer-firefighter-and-9-11-survivor-hikes-the-appalachian-trail-photos/

Newsday:

https://www.newsday.com/long-island/towns/rob-weisberg-appalachian-trail-tf4v9h33

Rob's Hike (On-line):

https://robshike.org/

Smithtown Messenger (Smithtown, NY):

https://messengerpapers.com/2023/03/emotional-sendoff-at-paws-of-war-weisberg-embarks-on-six-month-journey/

https://messengerpapers.com/2023/09/rob-weisbergs-appalachian-trail-hike-the-road-to-redemption/

USA Today:

https://www.usatoday.com/story/news/nation/2023/09/10/ny-firefighter-rob-weisberg-appalachian-trail-journey/70649601007/

The Virginian-Pilot (On-line):

https://www.pilotonline.com/2023/07/01/volunteer-firefighter-9-11-survivor-is-hiking-appalachian-trail-to-raise-money-for-those-with-mental-health-illnesses-its-saved-his-life-along-the-way/

<u>TELEVISION:</u>

60 Minutes Overtime (CBS National):

https://www.cbs.com/shows/video/dWjBOCvxXuYC5ZQgnoJeK XrCcX_BhRgZ/

ABC 7 (Sarasota, FL):

https://www.mysuncoast.com/video/2023/03/21/911-first-responder-hiking-appalachian-trail-work-through-ptsd/

ABC 10 (Bennington, VT):

https://robshike.org/2023/08/02/rob-weisberg-abc10-bennington/

Atlanta News First (Atlanta, GA):

https://www.atlantanewsfirst.com/2023/03/21/911-first-responder-hiking-appalachian-trail-work-through-ptsd/

CBS News (National):

https://www.cbsnews.com/newyork/news/rob-weisberg-hikes-appalachian-trail-to-raise-money-for-paws-of-war/

CBS News (New York, NY):

https://www.cbsnews.com/newyork/news/rob-weisberg-hikes-appalachian-trail-to-raise-money-for-paws-of-war/

CBS News (Philadelphia, PA):

https://www.cbsnews.com/philadelphia/news/911-first-responder-life-changing-support-ptsd-service-animal-paws-of-war/

FOX 5 (New York, NY):

https://www.youtube.com/watch?v=y5whAGvEitY

GNAT TV (Greater Northshire Access Television – Sunderland, Vermont)

https://www.youtube.com/watch?v=hGdlPoh6Z1s&t=38s

Inspiring Stories (Long Island, NY)

https://4vs.org/4VS-WatchNowPage3-InspiringStories-43.php

News10 ABC (Albany, NY):

https://www.bing.com/videos/riverview/relatedvideo?q=robert%20weisberg%20appalachian%20trail&mid=81507DF8A7832DB61C2881507DF8A7832DB61C28&ajaxhist=0

News 12 (Long Island, NY):

https://robshike.org/2023/03/22/hero-li-firefighter-to-hike-the-2200-mile-appalachian-trail-and-raise-funds-for-paws-of-war/

https://robshike.org/2023/03/22/hero-li-firefighter-to-hike-the-2200-mile-appalachian-trail-to-raise-funds-for-paws-of-war-night/

Newsmax:

https://www.youtube.com/watch?v=NYurNN6rUrE

THV11 (Arkansas):

https://www.youtube.com/watch?v=aGfvOqjvDuw

WPIX 11 (New York, NY):

https://robshike.org/2023/03/22/robert-weisbergs-sendoff-wpix-11/

https://www.youtube.com/watch?v=Enjq16kW2-k

WSB-TV (Atlanta, GA):

https://www.youtube.com/watch?v=El_NVlUvcCU

Scan the QR code above to see more pictures from my hike at
www.robsleepwalker.com

9 781968 404413